He fumed as he watched Holly drive away

Time to show Ms. Stephens who's the boss.

On impulse, Jared decided to drive by Holly's condo on Queen Anne. He told himself it was only a slight detour, worth it to see where the accountant-from-hell lived.

He'd memorized both her addresses from her résumé: the neatly typed home address and the handwritten address of the place she was staying right now. But even if he hadn't gotten it quite right, the yellow crime-scene tape across the front door and downstairs windows of the condo, incongruous in the upscale street, was a dead giveaway. There was no guard on the door, no one watching the property as far as he could tell. Looking at the darkened windows, Jared suddenly knew just how to annoy the hell out of Holly and at the same time solve her problem.

Just as she'd asked—no, *ordered*—him not to.

Dear Reader,

Have you ever been 100 percent certain you know someone and then discovered you were wrong? In *Whose Lie Is It Anyway?* Holly Stephens knows exactly what kind of guy Jared Harding is: a rule-breaking bad boy. But when Jared's the only person who can help her, she's forced to put her trust in him—and to get to know him better than she ever wanted. Is it possible to be both right *and* wrong about someone? And to love them anyway?

I'm always happy to hear from readers. Please e-mail me at abby@abbygaines.com and tell me if you enjoyed this story.

Abby Gaines

www.abbygaines.com

WHOSE LIE
IS IT ANYWAY?
Abby Gaines

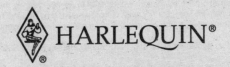

HARLEQUIN®

TORONTO • NEW YORK • LONDON
AMSTERDAM • PARIS • SYDNEY • HAMBURG
STOCKHOLM • ATHENS • TOKYO • MILAN • MADRID
PRAGUE • WARSAW • BUDAPEST • AUCKLAND

ISBN-13: 978-0-373-71397-4
ISBN-10:   0-373-71397-5

WHOSE LIE IS IT ANYWAY?

ABOUT THE AUTHOR

Abby Gaines wrote her first romance novel—and had her first taste of rejection—in her teens. It took some years before she got up the courage to try again. By then, thankfully, the PC and Microsoft Word had been invented, and getting rejected was a whole lot easier. Like all good romances, Abby's story had a happy ending, and a new beginning, with the publication of this, her first novel.

Abby lives with her husband and children in an olive grove. She says olive trees are the perfect outlook to inspire the funny, tender romances she loves to write. Visit her at www.abbygaines.com.

With love and thanks to Mum and Dad,
who always knew I could. Thank you for teaching
me what matters most.

Thanks to the FBI's Seattle field office for the
patient responses to my many questions.

CHAPTER ONE

HOLLY STEPHENS had decided to be late for work, so late she would be. The later the better. She steadfastly refused to glance at her watch as she sat in Seattle's rush-hour traffic, a chaos she usually avoided by starting early. Her old, uptight, anal-retentive self might want to know *exactly* how late she was, but the new, easygoing Holly Stephens didn't care.

She might even throw her watch in the trash when she got to the office. Or at least put it in a drawer for a couple of days.

Some folks might think being late for work didn't count when you were co-owner of the company. But anyone who made punctuality an art form, as Holly did, would know just how much it had cost her to lie in bed for an extra half hour. Dawdling as she got ready, making herself a proper breakfast, taking a longer route to work… Sheer agony.

But nowhere near as painful as being labeled Control Freak of the Year in a highly respected business magazine last week.

Even now, pain stabbed behind her ribs at the reporter's hatchet job. It was supposed to have been one of those glowing profiles—Holly had recently been named Washington Businesswoman of the Year, an incredible accolade for a twenty-six-year-old accountant. And to be fair, the journalist hadn't stinted on reporting her accomplishments. But his sidebar—A Day in the Life of a Control Freak—had detailed just how uptight, how controlling she was. Colleagues who called to congratulate her on the award studiously avoided all mention of the control-freak piece. But sooner or later each conversation reached an awkward silence, followed by a rush to get off the line.

She didn't blame them.

Because every word of that article was true. And now that she was forced to think about it, Holly didn't like what she'd become.

Over the weekend, she'd decided to let go of some of the behaviors that had served her so well in the battle to build her business in a competitive, male-dominated field. She would reinvent herself into a more relaxed, sympathetic person, one other people liked. One *she* liked.

Being late for work was a symbolic gesture of her resolve.

To her chagrin, relief fluttered inside her as she turned into the parking lot of the inappropriately named Greenglades Office Park. The flutter became a flapping of alarm when she saw the knot of people around the open doorway of the offices of Fletcher & Stephens, Certified Public Accountants. Surely her being late for work didn't warrant this much attention?

As she eased her Toyota into her parking space, Holly began sifting through potential explanations for the crowd's evident fascination.

The most palatable was that her assistant, Linda's, overly romantic boyfriend had once again filled the office from floor to ceiling with balloons. Holly shuddered. It could take days for three hundred heart-shaped balloons to pop. Any suggestion of a mercy killing— attacking them all at once with a very large needle— would be interpreted by Linda as a personal insult. And assistants who worked to Holly's level of detail were hard to find....

Holly flipped her visor down to check her makeup in the little mirror. Then she remembered she didn't worry about that kind of thing anymore and flipped it back up. As she climbed out, she directed her most carefree smile at the people milling around. No one smiled back.

She was headed across the narrow strip of concrete when a flash of insight hit her.

A fire alarm.

That would explain why everyone was out on the sidewalk. But why the ominous air? Unless it wasn't just a false alarm—could her office have truly been on fire?

Even more reassuring than the absence of fire trucks was her distinct memory of following her "old Holly" routine before she left the office late last night. She had turned the printer, the copier and everything else electrical off at the wall, and then stood on her chair and pressed the test button on the smoke alarm. These precautions made her business partner laugh, on the occasions Dave stayed late enough to witness them, but no way would Holly allow her office to burn down through inattention.

By the time she'd discounted the fire theory, she'd reached the sidewalk, and the crowd parted to let her through, their muted "good mornings" almost a sigh.

Holly had barely put one black pump over the threshold when a burly man with thinning, sandy hair materialized from the dimness of the office and barred her way. "You can't come in here, ma'am."

"This is my office," she said. "Let me through." Okay, that did sound just the tiniest bit controlling. "Please." She tacked on a smile of apology as she peered past the man to count at least five more of his ilk swarming the cream-and-gray interior.

"Are you Holly Stephens?"

"That's right."

"Special Agent Crook, FBI."

For a second Holly thought this was a prank—an FBI agent named Crook? Indeed, a snicker escaped her before she realized the badge he held in her face and his expression were both extremely serious.

This couldn't be about her being late for work. And as far as she knew, being the world's biggest control freak wasn't illegal. "Have we been robbed? I know I set the alarm yesterday, I always—"

"Ms. Stephens—" The interruption was barely civil and his tone snapped her attention back to him "—we're here to investigate a fraud. We have a warrant to search these premises."

Once again, the unfamiliar pieces of the morning's picture rearranged themselves, kaleidoscope-like. Holly struggled to make sense of them. She'd gone from balloons to fire to robbery to…fraud? Swiftly, she ran an inventory of the firm's clients. Which one had been stupid enough to try something illegal? And why hadn't she spotted it?

She drew a blank. "I'm sorry," she said to the FBI agent, "you're going to have to fill me in. Who exactly are you investigating?"

Special Agent Crook exhaled heavily. "You, Ms. Stephens. We're investigating you."

"MISSING?" AnnaMae Trimble leaned back in her chair and rubbed her chin. "The trust account that normally holds millions of dollars of your clients' money has been cleaned out, and you say Dave Fletcher is *missing?*"

Holly closed her eyes and pressed her slim frame farther into her friend's corduroy couch. "Of course he's missing. What would you have me think?" she demanded. "That he's run off with the money?"

"That sounds about right." AnnaMae must have noticed the rising pitch of Holly's voice because she softened her next words. "It's the most likely possibility. I don't want to believe it any more than you do."

"Liar." Holly opened her eyes. "You've never liked Dave."

AnnaMae dismissed that with a wave of her hand. "All the more reason why I don't want you going to prison for him."

"Dave's on vacation in Mexico," Holly said with exaggerated patience. "He flew out Friday night—the airline confirmed that to the FBI. Just because he's not at the hotel he said he'd be staying in, it doesn't mean he's a thief. He's due home in four weeks. He'll be back, you'll see."

AnnaMae met her gaze steadily, but said nothing.

"The investigation will prove I'm innocent." Holly twisted her fingers in her lap. "No one's going to lock me away."

"No jury will convict you, I grant you—not with that impossibly honest face." AnnaMae's lips twitched as she scanned the sedate navy business suit Holly wore with a peach silk top. "One look at Miss Goody Two-shoes and the FBI will be laughed out of the courtroom."

"It won't go to court," Holly insisted. "It's a mistake, that's all. The main problem right now is the inconvenience I have to suffer while they figure it out."

Inconvenience. That was putting it mildly. Holly had spent the whole day answering pointed questions from Agent Crook and his cronies. She could have howled when they told her she wouldn't be allowed back into her condo, not even to collect some clothes. They claimed to have been tipped off that she was hiding evidence at home. So the condo had been secured and would be searched whenever they got around to it.

She sat in AnnaMae's cozy cottage in the suburbs with a hundred dollars in her purse and her bank accounts frozen. AnnaMae was the only person who'd been sympathetic about last week's magazine article. She'd even called the journalist a lying creep, when both of them knew the truth. Now she had offered Holly a bed for as long as she needed it. But even if Holly could ignore the clutter her friend lived in—and she was trying very hard to do that—there was more to life than sleeping. She couldn't contact any of her clients while the investigation was underway, and no one would employ her in her present circumstances. No home, no clothes, no business, no money…

"I'm late for work just one lousy day," she said through gritted teeth, "and this is what happens."

AnnaMae's hoot of laughter drew a reluctant smile from Holly. Which was wiped off in an instant as a fresh thought assailed her. "The twins' college fees are due at the end of the month. The money's sitting in my bank account—there's no way I'll have access to it in time. What am I going to do?"

"How about you let your siblings pay their own way?" AnnaMae said, eyes wide, as if she hadn't suggested it a hundred times before.

Holly didn't intend to have that tired old argument with her friend again. They both knew she would dance naked down Columbia Street in rush hour before she would let the twins slide back into the mire of poverty in which they'd been raised. "Maybe I can get some work reviewing audits," she said. "Something back-room. Surely someone will accept me as innocent until proven guilty?"

"It's possible," AnnaMae said doubtfully. They sat in silence for a couple of minutes. Every so often, AnnaMae tutted.

The solution hit Holly with knock-out force. "Jared Harding!"

"Are you kidding? The man's a hood."

"You don't know he's done anything illegal," Holly said, though just last week she'd have said exactly the same. But she was no longer the kind of person who tried to force others into her own mold.

Besides, she was desperate.

"I know Harding sails close to the wind," she said. "And maybe he does stretch the law to its limits."

"He delights in bending the rules and making a mockery of people who play by the book. People like you," AnnaMae said.

"Some people would say that's just good accounting." It pained Holly to articulate an attitude she'd always despised. As far as she was concerned, there was right and there was wrong. You chose one or the other—you didn't mess around trying to prove that wrong could be right and vice versa. That certainty was the only thing she'd inherited from her mother.

"Why are you playing devil's advocate? *Your* clients don't have to go to court to prove the legality of their dealings. Jared Harding practically keeps the courts in business with the hearings his company has to attend."

"And he wins every single one," Holly pointed out. "You're right, he does push the envelope. But I happen to know that right now he needs someone who plays strictly by the rules. He's involved in a couple of sensitive acquisitions—he doesn't want even a sniff of complaint attached to them."

"Then he's hardly going to employ an accountant who's under investigation for fraud," AnnaMae said dryly.

"I could work out the deal and all the accounting implications to my usual standards, and Harding's people could present it to investors." She suspected the doubt chasing through AnnaMae's eyes was reflected in her own, but she persevered. "Jared Harding might not be my employer of choice, but this job is one hundred percent legit. And I'll bet I can name my price."

AnnaMae raised an eyebrow. "Just who are you trying to convince?"

"You know I've decided not to be so judgmental. To broaden my views."

"There's broadening your views, and there's sleeping with the enemy."

Holly recoiled. "I'm not talking about sleeping with him."

AnnaMae just shook her head.

"I'll be busy with the FBI tomorrow." Holly picked up the phone from the coffee table in front of her. "I'll ask Jared if we can meet Thursday."

AnnaMae raised her hands in surrender. "It's your funeral. But I'm not staying around to watch it."

After her friend left the room, Holly faltered. Working for Harding would test her resolution to its limits. She wouldn't contemplate it if she wasn't desperate. Besides, he would have every right to refuse to employ her. Not because of the FBI investigation, but because of what she'd said when he'd called her last month.

She'd never met the man—knew him only by reputation—and his call had come out of the blue. Holly couldn't imagine why he'd been so adamant that he needed an accountant with a reputation for scrupulous honesty. She'd turned him down.

But not before telling him that his questionable business values were incompatible with her client portfolio.

Which was nothing less than the truth—though she cringed at the recollection.

Jared had thanked her for her time and wished her all the best. Not the reaction she'd expected from the famously rough-and-ready Mr. Harding.

"Maybe he's not holding it against me," she said out loud.

Some hope. Behind Jared's smooth-as-silk words, Holly had detected a confusing mix of subtle mockery and cold steel. Would a man like him put himself in a position where she might reject him again?

But that didn't matter a damn now. She would call his personal assistant and get some time in Jared's diary, even if she had to beg.

Because if anyone in this city would hire an accountant who was under investigation for fraud, it was Jared Harding.

Holly consoled herself with the thought that working for him, without judging him and without compromising her own principles, would be a big step on her journey toward becoming a better person.

CHAPTER TWO

JARED STRETCHED elaborately, leaned back in his chair and swung both feet up to rest on the pale beech surface of his desk—and took pleasure in the shadow of disapproval that flitted across Holly Stephens's face.

Childish behavior, he knew, but the second she'd walked into his office, shoulders squared, chin high, lips pressed in a firm line as if she were here to perform some particularly distasteful task—namely, talk to him—he'd picked her as the type who would think worse of a guy just because he liked to rest his feet on a desk.

Her reaction proved him right. Score one for Jared.

His own satisfaction in this trivial matter needled him. He didn't need to get one up on a prissy accountant to feel good about himself. But somehow, the look of her had taken him back to the days when just about everyone looked at him like that—the days when he'd exulted in proving them right but winning anyway.

He hadn't known what to expect of Holly—but given her stellar reputation and the way she'd lambasted him the one time they'd spoken on the phone, it wasn't this woman whose navy suit bordered on frumpy, whose hair of indeterminate color was pulled severely back off her wan face. Nor had he expected when he shook her slim hand to feel a charged awareness that simply didn't make sense.

The confusion sparked by his physical reaction had provoked him to the kind of juvenile discourtesy he'd abandoned years before.

"So, Holly," he said, "what's changed?"

"I, uh, excuse me?" Holly cleared her throat, still trying to regroup the thoughts scattered by the searching intensity of his dark blue gaze. The moment she met him, she'd dived back into her familiar control-freak armor. At least that way she knew who she was, knew what she thought of him.

Because Jared wasn't at all what she expected. She'd seen his picture in the *Seattle Post-Intelligencer* many times. She'd acknowledged he was good-looking, even as she disdained the smile she deemed cocky and the arrogant tilt of his head. But the reality was altogether bigger, more forceful, more...male than any photo could convey.

It's his height, she told herself. He would easily be six-two, which made his broad shoulders seem just right, instead of hulking. She'd been right about the cocky smile and the arrogance, though—she eyed the black loafer-clad feet on the desk in front of her with disfavor. How could he expect her to take him seriously?

Yet she did.

"Could it be that my questionable business values are no longer incompatible with your client portfolio?" He quoted her earlier response to him.

Holly resisted an anxious urge to gnaw her lower lip. She looked him in the eye. "I shouldn't have said that, and I apologize."

His smile said he didn't believe her. "But you still feel that way."

"I—" She stopped, helpless. She wouldn't lie to him to get the job. "This isn't about my feelings. I need a job, you need an accountant."

"So you'll put aside your scruples?" He sounded almost disappointed.

"I'll do what I should have done earlier and reserve judgment." She thought she saw a flash of approval in his eyes.

"Why now?"

If their conversation had been difficult so far, it was about to get a whole lot harder. Holly kept her voice steady. "Before you offer me a job, I should tell you about my...less desirable attributes."

"Sounds intriguing." He brought his feet down to the floor, and leaned forward to scrutinize her. "Is that a mustache on your upper lip?"

"No, it's not," she snapped, her hand involuntarily testing the smooth and definitely hairless skin between her mouth and her nose. "Perhaps I'm the one who should be asking about *your* undesirable attributes."

"I'll tell you mine if you'll tell me yours," he wheedled. Despite herself, Holly smiled.

Jared blinked. Holly's lips, no longer tight with disapproval, emerged as full and perfectly shaped. The somber eyes he'd dismissed as unremarkable gray proved to have hints of forget-me-not blue when humor lit them. Which just went to show his male instincts— the ones that had been shocked at that handshake— were in full working order.

"You need to know," she said, "that as of last Monday I'm under investigation by the FBI for theft and fraud."

His shout of laughter was the last reaction Holly expected. Still, Harding was notoriously unpredictable. "You think it's funny?"

"Look at you." With a wave of his large hand he indicated her face, hair, clothes, demeanor. "You're the picture of innocence. You're even blushing, for Pete's sake. It's obvious to anyone with half a brain there's not a dishonest bone in your body."

He made it an insult.

"What about Babyface Malone?" she demanded, stung.

"Who?"

"Malone was one of the most heinous mobsters around, and he looked every bit as innocent as I do."

Jared snorted. "If you're trying to tell me you're with the Mob I'm not buying it. You're nothing but an honest accountant who's been wrongly accused." To his evident horror, tears sprang to her eyes. "Now what?"

"I…appreciate your judgment of me," Holly said, and added scrupulously, "however underinformed it may be." She meant it. News of her troubles had traveled fast within Seattle's accounting community, and two of the peers she'd phoned for advice before she turned to AnnaMae had made it clear they were assuming the worst. "You're right, I am innocent. So if you want to tell me about this job…"

He grinned. "I can think of nothing I'd like more than having the FBI's latest target handle the fine print on this deal."

Holly hated his smart-aleck attitude, but right now she couldn't argue. And this could be worse. Despite Jared's casual clothes, his office didn't appear to be a den of iniquity. The spacious corner suite wasn't as tidy as she'd have liked, but its high-tech equipment and minimalist furnishings exuded professionalism. *Give him the benefit of the doubt.* Besides, she had to admire his business acumen as he told her the bare bones of the acquisitions he planned to make with her help. It was a complex deal, involving asset swaps, share swaps and meaty taxation issues.

Fascinating, professionally speaking.

"So," he concluded, "do you want the job?"

Jared could hardly believe he was holding his breath as he waited for her reply. But accountants of Holly's ability, her creativity, weren't that common. The only reason her business wasn't ten times its size was that many chief executives were too fuddy-duddy to accept that a woman her age could be the best in her field. And most of the rest couldn't afford her. But Jared fit neither of those categories. He trusted her ability, and he could pay whatever she demanded.

He needed the integrity Holly brought to her work, the gold standard against which she would measure this deal. So what if she was under investigation for fraud— everyone who mattered knew she could spot a flaky contract a mile off and wouldn't allow anything remotely marginal in the eyes of the law.

Unlike her, Jared had been known to push the boundaries of legality. He hadn't overstepped them, but he'd done things others would consider unethical, if not illegal.

Because sometimes the end justified the means.

"I won't do anything illegal," she said. "And by that I mean anything that I personally consider to breach the spirit or the letter of the law."

He couldn't help smiling at the irony, given her current circumstances. "What you say goes," he assured her.

He couldn't afford to have it any other way. This was his chance to avenge the wrong done to his family, and it had been twenty years coming. This deal was big enough to attract the scrutiny of the IRS, the stock market and his competitors. And one person in particular would be watching closely. It had to look squeaky clean.

"I charge plenty, and I need a partial payment next week." Holly named a sum that startled Jared. He suppressed a grin—not many people would have the effrontery to demand that kind of fee when they were desperate—and agreed to pay.

But he wouldn't let her think she could walk all over him. So he said, "I still have one concern about you."

She bristled. "You said the investigation didn't bother you."

"Not that. I read an article about you last week."

For the first time since she'd stalked into his office Holly looked less than one hundred percent sure of herself. "I— You can't believe everything you read."

"So the glowing account of your illustrious career wasn't true?"

"Of course it was."

"But the other stuff—the control freak part—wasn't? I have to tell you, Holly, I don't work well with control freaks."

"I'm not—well, I guess I am a bit. That article was all my fault," she said in a rush.

Jared quirked an eyebrow.

"I should never have let that journalist trail me around. It was one of those days when nothing went right and I had to…well…take control of my staff and my clients more than usual. I got off on the wrong foot with the guy. Right at the start he asked how I'd achieved so much in just a few years."

"And you said?" Jared had a feeling he would enjoy her answer.

"I said…" Holly squared her shoulders and looked Jared in the eye. "I told him first impressions are important. That early in my career I could never have gotten away with dressing like he did, with his shoes all scuffed, his hair too long and his shirt hanging out. That no matter how good you are at your job, people will always judge you by appearance."

Jared made a point of inspecting his own shoes. They passed muster, by his standards at least. Who knew what level of shine Holly expected? "*My* shirt is hanging out," he said.

"Yours appears designed that way," Holly said stiffly. "In hindsight, it wasn't a clever thing to say, but he did ask. I gave him an honest answer."

"And you think he took such offence that he went back to his office and labeled you a control freak?"

"No-o," she said slowly. "I think he did that because I suggested he could write faster if he held his pen with the proper grip—I was only trying to help. And when it became clear the interview wasn't going well, I asked to see his copy before it went to press and threatened to sue if he wrote anything I didn't like. Which, of course, I have no grounds to do, as there was nothing factually incorrect in his article."

"You don't pull your punches," Jared observed, his voice bland.

"I got what I deserved."

Somehow the blue steel in his eyes—hard but not altogether unforgiving—strengthened Holly's backbone and impelled her to an openness she hadn't intended. "That article was a wake-up call for me. I've decided to be more tolerant of others."

His lips twisted, she suspected in cynicism rather than appreciation of her resolution. "So that's why you're here. I'm the lucky beneficiary of your newfound tolerance."

She nodded.

"That's good. Because I don't think I could work with the woman described in that article."

Holly gulped.

"So," he said silkily, "if you ever feel compelled to comment on the length of my hair or the state of my shoes, the way I hold my pen or the cleanliness of my desk—" Holly was certain he would discern from the guilt in her eyes that she'd already evaluated them all "—I suggest you run to the bathroom and tell it all to your reflection. Is that clear?"

"Perfectly," she said.

Jared stood and walked over to his filing cabinet. "I'll give you a copy of my standard employment contract. Amend the terms to suit yourself, and if I'm happy with it, I'll sign it."

He opened the top drawer and began to rummage through it. To stop herself from noticing how the drawer was stuffed higgledy-piggledy with papers, Holly picked up the cup of coffee Jared's PA had brought in. She took a sip of the now-cold liquid. As she put the cup back on the desk, a splash of coffee slopped over the side onto the polished beech surface.

On automatic pilot, Holly whipped a tissue out of her purse and mopped the puddle. Then she noticed a smear of dust all along that edge of the desk and ran the tissue over it.

"*What* are you doing?" Jared thundered.

Holly jumped. "I spilled coffee," she said. "I was just—"

"You were dusting my desk," he accused.

"No! Well, maybe a little. I happened to notice—" She stuffed the dusty, coffee-soaked tissue back into her purse.

"Perhaps I didn't make myself clear. In addition to the other things I mentioned, you are not to do any tidying or cleaning anywhere near me."

She nodded. "I understand."

"Do you?" He advanced toward her and Holly instinctively shrank back in her seat, even as she reached to take the contract from him. "Are you sure?"

He picked up her three-quarters full cup of coffee and slowly, deliberately, poured its contents over the surface of his desk.

Holly squawked and leaped to her feet, looking wildly around for a cloth, napkins—anything. Finding none, she dredged the sodden tissue back out of her purse…

And stopped. Jared was standing immobile, watching

her, impervious to the liquid spreading over his desk toward his laptop and the papers he had stacked on one end of his desk.

Holly swallowed. She dropped her tissue into the wastepaper basket, and forced her gaze away from the desk. "So," she said briskly. "When do I start?"

Jared almost applauded. Ignoring that mess was the exercise of an iron will—he was struggling himself. "I'll brief you over dinner tonight."

ONE PROBLEM DOWN, two thousand to go.

Holly peered in the mirror on her visor, stifling the memory of the last time she'd done that—had it only been Tuesday?—and then found herself barred from her office. It was unlikely she'd be refused admittance to the Green Room, Seattle's swankiest restaurant, if only because Jared wouldn't let it happen.

She knew that much, though she knew little else about the man. She'd spent the past couple of days surfing the Internet at AnnaMae's house, searching for information about her new employer. For someone who was never out of the headlines, the search yielded surprisingly insubstantial results.

Harding Corporation had succeeded where so many dotcoms had failed, creating a series of viable Internet businesses. The press had reported with a mix of admiration, envy and resentment the deals Jared had signed with companies and people no one else would touch. He'd cleaned some of them up and stripped some of them down for their dubious assets. He'd bought businesses for their possibly illegally inflated tax losses and offset them against his more profitable operations.

And rumor had it Jared hadn't paid a penny in personal or company taxes in five years.

It might be true. But Holly doubted it could be both true and legitimate. So he'd better have meant it when he'd said she could do as she wanted with this deal.

She walked the block from her car to the restaurant and pushed open the heavy wooden door with the brass handle. The maître d' made a dignified rush to meet her.

Holly followed him across the intimate space of the dining room. Jared rose to greet her and she slid into the booth-style seat that wrapped around two sides of the corner table.

Jared had changed his clothes. This morning he'd worn a casual gray shirt, which, as he'd pointed out, hadn't been tucked in to his dark pants. Tonight, a black polo and a zip-fronted jacket made him look too cool for words. Holly was still wearing this morning's suit.

"I would have changed, but I don't have any more clothes," she said, then clamped her mouth shut.

"I'd no idea things were so tough in the accounting trade."

"I wasn't allowed back into my home after the FBI searched it yesterday," she said. "And they froze my bank accounts, so I couldn't get any cash. And when the bank realized that, they canceled my credit card."

Her voice quivered. Holly bit her lower lip. She'd explained the situation to AnnaMae without shedding a single tear. Even lying awake in AnnaMae's spare bed the past two nights, she'd been shocked, but dry-eyed.

"You're not going to cry, are you?"

"Not in front of you," she said stiffly.

With overt relief he handed her a leather-bound menu. Thankfully she wasn't someone who lost her appetite under stress.

When they'd ordered, he said, "Since you're going to work for me, you'd better tell me about this investigation. Just the facts."

He was entitled to that much, Holly conceded. "David Fletcher and I went into business together two years ago, after we met at a conference. We were both unhappy with our jobs, and our different skills meshed well—he's good at client relationships."

"The schmoozing, you mean." Jared looked her up and down with that faintly insulting scrutiny. "I can see you're not a schmoozer."

"I'll take that as a compliment." She sat back in her seat while the waiter set her appetizer in front of her— a salmon kebab in a coconut curry sauce. It smelled divine, and she took a moment to inhale its spicy perfume, eyes closed.

That sensual gesture took Jared by surprise. Holly had ordered her food in a no-nonsense series of instructions—the waiter had practically saluted when she'd finished. Now she acted as if she'd dreamed of a meal like this her whole life.

Jared hadn't planned on wine with their meal. But if Holly really wanted to appreciate her salmon, he knew just the Sonoma Chardonnay to go with it. She didn't look worried when he ordered a bottle—just sent him an appreciative glance from beneath lowered lids, in a way he found curiously appealing. He shook his head. Holly Stephens was not his type.

For a few minutes, they ate in silence.

"How's your salmon?" he asked eventually.

"Superb. And this wine is great with it. How's your tuna carpaccio?" she asked.

"Excellent." Belatedly, he realized she was eyeing the wafer-thin slices of raw tuna with the anticipatory delight of a tax inspector scenting a scam. "Would you like to try it?"

"Yes, please." She pushed her side plate across the table toward him.

"What's that for?"

"Put it on there—the tuna." It was the same tone she'd used to give orders to the waiter earlier.

He forked a piece of tuna and held it across the table an inch from her lips. "Here."

She frowned. "Just put it on the—oomph!"

Jared had taken advantage of her mouth being open and pushed the fork right in. Involuntarily, Holly detached the tuna before she pushed the fork away. He was right, it was excellent. But that wasn't the point.

"What do you think you're doing?" she snapped. "No, don't answer that. Just quit playing games."

"You're the boss." Sarcasm edged his voice, and he said no more until he'd demolished the rest of the tuna without offering her another taste. With a satisfied sigh, he resumed the conversation.

"How do you think Fletcher got away with his crime, given you're so eagle-eyed?"

"You don't know Dave is to blame. He may be on

vacation just as he said. The Mexican authorities have confirmed that he flew into the country last Saturday."

"Who else could it be—if it's not you?"

"It's not," she said sharply. "The FBI suspects me because my PIN was used to transfer client funds."

"Who else knew your PIN?"

"No one." Holly grimaced. "As I repeatedly told Agent Crook before he revealed that my number was used."

Jared frowned. "You should have a lawyer with you to talk to the Feds."

"I didn't think I needed one. I didn't think there could be any evidence to link me to the crime."

Jared looked as if he might argue with her logic. Then he gave a small shrug. "So somehow Fletcher found your PIN?"

"I don't keep it written down," she said. "The only way he—whoever did this—could have found it would be with one of those security-cracking computer programs that reads your PIN when you enter it online, and e-mails it to the thief."

Jared nodded. He'd been offered those programs several times over the years—and had resisted the temptation, even when he would have dearly loved an inside track on the machinations of the man he planned to ruin.

"If Fletcher did do it," he said, "how come you never figured out what was going on?"

Holly's gaze centered somewhere above Jared's head. When she spoke, her voice was uncharacteristically diffident. "Dave and I became more than business partners over the past year."

Jared gave a low whistle. "Didn't anyone tell you not to mix business and pleasure?"

She scowled, and he figured that despite her intention of being more tolerant, Holly was mortified that Jared, a man she considered her moral inferior, was in a position to take the high ground.

"We got to be friends, that's all. But recently Dave said he wanted to take things further. I wasn't keen, so I avoided him, tried not to stay late at the office if he was there. I was less likely to notice if he was doing anything unusual."

"So you weren't sleeping partners?"

"Of course not." Her eyes widened as if the possibility had never occurred to her. "We worked well together, we enjoyed each other's company, we liked the same books and videos, but—"

Jared yawned conspicuously. "Give me a woman who doesn't understand me anytime. Did it occur to you Dave might have died of boredom—his body might be waiting to be found?"

"It did occur to me he might be dead." Holly's seriousness provoked an unwelcome twinge of guilt in Jared. "Leaving your ridiculous conjecture aside, I did wonder if someone blackmailed Dave, then killed him."

For an accountant, she had a good imagination. There was even a chance she could be right. But with the FBI tipped off that Holly was the thief, it seemed more likely Fletcher had done a runner and was trying to distract the Feds.

"Imagine for a minute you're wrong, and Fletcher did steal the money just because he wanted to." Jared grinned at Holly's frown. Imagining she was wrong obviously didn't sit well with her. "Where would Fletcher go? Does he have family?"

Holly's brow wrinkled as she tried to remember. "He has a sister in upstate New York. His parents are dead. His mother was from New Zealand—he may have family there."

"Did you tell the FBI that?"

"I didn't remember until you asked me. Anyway, I don't believe Dave stole the money, so it's not relevant."

Jared slapped his forehead. "Why are you so reluctant to admit you made a bad call going into business with him? Your clients' money is missing, your partner has vanished—" she opened her mouth to correct him "—and don't give me that crock about him being on vacation. Face it, two and two add up to four."

She sat still for maybe half a minute, absorbing his words. Then she said, "I went into business with Dave because I trusted him. The FBI thinks the evidence points to my guilt, but I know their two and two doesn't add up to four. So I have to give Dave the benefit of the doubt, too. This is about truth and…and justice and…and the American way."

"You're relying on *Superman* to get you out of this?"

She pinkened. "It's about playing fair."

Didn't she know life wasn't fair, that applying her high-and-mighty ethics to the situation wouldn't change anything? He'd learned the hard way that unless you fought against it, injustice would prevail. "If you want to find Dave, to set your mind at ease, I know someone who could help." But he was wasting his breath.

"Leave it, Jared," she said. "I don't need your help, or your private detectives, or your theories about the missing money. I'll fight my own battles, my way."

The woman was pigheaded to the point of impossibility, and bossy. Jared had never liked bossy women.

Given the way he planned to use her, it was better to *dis*like her. Better not to feel a thrill of challenge when she gave back as good as she got.

He switched the conversation to business. "You understand my own accountants will present whatever deal you work out to the market."

"Of course."

However much Holly got on his nerves, as they talked through some of the projects she'd handled, Jared could see why her clients loved her. Animation lit her face, adding to her feminine appeal. Had Fletcher really been attracted to her, before greed overtook him? Or had he been fooling her from the start, setting her up to take the fall? Jared may not be pure as the driven snow, but he was no Dave Fletcher.

Holly struggled to keep her mind on what Jared was saying, but his insinuations about Dave ate at her. She *wanted* to trust Dave. It galled her that she could have been wrong about him, when every day she relied on her instincts to steer her. Those same instincts warned her now to be wary of Jared. Yet here she was, working for him, confiding in him. Holly sighed as she licked the last of her roasted strawberry crème brûlée off her spoon.

"Coffee?" Jared asked.

She shook her head. "I have to get back to my friend's place and wash my blouse for tomorrow." She wished AnnaMae wasn't a petite size two. It would be so much easier if Holly could just borrow her clothes.

He gave her a pained look. "You mean, you're going to wear this outfit every day?"

"It's practical." She glared at him. "I don't dress to vamp up the office."

"Obviously."

"Do you want to give me an advance on my fee," she said, "so I can buy some clothes?" She could pop into Nordstrom for a new blouse and some underwear, at least. Beyond that, she'd need every penny she earned for those college fees.

He snickered. "Are you saying this is a cash job?"

"I will, of course, declare any cash advance for tax purposes," she said stiffly.

Jared got to his feet and waited for her to do the same. "I never doubted it." As they left the restaurant another idea struck him. "The FBI might let you collect a few things from your condo if a lawyer asks them. I could get my attorney to—"

"I'm in enough trouble as it is." Holly stepped away from him as if he'd just offered to deal drugs with her right there on the sidewalk. "Any lawyer who works for you probably brings up a red flag on the FBI's system."

Jared had taken plenty of insults in his life and never given a damn. So he couldn't explain why Holly's rock-bottom assessment of his character should leave him feeling sucker-punched. Not only was she rude, she was a hypocrite. She'd said she wanted to be more tolerant, then proceeded to label him little more than a criminal, right after eating an expensive meal that he'd paid for.

He fumed as he watched Holly drive away. *Time to show Ms. Stephens who's the boss.*

On impulse, he decided to drive by Holly's condo on Queen Anne. He told himself it was only a slight detour, worth it to see where the Accountant From Hell lived.

He'd memorized both her addresses from her résumé: the neatly typed home address and the hand-written address of the place she was staying right now. But even if he hadn't got it quite right, the yellow crime scene tape across the front door and downstairs windows of the condo, incongruous in the upscale street, were a dead giveaway. There was no guard on the door, no one watching the property as far as he could tell. Looking at the darkened windows, Jared suddenly knew just how to annoy the hell out of Holly and at the same time solve her problem.

Just as she'd asked—no—*ordered* him not to.

CHAPTER THREE

JARED COMMITTED TO his plan without taking even a moment to weigh it up. Weren't his best initiatives the product of pure gut instinct?

He parked around the corner on a quiet side street. Within seconds he was heading for the wrought-iron gate of the communal garden typical of these fancy complexes.

He tugged at the gate—locked. A card swipe mechanism on the brick wall blinked a red light, telling him he wasn't welcome. Jared took a closer look at the wall. It really wouldn't be too difficult to scale. He threw his jacket over—the need to retrieve it would be added incentive for success—and hoisted himself up. He went right on over the other side before any of Holly's neighbors could look out a window and alert the police to an intruder.

To his disgust, each condo had a small, private backyard, also walled. Holly must be raking it in to afford this. Unless, of course, she really had stolen her clients' money. No doubt the thought had crossed the Feds' minds.

As he judged the height of this second barrier, Jared considered the wisdom of what he was about to do. This wasn't just a wall he was about to breach. It was the boundary between his strictly business relationship with Holly and something…irregular. A degree of involvement in her problems that he didn't want. He dismissed the thought. No way was he chickening out.

He hauled himself over the smaller wall and started across her immaculate patch of lawn. He'd bet the Feds hadn't set the condo's alarm, so their people could come and go easily. But the back door and downstairs windows had more yellow tape across them. Best not to disturb it.

Jared climbed the fire escape to reach the largest upstairs window, which he guessed was Holly's bedroom. He draped his jacket over his elbow and smashed the glass. Too late, it occurred to him she was the sort of woman who would have dead bolts on her windows. He fumbled in the darkness to find the window catch. Yep, a dead bolt.

With the key in it. Suppressing an exclamation of triumph, he unlocked the window and slid it open. He stepped gingerly into the room, partly to avoid the broken glass, partly out of the crazy notion that the more carefully he moved the less likely he would be to trigger an alarm.

When he was sure the only sound he could hear was the thudding of his heart—surely breaking and entering hadn't been this stressful the last time he tried it?—he pulled the heavy draperies shut behind him and snapped on the bedside lamp.

Holly's bedroom was as neat as he would have expected. If the FBI had searched it, they'd done a good job of tidying up afterward. The white damask counterpane on the double bed was unwrinkled, with two square pillows propped carefully on single points against the light-colored wood of the headboard.

Twin matching nightstands flanked the bed, both surfaces clear of clutter. Next to the tallboy dresser, a small armchair was upholstered in a light-blue check. The walls, he guessed in the dim lamplight, were cream or off-white.

It could have been sterile. But it felt simply...honest.

On the wall opposite the bed hung framed photographs of two teenagers, a boy and a girl.

On the other wall, directly above the bed, hung something so out of place it had to be important.

An oil painting, unframed, in bold oranges and reds, measuring about a foot square. Behind all that color was a green-blue swirl of background, cold where the rest was warm.

With difficulty, Jared tore his gaze from it. He wrapped his jacket around his right hand so he wouldn't leave any fingerprints.

Ten minutes later he was done. He switched off the bedside lamp and opened the draperies. Light from the three-quarter moon provided almost as much illumination as the lamp had. As he prepared to exit through the window, a scratching sound froze him in place. Was it inside? A cat, maybe? After a moment he heard it again. He stepped out of the bedroom into the hallway, then moved to the top of the stairs.

The sudden wail of a burglar alarm almost sent him into cardiac arrest.

"Damn." Jared raced back into the bedroom, picked

up his load and headed out the window. Clambering down the fire escape was much faster than his ascent— every second he expected to be confronted by an angry neighbor or an unusually vigilant security company, the kind a woman like Holly would hire.

Holly's back gate wasn't locked from the inside, thank goodness. He sprinted across the communal area, praying all the way that the gate to the road would have a release button, rather than another card swipe. It did.

He threw the bundle into the car, hurled himself in after it and drove off, remembering to slow down as he hit the arterial road. Two hundred yards later, a security company vehicle passed him going the other way. A half mile farther on, a police car passed, lights flashing but siren off out of respect for the quality neighborhood.

The blood pounding in his ears, Jared drove all the way home right on the speed limit. He must be getting old.

BECAUSE SHE'D BEEN wide-awake since before six o'clock, contemplating her first day at Harding Corp with mingled dread and anticipation, Holly was first to the front door when the pounding started at six forty-five.

"Quiet," she muttered as she scrambled for the dead bolt key that, to AnnaMae's amusement, she'd hidden under the clay pot that held her friend's umbrellas. "You'll wake the neighbors."

She glared at the man on the doorstep. "Special Agent Crook. How are you this morning?" A thought struck her. "Is it Dave? Have you found him?"

He gave her a peculiar look, as if he didn't believe Dave actually existed. "Can I come in?"

That being a purely rhetorical question, Holly stepped back and tugged AnnaMae's tight spare robe, a satin concoction with a delicate floral pattern, closer around her. She followed Crook into the living room.

"Where were you at eleven o'clock last night?" he asked, accepting her offer of a seat.

"Right here, listening to a David Gray CD and having a cup of coffee with my roommate while my…blouse soaked in the tub," she said with careful precision that nonetheless omitted to mention she'd also washed her underwear.

"I'll need to confirm that with your roommate."

"I can vouch for her," AnnaMae said from the doorway. "She came in at ten-thirty, which I know because I asked her to wait a moment while my TV show finished. Then we had coffee, as Holly said. We both went to bed at eleven-thirty."

"Where were you before you came home?" he asked.

"I had dinner at the Green Room with a client," Holly said. "Is this about Dave? Is he all right?"

"Someone broke into your condo last night." Crook rolled his eyes when she gasped. "Your alarm went off at eleven. The security company got there five minutes later, but whoever did it was long gone. It doesn't appear anything was taken—TV, DVD and so on. I need to know if you had any valuables."

She shook her head. "Nothing, since you confiscated my laptop. Is there any damage?"

He ignored the question. "Did you keep any work files at home that someone might have tried to retrieve for you?"

"You think I organized someone to break into my own home?" Appalled, she stared at him. "I thought you already searched the place."

"We did. We cleaned out your home office."

She winced.

"But maybe there's a safe we didn't find." He scowled at her. "We will find it, so you might as well tell me now."

"There's no safe." Holly was still trying to absorb the news. "It must have been kids fooling around. How did they get in?"

"They broke an upstairs window, managed to get it open."

"I always lock my windows and hide the key."

Crook had the grace to look shamefaced. "One of our guys left the key in the lock."

"I'll expect you to compensate me for any loss or damage," Holly said, outrage overriding her instinctive respect for an officer of the law.

Crook grunted, a sound that could have meant either yes or no. Or more likely, *Get off my back, lady.* He hauled himself up off the sofa. "Call me if you think of anything else that might be relevant. We'll dust for fingerprints this morning." He looked her in the eye. "We don't think this was kids, Ms. Stephens. We think this is about whatever you're mixed up in."

When he'd gone, Holly sank into the spot he'd vacated on the couch. "Can things get any worse?"

"You need coffee." Her friend bustled out of the room.

Holly shut her eyes, clamped a hand to her forehead to ward off an incipient headache. She breathed deeply—in, out, in, out. A tap-tapping at the window jolted her out of her attempted trance. She screamed, and AnnaMae came running.

"What is it?"

Holly pointed a trembling finger at the window where a stick·topped with a white lace-and-chiffon bra tapped on the pane.

A minute later she snatched her bra off the end of the stick that Jared proffered from the living room doorway.

"Where did you get this?" She clutched the bra to her chest, then realized how suggestive that looked. She whipped it behind her back. "That's my bag."

"Nothing wrong with your eyesight." He advanced into the room and dropped the canvas overnight bag. "You'll find a few of your things in there."

"It was you! You broke into my home last night—for a panty raid?" She heard the beginnings of a shriek in her voice and clenched her teeth.

Uninvited, Jared sat on the couch. AnnaMae, agog with curiosity, propelled Holly to an armchair. She was about to take the space next to Jared herself, but Holly's glare deterred her. With visible reluctance, she left the room.

"You needed some clothes. I got them," he said.

She'd have to be stupid to believe he'd done it to help her.

"No need to thank me. The look on your face when I knocked on the window was all the reward I need."

That was the real reason. He'd derived puerile pleasure from her embarrassment. "How dare you break in—that place is a crime scene."

He raised an eyebrow. "And you had me convinced you're innocent."

"You know what I mean. The FBI taped it off. And how did you get into my complex? The gate's always locked."

He opened his mouth to answer, but she held up a hand. "I don't want to know. I'd probably feel compelled to report it to Special Agent Crook."

He snorted. "You can take law-abiding too far, you know."

"No, *I don't* know. This is exactly what I've never liked about you—"

"You've never liked about me?" His voice had gone dangerously quiet. "You hadn't met me before yesterday, but you *never* liked me?"

When he put it like that, it sounded unreasonable. "You're twisting my words. I said I never liked one thing about you, that you're known to deal on the fringes of the law."

"So much for your promise to suspend judgment," he snapped. "Since we're clearing the air, is there anything else you've 'never liked' about me?"

Well, he'd asked for honesty, her personal strength. "I don't like the deals you make that infringe on the rights of small shareholders. I don't like the way you mislead the market, distracting people from your shadier deals by feigning an interest in a legitimate one. I don't like the way you leak confidential information to the press when it suits you."

Jared's admiration for Holly grew. She was smart enough to sift through the business gossip, the newspaper articles extolling his successes, and figure out exactly what he was up to. Panic momentarily suffused him. Would she realize the role he'd set her up to play in this current deal?

With that extraordinary perception she seemed to have where he was concerned, she said, "In light of all that, I want you to promise me one thing."

"You're in no position to make demands," he reminded her.

"Promise you will give me an honest answer to any question. I won't work with you otherwise."

He briefly considered agreeing, then lying to her when he had to. But contrary to the low opinion Holly had of his personal integrity, he didn't break his promises. And he only lied when really necessary, which was seldom. "If I answer a question, you'll know it's the truth," he said. "But I reserve the right not to answer every question."

Because why he wanted this deal so badly was none of her business.

Holly nodded. "Now," she said briskly, "is there anything you don't like about me?"

For an incredulous moment he stared at her. Anxious to play fair, she was giving him a chance to insult her the way she'd just done him. He laughed loud and long.

"I mean it." Pink tinged her cheeks. "It's only fair."

Her steady gaze held his, but her tongue moistened those full lips—how could he ever have thought her plain?—in an anxious gesture.

"You're uptight."

"I know." She looked relieved that he'd stated the obvious.

He thought back over what he'd heard people say about her. It was human nature not to give unqualified praise, so those who admired her creativity, her technical precision, her intelligence, usually found something bad to say, as well. "You're stubborn and inflexible."

She was actually nodding, as if these were compliments. He had to play hardball. "You're condescending to those you consider your intellectual inferiors."

"I am not!"

Now he had her. Though the hurt in her gray-blue eyes made him feel like a heel.

"I admit I'm not a great people person," she said, "but I would never—"

"Hey." Jared cut her off. "You asked. You don't have to justify yourself to me. If it's any consolation, I've discovered one thing I really like about you."

"What's that?" she said suspiciously.

"Your taste in lingerie." He gestured to the bag between them. "For a lady who likes to dress so shapeless and dull, you've got some pretty hot stuff in there."

Holly felt her face flame. To hide her embarrassment, she leaned forward and pulled the bag toward her. She unzipped it and looked through what he'd brought. Most of her lingerie, and beneath it some clothes.

But not *her* clothes.

"I don't believe it." She rummaged through the bag again. "These are my sister's things—none of these clothes are mine." He'd obviously gone into the bottom drawer of her tallboy, where the overflow from the spare bedroom found a home. "I have a whole wardrobe full of suits and blouses. Why didn't you bring those?"

"I only chose stuff I liked," Jared said airily. "None of the rest came close. Besides, my office is casual."

"But I don't—" Holly counted to five. There would be plenty else to stress about in the weeks to come. At least she had fresh underwear and no need to spend a fortune on new clothes, assuming she was still around the same size as her sister.

"There's more," he said. "In the zip pocket on the end."

She felt the outline of something hard through the bag and opened the pocket. "Oh." Carefully, she pulled the painting out. Its bright colors shone in the dull of the living room. She blinked back tears. "I... How did you...?" She swallowed. "Thank you."

He dismissed her thanks with a wave of his hand. "It looked like it might be important."

"It is." She clasped it to her chest. "It's my father."

"You mean, he painted it?"

"My mother did. It's a portrait of my father." Holly's shaky laugh held equal measures of frustration and puzzlement. "I have no idea what Mom meant by it, but it's all I have left of him."

Jared narrowed his eyes. Could Holly not guess the meaning of a painting under whose warm, colorful surface lurked a cold, blue heart? Chances were, she couldn't. Abstract representations would be beyond this woman who lived her life in black and white.

Holly had no idea how many shades of gray there were in this world.

"Did your father die?" Dammit, he didn't want to get personal with her. He'd never have asked the question if he hadn't been in this bizarre situation, sitting opposite a woman whose underwear drawer he'd enjoyed riffling through far too much. Now she sat in front of him in the thinnest of satin robes, showing a tantalizing hint of creamy cleavage where the lapels met. He dropped his gaze to her bare feet, only to find they were—with their pale pink-tipped toes—troublingly, innocently erotic. Jared dragged his eyes back up to her face, which was no hardship.

Thankfully she didn't want to get personal, either. Her expression cooled as she laid the painting on the table. "No," she said briefly.

Fine by him. He got to his feet. "No need to thank me for getting your clothes." He grinned. Nothing was as much fun as pushing Holly off the moral high ground. "I'll see you at work. You'd better get moving, if you want to be on time."

He sauntered from the room, savoring the way she ground her teeth at his implication she might be late.

CHAPTER FOUR

HOLLY SQUIRMED in her seat. She just couldn't get·comfortable wearing casual clothes to work. No matter that everybody else in Jared's company was dressed equally informally.

She could see right through the heavy glass tabletop in the Harding Corporation boardroom to her sister's ultra-tight jeans. And the jeans reminded her of the appreciative and comprehensive look Jared had cast over them when she arrived at the office. At least the white cotton shirt she'd teamed with the pants was almost respectable.

But how she ached for a return to the ordered, peaceful life symbolized by her conservative wardrobe. Would she ever find her way back? She buried her head in her hands, blotting out the sight of the jeans, blotting out these surroundings she didn't want to be in, blotting out the man she didn't want to work for.

"Are you okay?" Impatience rather than sympathy edged Jared's words.

She took a breath that was unfortunately shuddery. "Tell me more about these deals I'm working on."

Jared paused a moment, presumably to see if she was about to dissolve into inconvenient tears. He stretched and clasped his hands behind his head, a movement that emphasized the lean length of his torso beneath his black knit shirt. Holly dropped her gaze back down to the papers in front of her.

"Two companies are involved," he said. "I want to buy Wireless World and merge it with one of my subsidiaries that isn't doing so well."

Holly nodded, his no-nonsense tone flipping her out of her black mood and into work. It wasn't unusual to put a highly profitable business like Wireless World together with one that was performing badly for the sake of tax benefits. In the up-and-down Seattle software industry, it happened all the time. "Any anticipated problems?" she asked, and was pleased that came out steady.

"One of the family stockholders has agreed to sell me his shares. I'll have a big enough holding that I can make life difficult for the rest of them if they don't sell me theirs."

"A hostile takeover." She couldn't blame the owners, a well-known family from Atlanta, for their reluctance to be bought out by Jared Harding. It would be like the three little pigs opening the door to the big bad wolf.

He grinned, as if he'd read her thoughts. "They'll come around."

"And if they don't?"

He blinked, and the humor was gone. "Too bad."

Holly gritted her teeth. "What's the other company we're looking at?" Did she imagine his hesitation?

"EC Solutions. It's a small software company, but it's made some significant overseas sales."

She leaned forward. "Tell me what you want, and I'll make sure you get it."

Jared had a few ideas as to how she could satisfy him—and they didn't involve balance sheets or calculators. When Holly had turned up in those skintight jeans this morning, he'd had the first inkling that choosing to liberate the least dull clothes in her condo might have been a bad idea. And though now she'd pulled her hair back into its usual unflattering style, in his mind's eye he saw it loose as it had been earlier. He'd realized then that what he'd taken to be no particular color was in fact a rich brown that, depending on the light, glinted red or gold.

"What do you want, Jared?" She pressed him, in the politest of tones.

He preferred women who didn't ask any question more difficult than "Can I get you a beer?" Holly would ask so many questions, he'd be forced to start thinking about the answers.

What did he personally want from this deal?

Revenge.

"I want," he said, "to win Wireless World without being plastered all over the newspapers as a predator and without doubts about the legality of the subsequent merger."

He didn't tell her what he really wanted—a deal so tight it would frustrate the hell out of anyone who wanted to outdo him. Would make them careless, ready to rush headlong into the next opportunity to beat him.

"And EC Solutions?" she asked.

"I'm not a hundred percent committed to that business." It was a form of the truth, at least. "Start the process and see how we go. It might get too competitive. There'll be other interested parties." *One other interested party.*

"I'll need a couple of days to familiarize myself with the companies and their accounts," she said.

"The bulk of your time should be spent on Wireless World." He was taking a risk getting her involved in EC Solutions at all. A necessary risk. If Holly couldn't unravel the web he'd set up, no one could. She was the ultimate test.

"There's one more thing," he said.

She lifted her gray gaze from the accounts she was studying.

"This deal is confidential."

Holly bristled. "I would never betray a client confidence."

He waved her protest away. "I don't mean that. I don't want anyone here knowing what's going on, either."

"You don't trust your own staff?"

"There have been a couple of leaks to the press."

She raised her eyebrows.

"Leaks that didn't come from me," he added. "This time."

"I won't gossip to your staff."

He moved on to the difficult part. "I don't want anyone here even knowing you're involved." She looked hurt, and he was annoyed to find himself reassuring her. "This has nothing to do with the FBI. It's a matter of internal security."

She frowned. "But I don't have an office, and all the resources I'll need are here."

"Come with me. Bring your stuff." He rose, waited the briefest possible time for her to pack up her briefcase and follow him.

They headed to the elevator. Instead of going down to the main office floors, Jared used his security card to allow access to the floor immediately above, the top floor of the building.

Holly stepped out. There were no offices here, only two numbered doors. Jared used his security card again to open Number Two and motioned her into a penthouse apartment—spacious, with fabulous views over Elliott Bay visible through floor-to-ceiling windows. Despite its luxurious furnishings, the apartment felt unlived-in.

"If anyone on my staff asks why you were in the office, I'll tell them you were looking for work but I turned you down." He ignored her indignant gasp. "You'll work here." He pointed to an office area in the corner of the living room. "This place is wired into the company network. I suggest you live here, too."

"Why would I—?" Her voice rose.

"It's a long commute from your friend's place to the city. And the amount I'm paying you, I want you working day and night."

Holly hesitated, and he tsked. "The sooner you get the job done, the sooner you get your money. Since I live right next door, it'll be convenient for us to work together in the evenings."

"You live here?"

"In Number One."

Holly bit her lip. She wanted to keep as far away from Jared as she could. But it was a big job on a tight time frame. And no matter how welcoming AnnaMae had been, Holly did like her own space.

"I promise I'm a good neighbor. No loud parties, no drugs."

"I don't like feeling I'm a prisoner," Holly said shortly.

"No one's saying you can't leave the building. If anyone sees you in the elevator, they'll assume you're working for one of the other firms with offices here. I just don't want you wandering around Harding Corporation. It's bound to trigger speculation."

Before she could argue, her cell phone started playing "America the Beautiful." "I'd better take this," she said. "It might be the FBI."

While she took the call, Jared walked over to the window that wrapped around the northwest corner of the building. Out one side he glimpsed the Space Needle, out the other the expanse of Elliott Bay. The Bainbridge Island ferry broke the surface of the blue water, and above the bay, traffic crawled across the West Seattle Bridge. Beyond the downtown office buildings and department stores stretched a clear blue sky. And beyond that, space. Cyberspace. When Jared had started his business, cyberspace had been the Wild West of the corporate world. He and others had tamed it to some extent, but its boundaries were still enticingly vague.

He imagined Holly would hate to operate in the virtual world he inhabited. She was bound by facts, realities. She thrived on—what had she said at dinner?—truth and justice. The American way. *Play by the rules and it'll be okay.* The woman's cell phone played a patriotic tune, for goodness' sake.

For Jared the American way meant freedom. Freedom to pursue vengeance to the ends of the earth.

Holly was arguing with whomever she was talking to, employing the superior tone that often sneaked into her conversations with Jared. The tone that drove a man to do things like break in to steal her underwear.

"You can't do that," she said. "I'm innocent, and I will prove—" She listened for another half a minute. When she spoke again, the assertiveness had disappeared from her voice.

"Just wait," she begged. "Please don't do this now."

When she ended the call, she turned to Jared white and stricken.

"What is it?" he asked. All the times they'd discussed the fraud inquiry he hadn't seen her look this shattered.

"That was the chairman of the Northwest CPA Association. They've revoked my membership."

For a second Jared thought he must have misunderstood. But she didn't say anything else, merely waited for his reaction. "That bunch of gray-haired, fat-bellied—" he grasped for a polite noun "—number-crunchers. Who gives a damn what they think? I thought someone must have died the way you—"

"This is a kind of death," she blurted out. "You may not have much respect for my profession, but it's…it's my life. If I'm not acceptable to the association, I'm not going to be acceptable to any client with ethics higher than pond scum. This will be the end of me."

Holly could have guessed Jared wasn't the sort to offer kind reassurances. But the anger that hardened his blue eyes took her by surprise.

"Don't you dare reduce your life to nothing more than your work," he snarled. "Damn well pull yourself together and get on with the job you're here to do. You can deal with those jerks at the association when this mess is over. In the meantime, stop your whining."

Holly's jaw dropped and she stared at him.

Jared unclenched his fists and said more calmly, "This thing with the CPA crowd won't affect your work for me, since you won't be the one signing off on the accounts. Now, are you going to live here or not?"

She nodded, the fight momentarily sucked out of her. She was still trying to figure out if she should feel shamed or enraged. And people said *she* was insensitive.

Before she could tell Jared what she thought of his people skills, the phone in her hand rang again, startling her. She read the display: Summer.

"It's my sister." She pinned a smile to her lips so she would sound cheery when she said, "Hi, there."

"What's with the fake happy voice?" Summer demanded.

So much for that idea. "Nothing," she said.

"Holly, tell me."

"Just a silly mistake. The FBI think I stole some money and I have to…deal with stuff."

"That's terrible!" Summer sounded even more shocked than Holly had been. "I'm coming back," she said instantly.

"No." Holly managed to inject her usual authority into the word. "I want you to stay where you are. You need that job."

"But I want to help," her sister protested.

"I know, and it's sweet of you. But there's nothing you can do. I just have to work through this. It'll be fine."

By the time she managed to convince Summer to stay in Portland, Jared was looking at his watch. Too bad. She wasn't about to apologize for talking to her sister.

"I have to get to work. Let's meet tonight and discuss progress," he said.

Holly seized the chance to wrest back some control. "I'll need more time to get up to speed."

"Tomorrow morning, then."

"Sunday night," she said firmly. "I'll spend the weekend thinking about your options."

"Are you charging me your exorbitant hourly rate for the time you spend thinking?"

"It's the most valuable time you'll get out of me," she said with no false modesty. "If you don't want to pay for it, I won't think about your deals and we'll go ahead with whatever any other accountant would recommend." She held the door of her apartment open. "In which case, yes, we can meet tonight and this job should be all over in a week."

Jared didn't budge for maybe half a minute. "Sunday, then." He handed her the key card. "This will get you in and out. I'll have Janine, my PA, collect your stuff from your friend's house and drop it here."

"I thought you said I could go out."

"If people see you arriving with your baggage, they might guess what's going on."

She scowled. "If you had this all worked out, why did you take my clothes to AnnaMae's in the first place? You could have brought them straight here."

"I couldn't bear to see you in that navy suit again." He grinned, dispelling the tension of a minute earlier.

"And I wanted to see your face when your underwear showed up at the window."

"Great," Holly said wearily. "A client with the mental age of a twelve-year-old."

And, damn him, he threw back his head and laughed.

AT EIGHT O'CLOCK that night, Jared tapped on her door with what he considered admirable restraint. She'd had ten hours. Surely she had something to show for them, no matter what she'd said this morning. He was curious to see how she'd got on—and warmed by the thought of exchanging more of the banter that both frustrated and elated him. He was certain Holly enjoyed it as much as he did.

He knocked again, tapping his foot as he waited, but again he got no response. He frowned. She wouldn't have gone out. She had all she needed for her work, and Janine had stocked the refrigerator. Maybe Holly was in the bathroom. He waited another minute before he struck the door with the heel of his hand.

When she still didn't appear, an unexpected wave of terror flooded him.

She wouldn't.

"This will be the end of me," she'd said about the call from the CPA association. *She didn't mean it like that.* Holly was strong. A survivor. But hadn't Jared thought the same about his brother?

The roar in Jared's head reached a crescendo and he pounded on the door. "Holly? Let me in or I'll break this door down," he yelled, loud enough for his words—and his fear—to penetrate the thick wood and the sound-proofed walls.

Just as he was about to make good on his threat, he heard the scrape of the chain. Another second and the door opened. Holly stood there, alive and well, blinking.

"Where the hell were you?" He pushed past her into the room, where a quick glance told him nothing sinister had happened. His fear dissipated in an instant, to be replaced by a surge of adrenaline, or relief, or just plain anger. He grabbed her by the shoulders, trembling with the effort not to shake her.

Holly had no idea why Jared was so mad. But the tremor in his powerful fingers told her he was struggling not to take it out on her in some physical way.

"Don't you dare," she warned.

"Don't *you* dare," he said, injecting the words with cold fury, "scare me like that again." Then he hauled her close and lowered his mouth to hers.

If this was a kiss, a small part of Holly's brain registered, it wasn't like any she'd had before. The rest of her brain struggled to deal with the instant response of every nerve ending to Jared's touch. But when she realized she'd already parted her lips to the invasion of his tongue, that now her hands had wound around his neck and into his thick, dark hair, Holly dismissed her brain and instead surrendered to the incredible experience that was Jared's kiss.

He devoured her with a hunger that should have horrified her. Instead she explored his mouth with a greed that equaled his, moved eagerly under his insistent hands, which pulled her against his hard length.

Then, as if sanity returned to both of them in the same instant, they sprang apart, Holly stumbling. Unable to meet Jared's eyes, she busied her hands tucking in her shirt, which had made its way out of her jeans, embarrassed to find she was breathing heavily. The only consolation was that Jared looked equally discomfited, tugging at the collar of his shirt, running a hand through the hair she'd mussed.

Now Holly noticed the pallor of his face, which emphasized the darkness of his eyes. But she could see he was more than furious; he looked positively spooked. So instead of castigating him for kissing her—and in all fairness, how could she when her response had suggested she was desperate for his touch?—she said in the mildest of tones, "What do you mean, *scare you?*"

Jared shut his eyes. When he opened them, the anger was gone, his voice was calm. But she sensed the huge effort that it cost him. "When you didn't answer the door I thought maybe you'd overreacted to this FBI thing and…done something stupid."

It wasn't like Jared to employ a euphemism when plain language was available. "You thought I'd killed myself."

He flinched. "You were upset this morning."

"You're right, killing myself would be stupid." Her acerbic tone seemed to reassure him, and he let out a breath. "I'm innocent and the investigation will prove it. So throwing myself out a penthouse window would achieve very little."

"Only a sore head," he agreed, sounding almost his normal self. "They don't open and the glass is extra tough."

She grinned at the release of tension. Jared smiled back. His relief added warmth to the smile, setting off a fluttering somewhere around Holly's midriff.

"What are you doing here?" she demanded before his charm overcame her resistance. "I told you I didn't want to see you before Sunday night."

"I'm ordering Chinese takeout. Do you want some?"

"No, thanks. I'll cook something here." There was an awkward pause. Holly figured Jared really wanted to know how her work was going, but she'd told him she wouldn't be ready to report back until Sunday, and she meant it.

"Why didn't you answer the door earlier?" he asked suddenly.

"I was concentrating. It can take a while to get through to me when I'm engrossed in my work."

Jared nodded.

"Why would you think I would kill myself? It seems…somewhat extreme."

In an instant, his expression shuttered. "I'll leave you to it." He made the distance in his tone a physical reality by heading for the door he'd so recently threatened to break down. As if the sight of it had triggered his memory, he turned on his way out. "By the way," he said carelessly, "that kiss—it won't happen again."

CHAPTER FIVE

WHO WOULD HAVE guessed that the mother of prosperous accountant Holly Stephens would reside in a second-rate trailer park?

Certainly not Special Agent Simon Crook, if he hadn't known her record. But the local cops had been bitter about their past encounters with Mrs. Stephens, so Simon had a good idea whom he was about to meet. And he was pretty sure he would find the answer to Holly Stephens's guilt or innocence right here. *Like mother, like daughter*.

The Stephenses' family home was no better and no worse than the other trailers surrounding it, with a couple of rooms tacked on the front. Venetian blinds obscured any view of the interior, and would have made the place look abandoned if not for the plants that flourished in the tiny front yard.

Special Agent Andy Slater dismissed the inhabitants of the trailer park an hour east of Portland in two words: *white trash*.

Simon frowned. Andy was a good agent, but he had trouble shaking off his Southern attitudes. "Some of these people work hard for a living," he said.

"This one doesn't." Andy gestured toward Mrs. Stephens's door. "Leastways, not so's we know."

He had a point. Crook knocked on the door, which shook in its flimsy frame, and waited. No answer. What a surprise. In his experience trailer-park dwellers were universally hard of hearing when the law came calling.

But they knew Margaret Stephens was at home. They'd stopped at the euphemistically titled Management Office on their way in, and the old guy there had confirmed it. "Don't often go out, that one. No car."

Crook knocked harder. "Mrs. Stephens," he called. "FBI. Open up." Silence.

"Break it down," Andy said laconically.

Simon assumed—hoped—Andy was joking, given they didn't have a warrant. Still, he was mentally judging where he would best apply his shoulder to the door if they did have one, when it opened.

"What do you want?"

For a second, he couldn't for the life of him remember why he was here. But Margaret Stephens's truculent greeting and the startling contrast between the hostile words and her husky voice weren't to blame for his momentary amnesia. No, it was Mrs. Stephens herself.

He'd expected a woman as scrawny as her daughter, but from poverty rather than fashion. Someone plain, like Holly, but made even mousier by her circumstances.

There was nothing scrawny and nothing plain about Holly's mother. Wild waves of thick, chestnut hair framed a face dominated by eyes as green as envy and a wide, full mouth that was positively sinful. He knew her to be forty-nine years old, but she was the most stunning woman he'd seen since…

Okay, so the woman was…voluptuous. But she was also a druggie and goodness knew what else.

"Mrs. Margaret Stephens? Can we come in? It's about your daughter."

She regarded them with suspicion. "Summer's working in Portland during her vacation."

"I'm talking about Holly."

"Holly?" Shock provoked her to take an instinctive step backward, and the two agents took advantage of it, stepping inside. "Is my baby hurt? Dead?"

"She's okay," Simon said quickly. "We just need to ask you a few questions."

The inside of the trailer was at first glance no more promising than the outside. Shabby furnishings—a couch that looked as if ninety percent of its stuffing had disappeared years ago, a threadbare rug, a Formica dining table with matching chairs so old-fashioned they were trendy again—all spoke of a woman struggling to survive.

If Margaret Stephens had made any money out of drugs, she must have blown it all.

Crook shifted his scrutiny from the furnishings—and did a double take.

"What the hell—?" Andy was also looking at the walls.

Not that a lot of wall was visible. Paintings, all sizes, covered just about every square inch. Crook surmised they were intended as art, given they were executed on canvas. But there any resemblance to the impressionist and modern masters he'd studied in high-school art class ended.

Some of the canvases bore swirling swathes of color,

others seemingly random splashes and splotches. A few comprised collections of tiny dots.

"My three-year-old paints better than this crap," Andy muttered, not quite under his breath.

Simon saw Mrs. Stephens's face redden. What did Andy think he was doing, antagonizing her before they had any answers to their questions? Not to mention being downright rude on a subject he probably knew less about than Simon.

"Shut up, Andy," he said. "Show some respect." He sensed rather than saw the woman's surprise, and took immediate advantage of it. "Mrs. Stephens, we need to—"

"It's Maggie," she interrupted him with quiet force. "I don't use Stephens much these days. Should've dumped the name when its owner dumped me."

The local cops had no record of Mr. Stephens ever getting into trouble. Maybe he'd had enough of his wife's shenanigans and gotten out of here, like any decent guy would.

"Like I said, ma'am—" he couldn't bring himself to use her first name "—we need to ask you—"

"What did you say your name was, Officer?"

Crook felt heat at the back of his neck. He hadn't introduced himself, a clear breach of protocol. "Special Agent Crook."

"I suppose your first name is Small-time?"

Beside him Andy sniggered, and Simon felt the heat intensify. "This here's Special Agent Slater," he persisted. "Mrs.—uh—ma'am, if you want to help your daughter, you'll answer our questions."

He'd hit upon the magic words. Maggie Stephens sat

on the worn-out sofa and gave them her full attention. She didn't invite them to sit, but Crook pulled a couple of dining chairs out and passed one to Andy.

In as few words as possible he outlined the theft Holly's clients had suffered and made it clear Holly was a suspect.

"Holly would never do that," her mother said. "She's honest, like me."

He frowned. He couldn't resist pointing out the flaw in her logic. "Ma'am, I understand you have several criminal convictions. Claiming Holly takes after you may not help her cause."

Maggie's remarkable green gaze didn't waver. "Holly is a woman of strong principles," she said. "She wouldn't betray those for money."

She said "money" with a genuine contempt that Simon envied. But with retirement looming he couldn't be complacent. And he wouldn't want to live in a trailer park....

"When did you last speak to your daughter?" He didn't imagine they were best buddies. Young Ms. Stephens looked as if she'd gone all out to get as far away—philosophically, if not geographically—from her upbringing as possible.

So he wasn't surprised when the mother said, "Maybe three or four months." Which probably meant six months.

"Does she ever talk to you about her business partner, David Fletcher?"

Maggie Stephens shook her head. "She mentioned him when they first set up the business, but not lately."

"What did she tell you about Fletcher back then?"

"Is your first name Murray?"

The unexpected question threw him off track. "What? No. No, it's not."

"It's just you look like a Murray."

What was that supposed to mean? *Most likely it means this woman's a fruitcake.* "We were talking about Dave Fletcher," he prompted her again.

"Holly said he wasn't particularly bright, but he was reliable and good on detail."

"You've got a good memory. She said that—what, two years ago?" Andy sounded plain skeptical.

"My daughter and I don't talk much." She addressed Crook as if Slater wasn't there. "So when we do, I hold on to that conversation for a long time."

"Then you should remember what you talked about last time you spoke," he said.

Maggie Stephens shrugged. "Is your name Horace?"

"No." Even as he willed himself not to respond to her provocation, he was faintly stung she would even suggest it.

"Wayne?"

An improvement on Horace, at least. Crook shook his head. He was more than familiar with delaying tactics. If he told her, she'd just think up some other way to bug him. "What did you and Holly talk about last time you spoke?" he repeated coldly.

She shrugged again. "She told me her business was going well, and the twins were doing okay at college, far as she knew."

"The twins?"

"Summer and River. They're nineteen. Holly is

paying to put them through college." Her voice was devoid of expression where Crook might have expected pride or gratitude. He left aside the subject of why Maggie might not be pleased her kids were going to college, and focused instead on the potential motive for fraud she had just presented.

"That's a big financial commitment for Holly," he said conversationally.

She saw right through that. "Holly is very generous with her money. Sensible, too. She doesn't spend what she doesn't have. And the only money she has is what she's worked for."

The questioning went around in circles for another fifteen minutes. While Crook didn't think she was lying, Maggie had been interrogated by authorities often enough that she knew how to annoy a federal agent, and how to say nothing that was of any use. Every so often she'd ask, "Is your name Kevin?" Or Peter, or John or whatever. Crook was pleased with the way he kept his cool, especially in the face of Slater's growing and ill-concealed amusement.

At last he figured he wasn't going to get any more out of her. He rose to leave, looking forward to getting out of the trailer, away from its shabby furnishings, its art-cluttered walls and the dominating presence of Maggie Stephens. With luck, he wouldn't have to speak to her again.

"Thank you for your cooperation, ma'am," he said, his politeness edged with sarcasm.

The glint of mischief in her green eyes told him she knew just how he felt. "My pleasure, Officer," she said.

And as he headed down the path behind Andy, she called, "Lucas?"

Crook stopped. She really thought he looked like a Lucas? The only Lucas he'd known had been the coolest kid in high school. Unable to help himself, he grinned at her. "Nope."

She stood in the doorway with her arms folded, a defensive stance. Her next words were diffident, almost shy. "You told your colleague to show some respect for my work. Does that mean you like it?"

He could have said yes, in the hope it would make the woman more inclined to help him. But generally he didn't lie, even to suspects. He had a hunch that a couple of small lies would put him on a road he didn't want to go down, and he might not find the way back again.

"No, I didn't exactly like them," he said. "Mind you, I didn't *dis*like them, either. I just...didn't get them."

He wasn't sure if her brusque nod indicated she'd taken offence or not. Not his problem. He raised a hand in farewell. By the time he and Slater were in the car, she'd disappeared inside.

"That woman is nuts." Slater didn't hold back his contempt.

Crook, who ordinarily had no problem ascribing varying degrees of lunacy to the people he met through his work, merely said, "She didn't give us much to go on."

That he hadn't given the ready agreement Slater was looking for irritated Crook. Maggie may not be nuts, but she was a criminal who in all likelihood had raised her daughter to be an even bigger criminal. He shouldn't defend her.

He flicked his turn signal as they pulled out of the trailer park onto the highway.

"So, Slater, is Holly Stephens innocent? What does your gut tell you?" It was a question Crook liked to ask his colleagues. Some agents made their best decisions on the promptings of their instincts. Others, like Crook, did everything by the book, followed due process, to figure out answers.

It hadn't always been that way. At one time, he'd employed what he considered to be an inspired blend of instinct and logic. But in recent years he'd become a process man. The process worked, but just sometimes he liked to hear what other agents' guts told them.

Slater shook his head. "Too soon to call."

For the briefest moment, Crook had a sense this case wasn't going to be as straightforward as it looked. Could it be his long-dormant instinct stirring at last? He dismissed the thought. The only thing his visit with Maggie Stephens had stirred was his hormones.

MAGGIE PACED THE CONFINES of her living room, unsettled by the intrusion of the two FBI agents. By one of them, at least.

How could she be thinking about a man when her daughter was in trouble? Even if that daughter believed Maggie had forfeited the right to worry about her long ago. What kind of a mother was she?

She knew the answer to that one. The kind of mother who always put her causes ahead of her family, and who'd probably do it all again, given the chance. With the possible exception of marrying Andrew Stephens.

After Andrew had left, she'd been thankful never to experience that powerful pull toward a man again. Until today. She couldn't explain—couldn't *believe*—the attraction she'd felt for the FBI agent.

And for no obvious reason. He wasn't good-looking—entirely average—and he was the sort of man who would despise everything she stood for. Life had taught Maggie long ago that respect was a scarce commodity. She sure wasn't going to find it in a man like Crook.

Though he'd surprised her as he left. Instead of lying to her and saying he liked the paintings, he'd given her an honest answer.

Maggie shook off the distraction posed by the man she'd met today. She couldn't be attracted to him after those accusations he'd made against Holly. *Holly.* The oldest of Maggie's children, but the one she always thought of as her baby, would be devastated to have her integrity questioned. She wouldn't welcome the phone call Maggie was determined to make. Maggie was under no illusion that she could comfort Holly, or help her. But she had to try.

She braced herself for the sneer of the park manager, who considered his tenants several rungs below him, and headed to the office to use the phone.

JARED FOUND HIMSELF unreasonably excited about his meeting with Holly on Sunday night. It was because the goal he'd worked toward for nearly twenty years was so close, he told himself.

It had nothing to do with Holly's razor-sharp analytical mind, which presented such an intriguing contrast to the sensuous, almost mysterious curve of her mouth. And definitely nothing to do with the hottest kiss in history, the one they'd shared Friday night.

They both knew he wouldn't do it again.

Tonight Holly opened the door promptly in response to his knock.

"Had a good day?" After an initial nanosecond scan of her person, Jared kept his gaze firmly on her face. The red leather miniskirt revealed gorgeous legs that Friday's jeans had only hinted at. Teamed with a white cotton blouse with off-the-shoulder sleeves, the overall look was one of sultry innocence. Very sexy.

But he knew she wouldn't appreciate his appreciation. And after his performance the other night, the last thing he needed was to get their first evening together—working together—off to an unpropitious start.

"A long day." She stifled a yawn—hardly the usual reaction Jared encountered when he arrived at a woman's home—as she led the way into the apartment.

Jared crossed to the office area. Apart from a small pile of papers on the desk, there was no evidence of three days spent on his deals. Could it be that Holly wasn't as thorough as everyone said?

He soon found it was more a matter of her being meticulously tidy. She'd gone over a ton of information since he'd last seen her, and she ran through his options with a thoroughness that lifted the hairs on the back of his neck.

Was there any hope at all that she might not figure out what he was up to?

"Jared?"

His eyes traveled over her slightly parted lips. Lips whose sweet, heated response he could recall without effort.

"What did you say?" he asked, annoyance seeping into his tone.

She bridled. "I asked if you want to hear my thoughts on pricing. But if you don't want to…"

"Go ahead." He got up and walked to the window, looked out at Elliott Bay instead of at Holly.

When she told him her conclusions, Jared was startled at how similar the numbers were to those he'd come up with, though her rationale was quite different. She knew her stuff inside-out—her only fault was that she explained things in such detail, he couldn't get a word in edgewise to compliment her.

They were so engrossed in their discussion that he didn't check his watch until hunger pangs reminded him they hadn't eaten.

"It's nine o'clock," he told Holly. "I'm starving. Let's get a pizza and keep working."

She wrinkled her nose, as if pizza didn't suit her, but agreed, so he went ahead and ordered. He poured two glasses of wine from a bottle he found in the refrigerator. When he looked up at Holly, she was rubbing the back of her neck with both hands. The movement lifted her breasts beneath the thin cotton of her blouse, drawing his eyes down to the high, rounded curves. He wondered which of those sexy bras she had on underneath. Maybe the transparent, gauzy white underwire with the front opening clasp. Or the—what was it, ivory?—with the imagination-stirring gold buckles on the straps.

Jared handed her a glass and raised his in a toast. "To you and your magnificent breasts."

When her eyes widened, he realized what he'd said. "Brain! I meant brain! To your magnificent brain."

He really had meant to say brain. Jared clapped a hand to his forehead and cursed silently. After last Friday she'd think he was hell-bent on seducing her.

He chanced a look at her.

The silence he'd taken as horror turned out to be helpless, silent laughter that shook her slim frame so hard, wine slopped over the rim of her glass. He grabbed it from her, and she used both hands to knuckle tears from her eyes. At last she got enough air in to make some sound, and her laughter bubbled out into the room and caught him up in it.

By the time he stopped laughing, Jared was weak with a sensation he barely recognized. Relaxation.

He wiped tears from his eyes. "I don't know how that came out," he said. "No doubt you'll slap a sexual harassment suit on me."

"Sure to," Holly said equably. "But I needed a good laugh, so thanks."

Her eyes, clear and honest, held his. As he handed her wineglass back, he saw something spark in their gray depths.

"So," he said, never a man to miss an opportunity, though he should probably pass on this one, "is there some guy who's going to punch me for what I just said?"

Holly took a sip of her wine and leaned against the

counter. Close enough and on the right angle for Jared to glimpse the swell of her breast where the top buttons of her blouse were undone.

"A boyfriend?" She shook her head. "My focus is on building my business. I don't have time for a relationship."

What was it with women and that word? "I'm talking about dating," he said. "Not a relationship. There's a difference."

"How interesting," she said sweetly. "What do your dates say when you tell them that?"

"I like to let them figure it out for themselves," he said. "When I don't call."

"Jerk," she said pleasantly.

He grinned, raised his glass in another toast, and downed a swallow of wine.

The man was impossible. The only reason she didn't despise him was because he didn't pretend to be something he wasn't, she told herself.

To remind herself he wasn't her type, she said, "So do you see yourself getting married one day? Having kids?"

He started as if she'd prodded him with a branding iron. "I'm not interested in playing happy family. I couldn't love one woman for the rest of my life, and I don't want to pretend I do."

"What hope would there be for the world if everyone shared your attitude?" Holly said. "There are some great marriages around." There'd better be. She was banking on living a completely different life from her mother's, and that meant making a happy marriage, one that would last.

"You're talking from personal experience, are you? From your parents' marriage?"

"Well, no, they're divorced." She scowled at his exclamation of triumph. "But I still believe in marriage. I want a husband and kids, and a house in the suburbs, complete with picket fence."

Jared shook his head in disgust. "I assume your parents split up, too?"

To her surprise he said, "My parents epitomize the suburban dream. They married when Dad finished college and have lived in the same house for nearly fifty years. I can scarcely remember them ever arguing."

"So what's the problem?" Holly asked, bemused. "It sounds perfect."

He looked as if he wished he hadn't started this conversation. "The problem," he said, "is that it's all built on a lie."

Before Holly could voice one of the dozen questions that sprang to mind, the buzzer rang from the lobby.

"That'll be the pizza." Jared made for the door with unconcealed relief.

While he was gone, Holly set out plates and silverware. She resolved not to pry further into Jared's background. A man who could twist the kind of normal family life that every American craved into some sort of tortured childhood had obviously made ingratitude an art form. Pandering to it would only make her mad—and would undoubtedly bring out the anger she sensed was barely contained beneath the thin veneer of Jared's occasional civility.

He arrived back and set the two pizza boxes on the table. "Plates," he said dubiously. "For pizza?"

"A small touch of civilization," she said coolly.

He shrugged, but gave up whatever point he was making as he started to unload slices of pizza onto the plates. Famished, they ate in silence for several minutes, by which time Holly's irritation had passed.

"This is great." She wiped a stray thread of mozzarella from her chin with her napkin and stood up to clear away an empty carton. "Fattening, but great."

Jared looked her up and down. Because if that wasn't an invitation to check out her slim curves, what was? "I don't think you're in too much danger of ballooning out."

She gave him a quelling look that inspired him to make his appreciation all the more overt. This time he ran his eyes blatantly over her and made fanning movements in front of his face. "Your sister has great taste in clothes. Does she look as good as you do in them?"

She disregarded the compliment. "Much better. These are more age-appropriate for her. And she's too young for you."

"You don't know how young I like my women."

Holly returned his frank appraisal. At thirty-five he had the irritatingly good looks of a man who would still be handsome, still attracting much younger women, when he was sixty. But for now, there was no trace of gray in the dark hair that was slightly too long. The faint lines of strain around his mouth and eyes robbed his face of any boyishness, but not of its charm. He grinned, and the contrast of white teeth against tanned skin almost took her breath away.

"What do you think?" he asked. "Do I pass?"

"I think a man like you must have better things to do with your evenings than work," she said. She herself often worked evenings and weekends. But she assumed Jared was the type to play as hard as he worked.

He chuckled. "The night is young. I'll get to better things later."

"Good for you."

"Sorry about the late hours." He sounded totally unapologetic. "But I'd like us to work most evenings. The sooner we're ready to start due diligence the better."

"I have nothing else to do." She shot a covert glance at him. His tan suggested he saw plenty of fresh air, but faint shadows beneath his eyes gave the hint of a lie to his vitality. He looked, she realized, jaded. Too much fast food, no doubt—he hadn't looked up the pizza number before he'd phoned.

"If you like," she said, "I could cook meals for us the next couple of nights. Something simple."

He couldn't have looked more horrified if she'd suggested they do cross-stitch during their coffee breaks.

"No." His face darkened. "No cooking. No...domestic stuff." He pushed his chair back and stood, as if to distance himself from the intimacy of sharing a table with her.

Although she barely knew the man, didn't even like him, it hurt. "Don't panic," she snapped. "It's not some plot to lure you into bed."

His expression lightened immediately, and he gave a wolfish grin. "You didn't say bed was part of the offer."

"It wasn't, and you know it."

"I have no objection to bed." He continued as if she hadn't spoken. "That doesn't count as domestic."

She looked at him, lean and dangerous, his eyes

hooded and mysterious. "I don't imagine it does with you," she said.

He grinned. "What *do* you imagine?"

"I...nothing." She threw her balled-up napkin at him in frustration. He caught it deftly with one hand before it hit.

CHAPTER SIX

RIGHT IS RIGHT, wrong is wrong. Holly had never wavered from that mantra, and she wasn't about to start now.

She'd broken one of her cardinal rules and gotten personally involved with a client. And it was wrong.

But she could fix it. She could get back on to a professional footing with Jared. All she had to do was avoid him in the evenings. The meals they'd shared so far had ended up more like a date than a business meeting. The conversation got way too personal and there were too many opportunities to really look at him. The man's physical presence would distract a nun.

From now on, she would keep personal contact to a minimum.

So when Jared turned up on Monday night, she told him she had a headache—which was true, she assured herself. The thought of behaving in an unprofessional manner toward a client really did make her feel ill. She handed him a sheet of paper with questions he needed to answer, told him to get back to her by morning, then shut the door in his face. At five o'clock Tuesday evening she handed him a proposed timeline for the negotiations, and once again told him to get back to her in the morning.

"You're not still unwell." His eyes narrowed as if his gaze could bore behind her temples.

"No," she said reluctantly.

"Then what's the problem?"

"There's no problem. You need to look at this timeline and you don't need to be in my apartment to do it."

He raised his eyebrows at the "my." "What if I want to clarify something?"

"My cell phone's on."

He leaned in closer to where Holly stood gripping the edge of her door, ready to shut it. Much closer. "Are you trying to get rid of me?"

He was near enough to feel his warm breath on her face, sending a shiver down her spine. Holly didn't let go of the door.

"You're being paranoid," she said snootily. "Now, if you'll excuse me…"

His burst of triumphant laughter arrested her. "What's so funny?"

"You're scared," he taunted. "You don't want me in there in case you give in to temptation and jump me."

"How dare you." She hoped the fire in her cheeks looked like anger. "Nothing could be further—"

He held up an admonishing finger. "Uh-uh, don't say something we both know isn't true. I expect nothing but total honesty from you, honey."

And before she could recover her presence of mind sufficiently to tell him what he could do with his expectations—and to tell him she would never be his *honey*—he'd turned and headed into his own apartment.

Holly closed her door at last, and leaned against it. That man had an ego the size of a...a—

A loud knock behind her sent her stumbling forward. So, he'd come back for more, had he? More innuendo, more insults.

"I am *not* scared of you, you low-down rat, and I am *not* going to jump you," she snarled as she hauled the door open.

"I guess that's bad news and good news, then," Special Agent Crook said.

Holly closed her eyes in the fervent hope that when she opened them again the FBI man would be gone. He wasn't. Thanks to Jared, she'd just hurled verbal abuse at a federal agent. She'd expected a visit from Crook since he'd called earlier to ask where she was. She just hadn't expected him right now. "I thought you were someone else," she mumbled.

"I've heard worse," he said with surprising good humor. "Can I come in?"

Holly stepped aside. "Have you found Dave? And how did you get up here unannounced?"

"The concierge unlocked the elevator for me—an FBI badge works wonders." He sat on the couch she indicated. "We haven't found Fletcher. We've asked the Mexican authorities to let us know if he checks into a hotel. But unless he's at a Sheraton or one of the other big chains, I'm not holding out much hope. By your reckoning Fletcher's away another two and a half weeks. Don't be surprised if we don't hear anything from him until he gets back."

If he gets back. "So why are you here?"

Crook handed her a sealed envelope. "In there's a

letter saying you're to be arrested for fraud. You need to turn yourself in to the U.S. Marshal's office tomorrow. They'll book you and get you in front of a judge for an initial appearance."

Holly sagged into an armchair. "You—you're charging me?" Her voice came out a near whisper.

"We have the evidence," Crook said. Did she imagine the faintest tinge of regret from him? "You told us yourself no one else has your PIN. We looked into your systems, but there was no sign of a hacker. Your assistant tells us you're the brains of the business and that Fletcher doesn't take a lot of initiative. There's no evidence he's involved, so that leaves you."

"If I were the thief, why would I be so stupid as to use my own PIN?" she demanded.

Agent Crook sighed impatiently. "One way or another, most criminals are stupid, Ms. Stephens. Makes my job a heck of a lot easier."

"If you're so sure I'm guilty, why don't you arrest me now?"

"I will if you want." Crook looked tempted to do just that. "But with fraud suspects we generally do it this way. Unless," he said, "you happen to be associated with gangsters or involved in violent crime?"

Holly shook her head.

"Then turn yourself in tomorrow, and plan on seeing a judge Thursday."

Holly faced the sickening truth. There was every chance she might be found guilty of a crime she hadn't committed, one that would send her to prison. She would be no better than her mother.

After Crook left, her first instinct was to go next door to tell Jared, to draw comfort from his scathing denunciation of the forces of law and order, and from the arms he would almost certainly wrap around her.

No.

He flirted with her mainly because it drove her nuts, and when she got upset or emotional, he made it plain he didn't want to know.

Jared was the last person she should turn to.

JARED WAS HALFWAY across the Harding Tower lobby at eight o'clock the next morning when he felt a prickle at the back of his neck. He turned around in time to see Holly step into the revolving door that would take her out onto Columbia Street.

What was the woman doing? She'd brushed him off two nights running, and now she was going somewhere in her frumpy suit when she should be upstairs working. He ignored the fact that the material she'd handed him last night proved she'd been working hard. Holly was up to something.

Could she have figured out Jared's deception already? Was that why she'd barely spoken to him for two days? He had visions of her gleaning evidence from his files and building a case against him for the Securities and Exchange Commission. They'd never win, of course, but they could tie him in legal knots for weeks while they tried to pin something on him.

"Like hell you will," he muttered, and he headed out into the street after her.

She was maybe twenty yards ahead of him, weaving

purposefully in her sensible shoes through the commuters crowding the sidewalk. As Jared sped up, he noticed out of the corner of his eye that the white-haired, gray-suited man next to him did the same. In fact, the guy's gaze was fixed on Holly. Why the hell would someone be tailing her?

Jared caught up to her first. He clamped a hand on her shoulder, startling her. She spun around in the street, then scowled when she saw him. "Could you leave me alone for five minutes?"

"Excuse me, are you Holly Rainbow Stephens?" asked the white-haired man.

In that polite but distant way of hers, she said, "That's right."

The older man held out a sheaf of folded pages, which Holly took. "You're served."

"Thank you," she said, but the man had melted into the crowd.

Thank you! Jared groaned. "You just thanked that jerk for handing you a lawsuit."

"I did?" Holly looked at the papers in her hand. Horror dawned on her countenance, and she dropped them as if they were contaminated.

Jared picked them up, grasped Holly by the elbow and steered her through the crowd to stand against the Bank of America Tower. Without asking her permission, he yanked the paperclip off and unfolded the pages, ignoring her hiss of annoyance.

He never would have guessed the name of the plaintiff. For a moment he wondered if this was some kind of sting, if Holly wasn't all she seemed. If somehow he'd become the patsy in his own game.

"Is Keith Transom a client of yours?"

Jared's controlled fury did not escape Holly. No doubt he was about to launch into an "I told you so," since the minute she'd left his precious apartment, she'd been slapped with a lawsuit. Of course, she now wished she'd never stepped out that revolving door herself....

"I'm asking you," he said again, "if you work for Transom. You found his ethics acceptable, but not mine?"

That old argument. If Holly hadn't known how insensitive Jared was, she would swear she'd hurt him by her initial refusal to work for him. "Keith was Dave's client before we went into partnership," she said. "I didn't want him on our books, but Dave wanted to keep him. So, yes, Fletcher & Stephens did some work for Transom. But he uses one of the big firms for most of his accounting."

She could understand Jared's anger, at least in part. Transom's fortune was reputedly ill-gotten, though no one had managed to pin any of his rumored indiscretions on him. By dint of his wealth and his legendary cunning, he was accorded a grudging respect by the business world, if not by Holly. But no matter what her personal opinion was, she couldn't have demanded that Dave dump him. Instead, she'd let Dave handle Transom's work, pleading client overload and gradually Transom's business had gone elsewhere.

But not all his funds. Scanning the legal document Jared held out to her, Holly saw that Transom was suing for the immediate return of funds held in the Fletcher

& Stephens trust account, and for damages relating to obstruction of his business.

"How did Transom know about the stolen money? And how did he find me?"

"No doubt the FBI contacted him, and he had one of his henchmen lean on a contact in the Bureau to get your address."

She skimmed the document again. "Obstruction? Is that legal grounds for suing?"

He snorted. "Doesn't matter. Transom will have you so tied up in legal bills that you'll settle without it coming to court. Either way, it'll cost you a fortune."

Court. That reminded her. "I need a day off tomorrow," she said abruptly. "The FBI are about to arrest me for fraud and I have a plea hearing."

He gaped. "What does your lawyer say?"

"I-I'm just on my way to see her. I never thought it would come to this. I figured they'd find Dave—or whoever did it or the money—by now."

Jared could have throttled her for that naiveté. "When will you understand that you, not Dave, are their number one suspect? These guys won't work any harder than necessary to get a result. Until Dave fails to return from his vacation, you are it."

Holly's face whitened, and she put a hand against the wall to steady herself. "I know."

"You're pleading not guilty," he said.

"Of course," she said without conviction. It looked as if Holly was finally aware of just how much trouble she was in.

Jared's instincts told him she wasn't working with

Transom. Any link between the two was irony rather than conspiracy. He didn't know who he was madder at: Holly for letting things get this far, and for having Keith Transom on her client list, or Transom for filing suit against her. But he did know he wasn't about to let Transom win another battle against an innocent person.

A warning bell sounded in his head. Getting embroiled in her dealings with Transom would be a step too far, would spell the end of any detachment he still had. He ignored the warning. This wasn't about him and Holly. It was about Transom, about Jared's family, about justice.

He didn't have a choice.

"I'm coming with you to your lawyer," he said.

That she didn't argue, that she merely swallowed and nodded, told him just how scared Holly was.

SIMON CROOK didn't want to drive to Marionville to tell Maggie Stephens he'd arrested her daughter. Why couldn't he just call the trailer park and have her brought to the phone?

"Because," Dan Pierce, Crook's boss, had told him earlier while a smirking Slater looked on, "it's got to be more than coincidence that the mother deals drugs and the daughter has stolen a truckload of money."

"Maggie Stephens's last conviction was six years ago," Crook protested. "And she was convicted of growing dope for personal use, not dealing."

Pierce gave him a look that said just because someone hadn't been caught in a few years, it didn't mean they'd gone straight.

"The money's been routed through a series of offshore accounts," Crook persisted. "Maggie Stephens couldn't do that."

"You don't know that," Slater chipped in helpfully. "This story has all the hallmarks of the Perretti case."

The Perretti family of crooked lawyers, doctors and public servants had led the FBI on several wild-goose chases in search of laundered cash. In the end it was pure luck that had led them to the real mastermind: the seventy-eight-year-old Perretti grandmother, resident in a nursing home.

Crook's boss was obviously determined not to expose his team to that kind of embarrassment again.

Crook didn't want to see Maggie Stephens. She persisted in breaking into his thoughts, like a stone that worked its way into your shoe. Crook heard himself whine as he said, "Can't Slater go?"

"Sorry," Slater said smugly. "I'm tracking down the business partner. Fletcher."

"Just go see the woman, Crook," Pierce said. "Take as long as you need to figure out her involvement."

"Have fun with Ms. Wacko." Slater snickered as Crook grabbed his keys and headed out the door.

So here he was, slogging all over the countryside on a lead that would most likely go nowhere, while the young guys got to stay behind and do the real detective work.

It was late afternoon by the time he pulled up outside Maggie's trailer. He got out of the car and fished his badge out of his pocket. This time, his meeting with Maggie would follow procedure to the letter. He wouldn't let her mess around. He eyed the bunch of kids kicking a ball around the parking lot. They eyed him back. A gangly boy, all muscle and sinew in a T-shirt with cutoff sleeves, spoke up. "You a cop?"

Crook locked his car. "Something like that."

"My dad doesn't like cops."

Crook would bet money the feeling was mutual. He thought about giving the kid the lecture that a few years ago would have been automatic. The one about the FBI being there to protect people, helping to make America a safe place for kids like him. He opened his mouth, then closed it again. It was bad enough that he had to talk to Maggie Stephens. He shrugged and headed up Maggie's path.

She opened the door before he reached it, and stood watching his approach. She was every bit as magnificent as last time, her rich russet hair cascading around her face, and her voluptuousness heightened rather than concealed by her faded jeans and man's striped shirt.

"Why, it's Special Agent Melvin Crook." She sounded almost happy to see him.

Already, following procedure to the letter seemed unlikely. He shook his head, refusing to be insulted. "I need to talk to you some more."

Inside, he took the chair she didn't offer him and waited while she settled herself on that lumpy couch.

"How's your investigation going?" she asked. "Have you found who stole Holly's money?"

So she hadn't heard about her daughter's arrest. Unless she was pretending not to know. But Crook didn't buy into the idea of Maggie as criminal mastermind, à la Perretti.

"It's not Holly's money," he pointed out. "It belonged to her clients."

Maggie waved a hand, slim with long, artist's fingers. "But have you found it?"

"No," he admitted.

"And you strike me as so conscientious, Sylvester," she said with a sorrowful shake of the head.

Ninety percent horrified, ten percent flattered that she was flirting, he looked down at the faded linoleum, then around the crowded walls. Anywhere but at the woman in front of him. He took a long moment to remind himself that female suspects sometimes played the flirtation card. When the staccato beating of his heart had returned to its usual measured pace, he chanced a glance back at Maggie. She was looking right at him, still with that curious warmth. His heart started drumming again.

He stood, paced across the room, then clutched at conversation. "Been doing any painting while I've been fighting crime?"

"You tell me."

He spent a minute looking. Then he pointed to a canvas with a mess of bright green swirls. "That's new."

Maggie stared at him. "You're right."

"Being observant is my job," he told her. But he'd surprised himself.

"Of course, you don't like my painting," she reminded him.

He shrugged. "Like I told you, I don't get it. But something about this stuff—" and now that he looked again he realized the jumble of shapes and colors had made an impression on him "—well, maybe it's got something."

"Which one do you come closest to liking?"

Crook knew his boss would see this as a chance to relax Maggie's guard. So he took his time, had a good look at each painting. There were a lot of them. Finally he walked over to a small, square canvas hung next to an age-speckled mirror. White paint, thickly applied, covered the canvas. Black lines crossed it at irregular intervals. And from the top-left corner, what looked like elongated drops of red paint fanned out, becoming sparse by the middle of the painting. "This one," he said, and turned to look at her.

There was no trace now of that flirty look. She knuckled one eye, took a deep breath. "Me, too. It's a portrait of Holly."

Well, he wouldn't have pegged that.

She smiled at his obvious puzzlement. "Holly is so determinedly pure—that's the white. But she puts these constraints on herself, so to me she never seems truly free."

"The black lines," Crook guessed, "are like bars." Like the bars Holly would find herself behind before long.

"That's right."

"What about the red…uh…spots?" he asked.

Maggie was silent a long moment. "Those are a mother's tears."

He wasn't ready for that. Wasn't ready for the tug inside his chest, the regret that made him reluctant to say what had to be said. He pushed the words out. "Maggie, I've come to tell you that Holly will appear in court at three o'clock tomorrow on fraud charges."

Maggie's face whitened and she sank onto the couch. "She didn't do it," she said angrily. "Why are you hounding her like this?"

"All the evidence points to her." He paused in case Maggie wanted to admit her own part in the crime, to save Holly. "An arrest gives us forward momentum. If she's not guilty, it's about now she'll give us anything she can to help us find the real culprit."

"You're telling me it's your job."

He'd known from the start she would feel like that about him, so why should her contempt trigger this scalding feeling behind his ribs? He scowled. "Yes, it's my job, and I'm good at it. But it's more than that. It's what I think is the right thing to do, and I'm damned if I'm going to duck out of that just because I have the hots for you."

Tell me I didn't just say that. Maggie was staring at him, a secretive smile playing on her lips. He'd said it all right. He'd said it, without even knowing he felt it.

But he couldn't feel that way, not about Maggie Stephens. *It's been so long, that's why I let her get under my skin. It's a physical thing. Like an itch. Now Maggie's going to lay a complaint against me. Or else milk this for all it's worth.*

Her next words confirmed his suspicion.

"I need to go to Seattle," Maggie said. "I need to be there for Holly. Can I ride back with you?"

He should say no outright—knock this thing on the head right away. "It's not a trial, just an initial appearance where the charges are read out and she applies for bail. Wouldn't she have told you if she wanted you there?"

Maggie's mouth set in a firm line. "She needs me, she just doesn't know it."

Simon grappled with the suitability of driving a

woman he'd just admitted to lusting after all the way to Seattle. Maggie could claim anything, and it would be his word against hers. On the other hand, the boss wanted him to spend more time with her. And he was a whole lot more comfortable in his car than he was in her trailer.

"If you won't take me, I'll hitch. I'd better start now. It may take a while to get a ride."

Crook groaned inwardly. As if he was about to let her hitchhike. He'd doubtless find himself investigating her murder at the hands of some interstate psycho tomorrow. Wouldn't his boss just love that?

"Forget it. I'll take you." He looked at his watch. It was nearly six. "How soon can you be ready?"

"Fifteen minutes."

True to her word, a quarter hour later she stood in front of him, carrying what looked like a large purse, but which he assumed contained all she'd need for a couple of days away.

By that time Simon had his strategy worked out. She could sit in the backseat of the car. He would use the time to question her about Holly, and as soon as they got to Seattle he would write up his notes. So if later on she accused him of anything, he would have ammunition to fight back with.

Simon preceded Maggie down to the car and opened the rear door. "Hop in."

"Uh, I don't think so."

Simon gritted his teeth. "You have to go in the back, it's FBI policy."

She pointed down. "I don't think we're going anywhere."

The front tire was flat. And it didn't take twenty-twenty vision to see the jagged gash that had destroyed it. Simon cursed, then cursed again when he realized the rear tire was the same. The other side of the car was okay.

"Those kids," he muttered, remembering the youth with the cut-off T-shirt and the cop-hating father.

"I'm sorry." Maggie's regret sounded genuine. "Most of those kids are fine, but one or two…" She kicked at the tire with one of her sandal-clad feet. "What are you going to do?"

"You mean, after I find that kid and have the cops arrest him?" Simon closed his eyes. It wasn't worth the aggravation.

Better to concentrate on getting the tires fixed. Which would mean reporting this to the office. Slater was always dropping hints to Piérce that Crook was off the pace. Pierce would probably think Crook was past it, that if he'd scared the heck out of the kids over those smart-aleck remarks about cops, this would never have happened.

That shouldn't matter since he was about to retire. But he had his pride. He opened his eyes to find Maggie still watching him. "You go inside, while I find that kid."

AN HOUR LATER Crook had scared the kid and his mother—the father didn't live there—enough that they offered to replace the tires. The boy's uncle owned a tire shop, but he wouldn't be able to get ahold of the right ones until morning.

"I'll find a motel in town," Crook told Maggie when he got back to her trailer.

ABBY GAINES 95

"You won't get a room," she said. "It's the American Rose Growers' annual convention. They book the town out every year."

She was right. He borrowed a phone directory from the management office, only to find there wasn't a room to be had.

"You'll have to stay here," Maggie said.

"Here?" Surely she didn't mean…

"In the kids' room," she said, and her eyes gleamed with the knowledge of what he'd been thinking.

He couldn't stay here. Could he? If spending hours in a car with her was fraught with risk, spending a night in the dump she called home would be like rolling around in dead fish then jumping into a pool with a shark.

He looked at her, at the abundant auburn hair he now admitted he wanted to run his hands through, at her womanly figure, at her intelligent eyes. And found himself unable to articulate the reasons he shouldn't stay.

Maggie did it for him. "You don't trust me," she said. "You feel bad about what you said before, and you think I'll take advantage of it."

He acknowledged she was right with a slight nod.

"Nothing is more important to me than getting to Seattle to support Holly." Maggie stuck out a hand. "Let's call a truce, Marvin. I won't accuse you of anything improper, and you'll drive me to Seattle in the morning." She gave a wry smile. "If you're lucky, you'll never see me again."

She meant it. He may not have much left in the way of instincts, but Simon did know Maggie intended to stick with the truce she'd proposed. They could make this work. He would look on it as an extended interview, a chance to question her further about Holly. A growl from his stomach reminded him he'd skipped lunch.

"What's for dinner?" he said, the implied acceptance of her invitation coming easier than an outright yes.

Maggie looked flustered, the first time he'd seen her less than sure of herself. When she stuttered, "I—I can do beans on toast," he realized it was a lack of confidence in her culinary ability. A justifiable lack, by the sound of it.

Crook thought of the meals Sally had cooked him every night through fourteen years of marriage. Then of the microwave meals he mostly dined on alone since Sally died. Life would indeed be spiraling downward if he descended to beans on toast. "I'll take a look at your kitchen," he said, dignifying the cooking alcove with a title it didn't merit.

He found eggs, a couple of soft but not unusable potatoes, milk and a can of tuna. "Got any herbs?" He asked the question without much hope, but Maggie disappeared outside and came back with a handful of freshly picked thyme.

He was chopping it when he spotted the envelope on the crowded counter. The letter was addressed to Maggie. But it was the sticker in the top left-hand corner, bearing the address of the sender, that caught Crook's attention.

He picked it up. "You have a letter from Holly," he said.

Maggie turned from her halfhearted attempts to straighten the room. "It's been there a couple of weeks."

"And you haven't opened it?"

She shook her head. "I'm not planning to."

"Mind if I do?"

Maggie lifted her shoulders, and Simon took that as permission to tear the envelope open. Inside was a single piece of paper, a check. His eyes widened when he read the amount. Was this the link between Maggie and Holly and the missing money? "Do you know what this—?" But he could see from Maggie's closed expression that she knew exactly what he held in his hand.

"Does Holly often send you this much money?" he asked.

"About once a month." She pointed to a shoebox on the shelf above the sink. "Put it in there."

Crook opened the box, to find it stuffed full of checks, all from Holly, all, as far as he could tell, for the same generous sum. "So you're not going to cash this," he said. Maggie didn't reply, and he put the check in the box, then slid it back onto its shelf. He'd noticed the checks dated back several years, so they must have nothing to do with the missing money. If Maggie didn't want to talk about her relationship with her daughter, Crook wasn't going to press the issue until he thought it vital to his investigation. Which right now he didn't, no matter what his boss said. He picked up his knife and went back to chopping.

He made a frittata, a simple, satisfying dish that Sally used to make for supper on nights when he worked late and didn't want to go to bed overly full. Maggie stayed out of his way, but sent curious glances in his direction every so often.

They sat to eat at the Formica table. Crook would

have killed for a beer, but it turned out Maggie didn't drink, didn't keep alcohol in the house.

"This is great." She put her fork down after the first mouthful. "You made it look so easy."

He chuckled, pleased with his own effort. "It's not much harder than beans on toast."

Over dinner, the conversation circled. Crook would ask something about Holly, Maggie would give a minimal answer then change the subject. Other times he would start off on an apparently unrelated topic, then turn it back to Holly, hoping to take Maggie unawares so she might let something slip. Such as when he asked if she'd ever thought about selling her paintings. "Some people like that sort of thing," he said, before he realized how tactless that sounded.

"Incredible," she said, and he began to apologize, until she laughed. "I do sell the occasional painting. There's a second-tier gallery in Portland that takes my stuff, and a café here in Marionville that gets some passing tourist trade. It's only a few hundred dollars at a time, but it makes a difference."

"Is that your only income?" He tried to keep his tone neutral, but she saw right through it.

"I'm not selling dope on the side, if that's what you mean. But actually, marijuana did get me into a business."

"What's that?"

"I used to grow dope out back." She gestured toward the rear of the trailer. "Just for my own use, but I was good at it. When I decided the weed was killing off too many brain cells and it might affect my painting, I ripped it out and planted herbs instead."

"The thyme we had tonight," he said.

"And rosemary, mint, cilantro, basil. The restaurants in Marionville take whatever I can produce. I've been selling my herbs for three years."

"So between that and the painting, you make enough to live on."

"More than enough." Seeing his obvious doubt, she added, "I even put a little money aside each month."

"What for?"

She shrugged. "In case my kids ever need it…. But I don't suppose they will. It's only a couple thousand bucks. One day I'll buy a plane ticket to Italy."

"Italy?"

"You know, that place where all the best painters came from. I've always thought when I run out of ideas, that's where I'll go. Get a top-up of inspiration."

"You mean, for a vacation?"

She shrugged. "Maybe a few months, maybe a few years. I'll wait tables or something, and paint in my spare time."

"But you wouldn't get a work permit."

The look of utter bafflement she sent his way reminded Crook just how different they were. No matter how easy it was to share a meal with her, how easy it was to imagine kissing her—and more than once he'd had to forcibly steer his brain away from that direction—she might as well be in Italy right now, for all the common ground they shared.

IT WAS ONLY nine o'clock by the time they'd tidied the tiny kitchen, but Crook felt wiped out. A man could only handle so much of Maggie's full-on presence.

"Guess I'll hit the sack," he said. Turning, he found himself chest-to-chest with Maggie. "Uh, good night," he said awkwardly.

Once again, she shocked him. She leaned in and kissed him hard on the lips. "Thanks for dinner. Good night...Harry?"

He wanted to be angry about the kiss, to tell her she'd breached their truce. To tell her if she tried anything like that again he'd arrest her for obstruction of justice.

Instead, light-headed, he shook his head to let her know she still hadn't figured out his name.

CHAPTER SEVEN

WHEN THEY LEFT for Seattle the next morning, Simon felt he was driving a perilously thin border between his own legitimate life and the wacky world of Maggie Stephens. For a start, he still hadn't told her his name, though he'd spent nearly twenty-four hours in her company. That was weird in itself. But even weirder was that Simon derived some comfort from this anonymity. After all, he couldn't be getting too interested in a woman if she didn't even know his name.

Maggie didn't make it easy to be with her. He could handle the whole-wheat toast and herbal tea for breakfast. He could even handle the tepid shower in the tiny bathroom that doubled as a laundry. But when she told him about her interstate phobia he began to wonder if he was losing his grip.

"What exactly is 'fear of the interstate'?" he asked, having pulled off the road at her urgent request just as they were about to hit I-5.

"I can't drive on those big roads," she said. "It's not just me. Thousands of people feel the same."

Crook rolled his eyes, catching a glimpse of thousands of nonphobic people on the freeway above them as he did so. "You're not driving. I am."

"I can't be on it at all. It's tachophobia, the fear of speed," she elaborated. "That's what Holly says. Though I'm not scared of all speed, just interstates."

Any other man would have dumped her at the side of the road and let her hitch, psychos or no psychos. Crook counted to ten, making sure to breathe evenly. "So what do we do?"

"There's another road. Highway 101."

He knew the road, though he'd never driven it. It would probably add an hour to their trip. With a sigh, he pulled back out into the traffic, headed away from the interstate.

"Thank you, Matthew."

Simon shook his head. This was going to be a long trip.

An hour into the drive, a thought occurred to him. "Will your fear of speed stop you from flying to Italy?"

"I've flown before without a problem," she said. "I met Andrew, Holly's father, when we were both in the Peace Corps in Tonga. Flying was the only way to get there."

"So your husband was something of an, er, idealist, too."

"Maybe," Maggie said. "I'd been with the Corps for three years when we met. It was Andrew's first project and he left early, when my stint was up. I took it as a sign of his love for me rather than a lack of commitment to the cause." She gazed out her window, as if intent on the view of the Columbia River. "Sometimes you ignore things that give you a clue to a person's true nature. Maybe you just don't want to know. But in your heart, you know the truth."

She might be talking about hearts, but Crook knew she

meant instinct. The thing he struggled with. If he had to go with his gut now, what would it tell him about Maggie?

She's okay.

That's not your gut, that's your libido.

"You know, Crook, you're not a bad guy." Maggie's husky drawl sent a shiver down his spine.

It seemed her thoughts had been running along the same lines as his, evaluating him as he tried to evaluate her. "I'm one of the good guys," he reminded her. "On the side of right."

"You're on the side of the law. It's not always right."

He couldn't in all conscience disagree with her. Hadn't he seen instances where the law had prevailed and the outcome had been just plain wrong? Still, he didn't want to give that much away, so he grunted.

"You could have refused to bring me along today," she said.

"You mean, I had a choice?"

She smiled. "You did a good thing. Maybe not the right thing, but a good thing."

"I wanted to question you, find out more about you and Holly." He couldn't let her believe he'd given her a ride just because he was a nice guy.

"I know. But you could have insisted on taking the interstate."

"You might have done something stupid, like jump out of a moving car."

Maggie closed her eyes and smiled. Crook's unassuming nature appealed to something inside her. She reminded herself that any flirtation with the FBI agent was merely a distraction. She could throw as many phobias and other delays into this journey as she wanted, but it didn't change the facts. At the other end was the daughter who Maggie was certain would reject whatever she offered.

The daughter who needed her.

"IT'S ONLY A PLEA hearing." Jared's rough whisper told Holly she was losing her grip.

She took a slow, deep breath, squared her shoulders and lifted her chin from where it almost grazed her chest. Yes, she was in a courtroom. But she'd done nothing wrong. She was not her mother.

"Attagirl," Jared said.

She frowned at him. "Don't patronize me. I have nothing to feel guilty about—I'm not the one parked illegally right outside the courthouse."

He grinned. "That's more like it."

Her attorney made a shushing sound as the judge entered the courtroom and they all stood.

Special Agent Crook outlined the case against Holly, who pleaded not guilty, and her attorney promised, more out of hope than certainty, a compelling case that would prove her client's innocence.

"I presume there is no custody requirement?" the judge asked.

Holly sucked in a breath. Her lawyer had assured her she wouldn't be taken into custody, but still, hearing the question was a shock.

"Your Honor," the prosecutor said, "we consider Ms. Stephens to be a flight risk, and that remanding her into custody would be the best—"

"Your Honor." Holly's lawyer was on her feet. "My client is prepared to meet whatever bail conditions the court requires. She is determined to defend herself against these charges, of which she is completely innocent."

The judge took a moment to scrutinize Holly. Just when she thought he was going to have them drag her away to a cell, he gave her a small smile and then his face resumed its former stern lines. "I am prepared to accept the defendant is not a flight risk, but the public expects those accused of financial crimes to be treated no more leniently than anyone else. The defendant is charged with stealing a sum beyond the imagining of most Americans, so is released on bail of five hundred thousand dollars," he declared.

Half a million dollars! How could she pay a bond on that sort of bail when her accounts were frozen? Holly opened her mouth to argue, but Jared's hand on her arm stayed her.

"I'll pay the bond," he said.

"You can't do that."

His response was impatience rather than anger at her ingratitude. "I want to get this job done. I need you at the office."

Holly knew there was more to it than that. She might be the best in her field, but Jared could get someone else if he had to. Right now she would accept his explanation, in the interests of getting as far away from this courtroom as possible.

The court was dismissed and, as they turned to leave, Holly's gaze traveled the length of the room. She groaned. "What's *she* doing here?"

"Who?" Jared looked around.

"My mother." With the tiniest movement of her hand, Holly indicated the back row.

As they watched, a woman with thick chestnut hair pushed back behind her ears got hesitantly to her feet and stepped into the aisle. Jared could see that her dress, though clean and pressed, was somewhat shabby. Holly's mother was on the heavy side of curvy, but she still had great legs and slim ankles. She was an attractive woman, though Jared found her obvious charms far less inspiring than Holly's repressed sexiness, which turned him on so painfully.

Holly stopped when they came level with her mother. Jared sensed that if Holly could have, she'd have walked right on by. But it seemed the maternal bond overrode her ability to be incredibly rude, something she reserved for Jared.

"What are you doing here?"

Jared winced at Holly's blunt question, and revised his view.

"Baby, I'm so sorry this is happening to you." Holly's mother wiped her palms on her dress.

"I didn't steal the money," Holly said sharply.

"You don't have to tell me that." At her mother's evident shock, Holly's expression thawed.

"Thanks." Her voice was gruff.

"Is there anything I can do? If you need money, I have—"

"I'm okay, really. I just need to work through this process. They have no evidence. I won't be found guilty."

Her mother looked dubious. "Okay, baby," she soothed.

"Ms. Stephens." Holly turned, but her relief swiftly evaporated. It was a young man, whose thin curls and wire-framed glasses were familiar.

Ed Kelly, the journalist who'd written the Control Freak of the Year piece.

Kelly's expression bore none of the sycophantic admiration he'd started with the last time they met. Which had lasted about ten minutes, until she started to criticize him. His smile had an unpleasant edge, and avid curiosity lit his pale blue eyes behind the glasses.

"Ed." Holly shook his hand warily.

The young man launched right in. "When did you learn about the missing money? How do you intend to prove your innocence?"

"I'm sorry, I can't discuss anything with you," Holly replied with dignity, and felt an approving squeeze of her elbow from Jared.

The journalist turned to the man who'd just offered to hand over half a million dollars if Holly absconded. "What's your involvement with Fletcher & Stephens, Mr. Harding? Are you a client…or a partner?"

For a moment Holly thought Jared might stoop to talk to the journalist—he appeared to be contemplating the question. Then Jared leaned his face so close to Kelly's it could only be called an invasion of personal space. He spoke quietly, but with a controlled fury that had the younger man paling to the same shade as his notebook.

"Stay away from me and stay away from Holly Stephens."

"I'm only doing my—"

Jared swept Holly past the man without another word.

"You shouldn't have threatened him. He'll probably report you," Holly chastised him as they made it to the foyer with Maggie following close behind. "Someone at the FBI must have leaked the story. How else would he have known to be here?" She paused. "Which is totally against the rules—I'm going to file a complaint."

Jared let out an exasperated groan. "There are more important concerns," he said. "Such as your professional reputation."

"I'll be vindicated by the investigation."

"Oh, come on." He jerked her to a stop. "Even if they find Fletcher and the money, there'll be a lot of people only too willing to believe you were involved. It'll be damned hard to pick up the pieces."

Maggie nodded her agreement, and for a moment Holly wavered. What Jared had said held an unpleasant ring of truth. "I'll ask the FBI to issue a statement that I'm innocent. One that's unequivocal."

He snorted. "You're talking about a government agency. They don't know the meaning of the word. We have to get you away from here."

She looked at him, startled. "Why?"

"Kelly was just the start. White-collar crime is hot these days, and with your stellar track record, your fall from grace is too good a story to resist. We already know there's a leak somewhere on my staff, and someone may have seen you going in and out of the building. Transom found you without any trouble—it's only a matter of time until the media track you down."

"Where would I go?" She sounded lost, vulnerable.

Jared stepped back.

He turned to Holly's mother and extended a hand. "I'm Jared Harding, a friend of Holly's."

Holly annoyed him, infuriated him and turned him on, yet somehow he did consider her a friend.

"Maggie Stephens." The older woman met his firm grip with her own.

"You painted the picture Holly has of her father, didn't you?"

He definitely wasn't imagining Holly's annoyance. She made a small squawk of protest. Maggie looked equally uncomfortable, her arms folded defensively across her chest. "I did paint several pictures of my husband. I didn't know Holly still had one."

There was a swift exchange of glances between the two women. Jared discerned coolness in Holly's gaze, pleading in Maggie's.

He pulled Holly aside and asked her quietly, "Where does your mom live?"

"In Marionville, near Portland. I'm not going with her."

"You need somewhere out of town, and you should be with people who'll support you." Jared put a warning hand to her lips. "Listen to me, Holly. The press will be all over you—think Martha Stewart."

She shoved his hand aside. "Martha Stewart is an icon."

He continued as if she hadn't spoken. "If you leave town now, after a day or two you'll be out of sight, out of mind."

"Holly, come stay with me." Maggie had overheard that part, and her quiet urging led, Jared thought, to a softening in Holly's expression.

"I can look after myself."

But Jared heard the yearning, and he guessed Maggie did, too. She reached out and put her arm around Holly's only slightly tense shoulders.

Then Maggie started as she looked past Holly. "Summer's here."

Jared wondered what that had to do with this mess. And besides, September was just around the corner. Summer was almost over.

Ah. A girl was hurrying across the lobby toward them. Jared recognized her from the photo on Holly's bedroom wall.

"Summer." Holly threw her arms around the girl. "I told you not to come."

"Of course I came," Summer said. "I didn't know where you were, so I went to AnnaMae's and she said you'd be in court."

"I didn't want you to worry."

Jared cleared his throat, reminding Holly of his presence.

"This is my sister, Summer," she told him.

Summer was a younger, prettier version of Holly, with dark hair cut spikily short. She wore the briefest of sundresses—she must be freezing in this air-conditioning. Because he knew it would annoy Holly, and he owed her some annoyance, Jared gave the girl an openly appreciative look, even though he found her over-made-up face somewhat vacant. "Pleased to meet you," he said, lowering his voice to the drawl women told him was irresistible.

Holly, clearly able to resist anything he might throw

at her, glared. But Summer, with the easy distraction of youth, forgot her sister's troubles long enough to return his appraisal with equal appreciation, her grin openly flirtatious.

"Hey," she said, and held out a manicured hand.

Her touch did nothing for him, he was relieved to find. It was bad enough that Holly turned him on; he'd have been seriously worried if he'd started lusting after teenagers.

"Summer, this is my *current* employer, Jared Harding."

He figured the emphasis on current was meant to make it clear Holly didn't plan to work for him a moment longer than necessary.

Summer said, "I've come to tell you I'm dropping out of college. You can't afford to pay our fees as well as a lawyer and…and goodness knows what else you have to pay for."

Holly paled. "You are *not* dropping out of college." She grabbed Summer by the elbow and pulled her closer. "Don't worry about the money," she whispered, but not so quietly that Jared couldn't hear. "Jared's paying me a ridiculous amount, and I'll pay your fees on time."

A ridiculous amount? He'd thought the number sounded a shade high—he hadn't realized she was taking him for a ride. And all to pay college fees for a kid who planned to drop out.

Summer was close to tears as she said, "It's not about the money. I shouldn't have said that. I wanted to tell you, only I didn't have the guts, and I thought you might be pleased to have the financial pressure off now that…"

She tailed off, then took a deep, refueling breath. "Hol, I don't want to go to college. I want—"

Whatever Summer wanted was lost as Holly rounded on her mother. "You did this," Holly accused Maggie. "You never wanted her to get an education and now you've talked her into quitting. You can't bear the thought of anyone having a normal life, making something of themselves."

"Baby, that's not true." But the glimmer of hope in Maggie's eyes had been extinguished. "If you really believe that, it's best I go now."

For half a second Holly hesitated. Jared thought she might withdraw the accusation. But then she nodded coldly.

Maggie caught her breath. "I love you." She turned and walked away. Before she'd gone far, Agent Crook detained her with a hand on her arm, and they stood talking.

Holly watched the exchange. "What's my mother saying to that FBI agent? She's so naive, he's probably taking advantage of her to incriminate me."

But Jared noticed the way Crook and Maggie stood very close to each other, and their intent focus. "I think your mom and Crook have something else on their minds. Something personal."

Holly glowered. "Don't be silly." She turned her back on her mother.

Jared sighed. The Stephens family reunion had been about as prickly as he might have expected where Holly was involved. But then, in his experience, family was always more trouble than it was worth. When Crook and

Maggie had moved out of sight he tugged Holly toward the exit. "I'll take you back to the apartment," he said, and added to Summer, "You'd better come, too."

JARED LEFT THEM on the couch while he made coffee, but he was close enough to hear every word of their argument.

"You have to go to college. How else will you get a good job?" Holly demanded.

"I've already found a job—the place I've been working during my vacation."

"A *beauty parlor*."

Holly would have used the same tone to say, "*a brothel,*" Jared figured.

"That's what I want to be. A beautician."

"*No.*"

Jared had to struggle not to laugh. Beautician was so clearly the right job for Summer, and Holly was acting as if her sister had just scuppered her own chances for a Nobel prize.

"Summer, you're too smart for that," Holly said.

"I'm not smart. Not like you are. I've hated every minute at college. My grades are awful." Summer screwed up her face in apology. "I love it at the beauty parlor, Hol, I just love it."

As he took the coffee through, Holly made a visible effort to pull herself together.

"I understand you're not happy," she said in calm understatement. "Let's talk to River about this."

"There's no point," Summer said. "He should be here, too, only he didn't have the guts to tell you himself. He's quitting college, as well."

Holly felt the breath leave her body and she couldn't find any air to suck in. She was aware of her mouth opening and closing while she tried to process the information.

"River wants to be a beautician, too?" she asked stupidly.

Summer tittered as she edged away from Holly, who appeared to be losing her mind. "He wants to be a chef. He's taken a job as short-order cook in the café down the road from Mom."

Holly shut her eyes. She had worked so long, so hard, to give Summer and River a chance to escape the shoddy life their mother had forced on them.

"Holly, are you all right?"

Jared sounded very close. She opened her eyes to find his brilliant blue gaze inches from her face. She read concern in it. And something else. Pity.

She had to say something, anything, to erase the pity. "Okay, Summer, if that's what you guys want—well, I guess I can buy a new car now." Oh, yeah, convincing. Her voice had emerged thin, reedy with unshed tears.

Jared put a hand on her shoulder, and restoring warmth flowed into her. "Holly's going away for a while, Summer. You can call her on her cell phone, but for now you'd better leave."

Summer gave him a glare that would have been worthy of Holly. "I'm not going just because you say so."

Holly patted her sister's hand. "It's okay. You should go. I have a lot to think about."

Still, Summer hesitated.

"I'm fine about the college thing," Holly said. For a

moment Jared thought he'd caught her in a lie. Then she corrected herself. "I *will* be fine, just as soon as I get used to it."

After Summer left, Jared said to Holly, "Pack your stuff. We'll leave after lunch tomorrow."

He strode out the door before she could ask where they were going.

CHAPTER EIGHT

NEXT MORNING, Jared dialed the number that had come in handy on more than one occasion when he'd been setting up a deal that required extra information—special information. Colonel Briggs was available immediately and could be at Jared's office in fifteen minutes. A man who appreciated which side his bread was buttered on, unlike a certain female accountant Jared could name.

Jared spent the time writing down the essentials of the case. The Colonel would take his own notes, but Jared might as well be sure they were on the same wavelength.

When his assistant tapped on his office door, he rose to greet the visitor.

"M'boy." The Colonel's grip was as fierce as ever.

"Colonel." Jared always enjoyed meeting with the retired British soldier. It was refreshing to be able to skip the small talk without being considered rude.

They sat at the meeting table in one corner of the office, and Jared briefed him.

"If I may clarify…" Colonel Briggs launched into a recap of his client's instructions. "This David Fletcher has absconded with around six million dollars. You want me to track him down and report to you on his where-abouts. Will I be treading on anyone else's toes?"

"The Feds are investigating, but they're focusing on Fletcher's business partner for now." Jared passed over the photo of Holly he'd torn from the control-freak article.

The Colonel gave a dignified snort. "Can be an asset to a criminal, a face that honest."

"She's innocent."

"Common name, David Fletcher. Do you have passport details, any information about contacts over-seas?"

"No passport details." Jared suspected Holly would have them, but she was unlikely to cooperate in an un-official investigation. "His mother came from New Zealand. He may have dual citizenship, or at least have contacts there he could hide out with. You'll find his photo on the company Web site."

Briggs harrumphed. It was more information than Jared had given him on other jobs. "And the budget?"

"Whatever you deem necessary." Jared knew the in-vestigator to be frugal, preferring the anonymity of chain motels and restaurants to the chance to splash money around. "Just keep me informed. I'm heading out of town this afternoon, but you can get me on my cell phone."

There was nothing left to say that mattered, so the Colonel departed. Jared expected to hear no more until the older man had some concrete progress to report. No point mentioning this to Holly until then.

WHEN HOLLY CLIMBED into Jared's Saab on Wednesday afternoon, he handed her the *Seattle Post-Intelligencer*.

The front-page headline jumped out: CPA In FBI
Probe. And beneath it ran her photo, the one they'd
used when she was named Washington Businesswoman
of the Year.

Just her luck that Ed Kelly would freelance for Seattle's
top newspaper. Thankfully she hadn't said enough to the
journalist to be quoted directly, but the disappearance of
millions of dollars of clients' funds made ugly reading.
And though Dave Fletcher was named in the report, too,
it was Holly's photo plastered across the page. "Stephens
would not comment, and the firm's clients refused to
discuss the matter," the article concluded.

That last was not out of loyalty to the firm, Holly suspected, but out of a desire not to show themselves stupid
enough to have invested with a crooked accountant. She
bit her lip, suddenly relieved that she'd given in to
Jared's order to leave town. Only he and the FBI would
know where she was.

"Where are we going?" It was a measure of her pre-
occupation that the question hadn't occurred to her
before now.

"To Kechowa, over the North Cascades. My parents
live there."

"Your parents!"

"It's not my idea of a good time, either, but I was due
to visit next week, anyway, so I thought we'd head out
a few days earlier."

"What do they think about my coming with you?"

"They don't know." At her outraged gasp, he added,
"They're used to me bringing a woman along."

"I am *not* a woman."

"I wondered about that myself, the way you're so—"

"You know what I mean. I'm not the kind of woman you…date."

Jared eyed her purple bustier-style dress with its short skirt and laced-up bodice. He fought the inevitable rise in blood pressure. "In that getup, you're not too far off the mark."

"Gee, thanks." Holly sank back into her seat in disgust. "We'd better stop on the way so I can buy some clothes. I can't wear Summer's stuff out in public."

Jared didn't bother to answer that. As he turned onto I-5 north and put his foot to the floor, she craned toward him. He realized she was trying to see the speedometer.

"The limit is sixty until you get out of town. Slow down," she ordered.

He pressed down harder on the gas and heard her mutter something that might have been, "Pathetic."

He grinned as he shot into the fast lane and headed north.

JARED SPENT the first two hours of the three-hour drive to Kechowa wondering if he'd made a big mistake, bringing Holly with him on a trip that was bound to be fraught with tension.

He didn't have time to play nursemaid to Seattle's most wanted woman, and he didn't want to be in a position where he owed his parents anything. And he hated the fact that returning to the mountain town where he'd grown up still gave him the heebie-jeebies.

He glared at Holly, who, oblivious, was showing an obscene disregard for the perils of motion sickness by reading EC Solutions' financial accounts. Just glancing at her as she read made Jared feel queasy on this winding stretch of the North Cascade highway. Still, at least she didn't want to talk.

He'd bet her intense focus on her work was designed to stop her thinking about the twins dropping out of school, which for some reason seemed to matter even more to her than being charged with fraud.

Jared wondered why he should feel angry on Holly's behalf. He was all in favor of people, in this case Summer and River, making choices to suit themselves rather than the expectations of well-meaning traditionalists, in this case Holly. That he should now be siding with Holly, even applying the word "ungrateful" to her siblings, was galling.

"You were mean to your mother yesterday," he said, to remind himself she deserved all she got.

It took around ten seconds for his words to seep through her concentration. The way Holly's head belatedly jerked up was almost comical. "I was not."

"Yes, you were."

"If I was—" Jared had known her honesty wouldn't let her deny it again "—she deserved it."

"Why?" he asked. "I can see she might not have been the kind of mother who stayed in the kitchen baking cookies." There had been something too untamed about Maggie Stephens for that. "But she seemed nice enough."

"You're wrong about the cookies." Holly gave him a hard, bright smile. "My mom's specialty was hash cookies."

"Hash cook—as in marijuana?"

"Uh-huh. But to give credit where it's due, she didn't let us eat them."

"Wow." Jared absorbed the news of Maggie Stephens's unusual culinary habits. "So she ate them herself?"

"Sure did. She and her friends would sit outside the trailer on a summer's evening and they'd eat their hash cookies."

"I suppose she drank wine from a bottle in a brown paper bag, as well?" he asked, wondering if Holly was spinning him a line. He found it hard to believe she'd lived in a trailer.

She smiled faintly. "Mom's a teetotaler. And before you ask, there were no 'uncles' around, either. At least, not when I was there. Dope is her only and occasional vice, in the accepted sense of the word."

"But you consider she had other vices."

Holly couldn't voice the bitter memories that colored her childhood. How strange that she couldn't bring herself to betray her mother when she had no respect and little love for the woman. She decided her reluctance stemmed from fear that Jared would pity her.

"There are some things that matter to Mom, and some that never will," she said at last. "She didn't care that we didn't dress like other kids, didn't eat like them, didn't have a father around after Dad left. Actually, I don't think she even noticed. She was always in her own world."

Holly leaned forward and fiddled with the vent until she got the air flow just right.

"But she cared a lot about her causes. The threat of

nuclear war under Reagan in the eighties was a biggie, then the Rwanda crisis. Mom would head to L.A., D.C., wherever, to join protest marches."

"Did she take you guys along?" Jared tried to imagine Holly on a protest march.

"Uh-uh. From when I was twelve, she'd leave me to look after the twins. I guess they were four or five years old."

He frowned. He didn't know much about kids, but twelve sounded young to be babysitting for days at a time. "Did you cope okay?"

"Barely. I could do the basics of putting food on the table and getting us all to school. But I felt so...alone. Not knowing where Mom was, not able to get ahold of her in an emergency." She shivered. "At nights, after the twins were in bed, I'd get scared. I'd sleep in Mom's bed and I always wanted to pull the covers right over my head, but I was afraid I wouldn't hear the twins if they called."

"What about your father? Grandparents? Couldn't they look after you?"

"Mom had argued with Nana—her mother—and didn't want her involved. She wouldn't let me tell Nana when she was going away." Holly shrugged, stared out the passenger window. "Nana died when I was fourteen, anyway. And Daddy..."

She used the childish name, her memories of her father suspended when she was eight years old. "He was an accountant." She smiled a wry acknowledgment of Jared's raised eyebrows. "He left on my eighth birthday and he never came back. He said he'd call me, but..."

Jared's mouth twisted. "Why did he go?"

"He couldn't cope with *her*."

That one word—*her*—had a thousand meanings. The disgraceful state of their clapboard house. The endless hours Mom spent painting. And her refusal to look after Daddy. The twins he'd always said he'd never wanted, but Mom had gone ahead and had anyway...

So when her father didn't call, didn't come back, Holly had known exactly who to blame. And when they'd had to move out of the clapboard house and into Nana's house. And later, after Mom argued with Nana, when they'd moved to the trailer park.

Without their father, the thin glue of normalcy that held them together evaporated. With no one to call time on her, Mom retreated further into herself. And the less regular the meals, the less ordered their existence, the more Holly drew on her diminishing store of memories of her father.

Daddy said I must always do my homework. Daddy said if you're good at math, you're good at life. Daddy said a healthy body means a healthy mind. When she'd first started parroting his views, she hadn't known what they meant, only that they brought routine to her life. By the time she understood, they were her lifeblood.

"The twins and I never fit in at school," Holly told Jared. "We dressed oddly, everything a couple of sizes too small, falling apart. Other kids notice that stuff. So do their parents. I...found it difficult. Knowing I had a normal father out there somewhere helped." Helped when Mom had turned up at school an hour late for her teacher interview, wild hair uncombed, bedroom slip-

pers still on her feet, only to bawl the teacher out for
"not teaching these kids a damn thing about how to
look after the world they live in."

"Your mom took it hard, then? Your dad leaving?"

Holly noticed the forest was thinning and glanced at
her watch. They must be getting close to Kechowa. "I
guess she did." She hadn't really thought about it before.
"Yes, she was upset. She'd painted lots of pictures of him.
I remember her breaking them up and burning them."

"But you still have one."

"I hid it under my mattress. Mom wasn't the sort of
housekeeper who'd ever find anything there. I know
Dad was in contact with her after he left, but she didn't
tell me where he was."

And Holly had never forgiven Maggie, for that or for
robbing them of a normal life.

"Your dad's never made contact with you directly?"

"Not even when Mom went to prison."

"Prison!"

She chuckled. "Just for a week or two at a time. She
was arrested during protest marches a few times, charged
with disturbing the peace and smoking dope. We never
had any money to bail her, so she'd be in for a few days
until whatever organization she was protesting for paid
her fine. I looked after the twins, and we never told
anyone she was gone. But I did wonder if my father
might read about Mom's convictions in the newspaper."

"No wonder you're screwed up."

"I am not screwed up. I just happen to prefer a more
orderly existence than my mother's."

"Did you ever try to contact your father?"

Holly hesitated. "I guess after so long I chickened out."

"Holly Stephens chicken? Never."

She ignored the warm glow his assessment kindled. "Well, whatever the reason, I didn't. And chances are, he'll have read that I'm under investigation." She'd hoped he would have read about her being Businesswoman of the Year. If he had, it hadn't spurred him to contact her. She didn't need to state the obvious about the conclusion her father would draw from the latest reports. Like mother, like daughter. She couldn't even think about finding her father until she'd cleared her name.

THEY DROVE OVER the riverbridge into Kechowa at four o'clock. Holly pressed the button to lower her window and breathed in the fresh mountain air.

"It's hot," she said, surprised.

"It's often up in the nineties, sometimes over a hundred, here in summer."

"Remember, I want to stop and buy some clothes," she said. "Just a skirt and some pants, a couple of blouses."

"Just tell me when you see a store you like the look of," he said, unusually helpful.

She soon saw why he could afford to be helpful. The main street was cute, with its wooden boardwalks and frontier-style buildings, but it was no shopping mecca. A couple of stores displayed souvenir T-shirts and baseball caps, and an old-fashioned candy shop tempted her, but for the wrong reasons.

No Nordstrom, no Gap… Just a menswear store, and one called…

"Schott's Bicycles and Lingerie." Holly stared at the

fancy red stenciling over the top of the window. "That's kinky."

"I would have thought it's your kind of store," Jared said.

"But what's the connection between bicycles and lingerie?"

His gaze flicked over the low-cut neckline of her dress. "I'm sure I could think of one, given some encouragement."

Holly folded her arms across her chest. "You knew there'd be nowhere for me to buy clothes here. You should have stopped before we left Seattle."

He grinned. "But, honey, I like you just the way you are."

By the time they reached the far end of town and turned into his parents' dead-end street, the lightness of his banter with Holly had evaporated and Jared's mood was black. The paneled front door of the two-story brick house, the last house on the road, opened before he'd turned off the engine.

His parents appeared to battle briefly in the doorway for the privilege of being first to welcome them. It was Dad's innate courtesy, Jared supposed, that allowed Mom to win and to jog down the front steps ahead of him. Jared scowled. What was the big hurry? They all knew this week would be torture.

He wiped the scowl off his face as he got out of the car. He wasn't here to argue with his parents. He would keep his distance, emotionally if not physically, get through this annual ritual, get some work done, then get the hell back to Seattle.

Holly figured it would be a waste of time to wait for Jared to come around and open her door. She clambered out and stood next to the car while his mother hugged him and his dad slapped him on the back and pumped his hand. She noted the lack of enthusiasm in Jared's response.

"Mom, Dad, this is Holly Stephens." Jared motioned her forward.

Mrs. Harding, who had the kind of compact, rotund figure so many short women end up with later in life, blanched as she took in Holly's attire. It was hard to get beyond that fashion statement to Holly's face, but eventually the older woman managed it. She looked Holly hard in the eyes, and a flicker of relief crossed her face. And when Holly extended her a hand, Mrs. Harding ignored it and enveloped her in a rose-scented hug.

Holly began the process of easing back and reclaiming her personal space as soon as she decently could. "Nice to meet you, Mrs. Harding."

"Call me Beth. It's wonderful to meet you." Beth's blue eyes, a warmer version of Jared's, sparkled in welcome.

"It's kind of you to have me," Holly said stiffly, unsure if Jared was about to spill the story of her court case and why she was here in Kechowa.

"I can't remember the last time Jared brought a girl home."

"Mom, Holly works for me. This is business."

So he wasn't planning to tell them. Yet. Holly let out a small breath, relieved.

"Of course it is, sweetie." Beth blew him an airy kiss. "But she seems very nice. Are you sure—?"

"Quite sure," Holly said quickly, certain the sound behind her was Jared grinding his teeth. "We have a lot of work to do, and we need somewhere quiet."

"As the grave," Jared chipped in sourly, ignoring his mother's hurt look.

Beth showed Holly to an upstairs bedroom with a large single bed covered by a blue-and-green-striped counterpane. Football trophies ranged along the wooden bookshelf, and pennants, faded with age, adorned the light-blue walls.

"This is Greg's room," Beth said. "Our oldest son."

Holly struggled to equate this picture of suburban normalcy with the Jared she knew. A middle-class home, two evidently loving, straight-up-and-down parents, a college-football-star older brother. How did this environment produce a man who acted as if normal was a dirty word?

Jared had disappeared with his bag into the room next to hers. His old bedroom, presumably. She stifled the sudden consuming desire to know what story his walls would tell.

After Beth left, Holly unpacked her things, then took her toiletry kit along the hall to the bathroom.

"Oh." She stepped into the small room before she realized it was occupied. Jared had also decided to freshen up, which in his case involved taking off his shirt. There was about a foot of space between Holly and his bare back. Worse, when he turned to face her, she was eyeballing his chest.

Which was, quite simply, the perfect male chest. Muscled, firm, broad where it should be and tapering down over abs a gym addict would envy.

"Sorry. I didn't know you were in here," she said, addressing his nipples.

"You could try knocking," he suggested.

"You could try locking the door."

"I'll be done in a minute, if you want to wait." He looked at his watch and the movement distracted Holly enough that she could bring her gaze up to his face. "Dinner's at six."

His tone made it clear he thought eating dinner at six o'clock obscenely early. So did Holly, but she wasn't about to agree with him.

OVER DINNER—roast lamb scented with garlic and rosemary, just the kind of comfort food Holly adored—she answered the senior Hardings' questions about her business. Since they didn't actually ask, "Are you being investigated by the FBI?", she didn't feel obliged to mention that.

"Your parents must be very proud of you," Beth said. "Having your own firm and doing so well."

"No—well, maybe—I don't know." Her dithering caused an exchange of concerned glances between Jared's parents, and Holly rushed to change the subject.

"You must be proud of Jared," she said. And because his mother's instant and unqualified agreement elicited something like a faint snort from the man himself, Holly hurried on. "What about your other son, Greg?" she asked. "Is he in business, too?"

For a second the silence filled the room.

"Greg has passed on," Beth said. At the same time, Edward said, "Greg's not with us anymore."

But Jared's stark declaration overrode both of them. "Greg's dead."

CHAPTER NINE

HOLLY CLAPPED A HAND to her mouth. "I'm so sorry."

"You couldn't have known," Beth said kindly. "And you haven't upset us. It's been twenty years now—Greg was a lot older than Jared. We never stop missing him, but after so long the pain isn't as sharp."

There it was again, that faint snort from Jared. What was he playing at? Couldn't he see the hurt in his mother's eyes, the stiffening of his father's shoulders?

Holly was at a loss for what to say next. "I'm so sorry," she finally said again, feeling inadequate. To her relief, Beth started clearing plates.

"Come help me serve the cheesecake," she invited Holly.

NEXT MORNING Holly and Jared set up in the office, a second-floor bedroom that had been converted to a working space. It faced east, so the morning sun streamed through the windows, picking up dust motes in the air.

Holly opened her laptop on one side of the large desk, while Jared did the same with his on the other.

"We have everything we need here—printer and Internet connection," he said. "I keep this place set up for when I'm visiting."

"Do you come here often?"

He grinned at the old pick-up line. "Once a year."

She raised an eyebrow. "The town looked beautiful when we drove through it. With the mountains all around, I'd have thought it would be the perfect place to de-stress."

"I don't get stressed."

If that was true, why did his repressed rage seem even more apparent here in Kechowa?

"I like your parents," she said.

It was true. She'd liked Beth right away and she felt an affinity with Edward's more cautious manner. Jared's father was tall and dark like his son, but that's where the resemblance ended. Though they'd only been here a day, Jared moved about his parents' house with an edgy restlessness. In contrast, Jared's father seemed to measure each pace. Both men had confidence—Jared's in himself, Edward's in the orderliness of his world.

But while Jared's warmth inevitably seemed fueled by impatience, anger—or desire—Edward's warmth came from a shy cordiality. He'd been reserved to start off, but by the end of the previous evening he'd been chatting freely.

Edward didn't deserve the hostility directed at him by Jared every time he spoke.

"Why are you so horrible to your father?" Holly demanded. "He's a sweet man."

Yeah, that was Dad, all right, Jared thought. Sweet as sugar and just about as good for you.

"I'm not horrible," he retorted. "We're just not close. You of all people should understand that."

"Your parents are very close to each other," she said. "I don't know what went wrong with you."

"When two people have been married that long, I guess they turn into clones of each other," Jared said. "If that's what you mean by close."

"I mean, they seem to communicate in some kind of secret language. *That's* what I call close."

He stared at her, baffled. "What are you talking about?"

She sighed with exaggerated patience. "Your father talks to your mother without words. He says something with his eyes and she says something back. Surely you've noticed?"

"I've noticed they don't talk much," he said. "I think you'll find that's because they've run out of things to say. Not because they have some imaginary secret language."

"Oh, brother. You really are—"

"We're not here to talk about my family," he said, angry. "If you've got anything to say about the Wireless World acquisition, go ahead. Otherwise, shut up."

"I do have something to say about Wireless World, as a matter of fact."

She had that crusading light in her eyes again.

"Go ahead," he said wearily.

"The Greersons have built this business into the dominant player in the South—"

"I know. That's why I'm buying it."

She ignored the interruption. "There's no doubt they have considerable skill on both the technical and operational sides. As far as I can tell, they've only made one mistake."

Leaving Wireless World vulnerable to takeover by

Jared. He made winding motions with his hand, to give her the idea she should skip the details.

She pursed her lips. "They won't welcome your acquisition, and I daresay you're planning to fire the lot of them."

So she was familiar with his standard practice. Big deal.

"Family stockholders take this kind of deal too personally," he said, irritated that he felt obliged to justify his course of action. "It clouds their judgment and they end up sabotaging the business."

"The Greersons wouldn't do that. They've put everything into that company."

"However unintentionally," he continued, "they end up causing trouble. I don't need that during the transition."

"Why not give them a chance?" She pushed a piece of paper across the desk to him. "I've had some thoughts about how you could employ various members of the family. You don't have to keep them in the same roles they have now, but you could still benefit from their knowledge."

His face darkened. "You're not my personnel manager, and I'm not paying you to develop your own pet theories. If you've got something useful to say, say it. Otherwise—"

"Shut up," she supplied for him. "I just thought—"

"This isn't a movie where the softhearted, beautiful accountant persuades the hard-bitten executive to give up his callous plan and everyone comes out happy. This is business. Being nice doesn't come into it."

Holly opened her mouth to protest, then closed it

again. Had he just called her beautiful? Flustered, she changed the subject. "About EC Solutions."

Jared was reluctant to pick up on her cue. Trouble was, even if he did fool her and he got his revenge on Keith Transom, the day would come when Holly would realize exactly what Jared had done, and the part she'd played in it. Worse than her fury would be the betrayal she'd feel.

Because although Holly might have come into this project thinking him a sleazy jerk, Jared knew he'd earned her respect. But what he was planning to do with Transom went well beyond even Jared's own ethical boundaries.

For that, Holly would despise him.

Jared looked across the desk at her, where she sat seemingly oblivious to his scrutiny, eyes focused on her screen, her lips pursed.

The room seemed suddenly stifling, and he had to escape. "Come for a walk. Let's get some air."

Holly took it as an olive branch—damn her—and her mouth curved into a generous smile that sucked the air out of Jared's lungs. "Sure," she said, and she was out the door ahead of him before he could tell her he'd changed his mind, he'd rather go alone.

They walked through the woods that started at the end of the backyard, where oak trees gave way to dense stands of pine and maple. The ground beneath their feet was dry, and sunlight filtered through the canopy above them. Holly took a deep, appreciative sniff of the pervasive, cleansing scent of pine.

"Don't you just want to bottle this and take it with you?" she demanded.

"That's what Greg used to say." Jared could have kicked himself. He didn't want to talk to Holly about his brother.

When she didn't speak for a full half minute, he thought maybe she hadn't heard.

"Were you close to your brother?"

No such luck. She'd obviously been worrying about the best way to broach the subject.

"Close enough," he muttered. Above his head, the low-pitched caw of a raven mocked him.

"Did you play football, too?"

"One quarterback in the family was enough."

"You were jealous of Greg." It wasn't a question.

"I was *not* jealous." He saw her lips press together in a determined effort not to contradict him. "Okay, I admit I had some…younger brother issues. Show me the family that doesn't. Greg and I were very different kids, but Mom and Dad accepted that. Greg was fifteen years older than I was."

And that made Jared an afterthought. Why had his parents needed a second son, when the first was all but perfect? No wonder they'd never expected Jared to live up to Greg, never encouraged him to go into football or taken an interest in his passions. Okay, so maybe he had been somewhat jealous. "The age gap meant we weren't best buddies. But I…loved him."

Holly scuffed through the undergrowth. "How did he die?"

Jared took his time before he answered. "He killed himself."

"Oh, Jared." In her voice, he heard a wealth of sorrow. To his surprise, she took his hand in hers, squeezed it. When she would have withdrawn, he laced his fingers through hers and held on. For maybe another minute they walked like that, hand in hand. And because she didn't ask how, why, he wanted to tell her.

"Greg was brilliant at everything. A scholar, football player—and when he'd finished his degree he got a job with IBM. Blue chip, that was Greg."

They came to a clearing, and Jared guided Holly to a picnic table in the center. The rough, bird-stained surface didn't look as if anyone had lunched there in a while. They sat on the bench seat, side by side.

"Greg was ambitious, so after five years at IBM he went out on his own, started a software company. Did great, of course. Better than anyone expected—though I always knew he'd make it."

"Then what?" Holly said at last.

"He started the business with financial backing from a private investor—a loan, rather than a stake. If there was going to be a huge financial gain, Greg wanted it all for himself." Jared shook his head. "It's not as if his problem wasn't anything that millions of companies haven't gone through before."

"Cash flow."

"Yep. He made a couple of huge sales—they would be worth millions when the dollars came in. But the product needed refinement first. That cost money, and Greg didn't have it."

"And banks are reluctant to lend money for software development without concrete assets to secure the loan," Holly said. There wasn't an accountant in Seattle, home to software legends such as Microsoft, who hadn't learned that.

Something skittered among the trees behind her, and she twisted in alarm.

"It's just a squirrel. Or a weasel," Jared said, putting his hand over hers. "Greg went to his original backer, gave him the projections, asked for more money. And the guy came through. Greg was over the moon. He didn't read the loan agreement too carefully."

Despite the fact that it had already happened, that the course of history wouldn't be changed by this recounting, dread pooled in Holly's stomach. "What happened?"

"As soon as Greg spent past the point of no return, the guy recalled the new loan. And the original one, too."

"Oh, no."

Jared nodded grimly. "The banks didn't want to know. Overnight, the business was gone, taken over by Greg's supposed backer."

"And that's when—?"

"He didn't have to do it!" His fist thudded into the brittle wood of the table. "Why kill himself over...what? A bunch of programmers and a few lines of code? Greg could do anything. He wasn't even thirty years old. If he'd started again he'd have been back up there in no time."

He took a minute to collect himself; Holly stared at the whorls of a knot in the pine table. "It was the first time he'd failed. Nothing in our perfect family life had prepared him for it, and he didn't know how to handle it."

From the flatness in his voice, Holly could tell Jared had been over his brother's death a million times until he'd salvaged this explanation, poor though it was.

"Is that what your parents think?"

He shrugged.

"If they do, they may blame themselves," she suggested.

"Sometimes," he said slowly, "I wonder if their love for him died when his business failed. If it was so out of character for him to disappoint them, that they couldn't handle it."

"You can't mean that." Not when Holly had seen the still-raw hurt in Beth's eyes.

"They were so calm, so accepting of his death. It wasn't natural."

"What else could they have done?"

"They could have gone after…the guy who called in the loan. Sued him. Not for the money—" he forestalled Holly's next comment "—but for the principle. That bastard drove my brother to suicide, and was rewarded with a juicy business he's made millions off. Why should he have gotten away with it?"

"Have you talked to them about it?"

He shook his head. "I was fourteen when Greg died. I ranted and yelled, but they didn't listen. So we stopped talking, all of us." He scowled. "Which suited Mom and Dad just fine. They couldn't stand the stigma of having a kid who killed himself—knowing that everyone was talking about it. They were happy to forget Greg ever existed."

"But—"

He cut off her protest. "I went away to college a few years later and we haven't discussed it since."

"You going into the Internet business," Holly began tentatively. "You were following in Greg's footsteps?"

He shook his head. "That's where the similarity between me and Greg ends. After he died, I went off the rails awhile—petty theft, stuff like that. I think I was trying to tell Mom and Dad not to expect me to fill Greg's shoes, that I'd never be the golden boy."

"What got you back on track?"

"Believe it or not, I didn't have it in me to be really bad." He ran a hand through his hair, tipped his face up into the sun. "I guess like anyone who's behaving that way, it dawned on me it wasn't making me happy."

Holly knew the hopelessness of that realization. You put all your effort, your focus into one thing, only to wake up one day and realize it would never be enough, that something of supreme importance was missing.

"Wh-what does make you happy? Your business?"

He looked at her almost with dislike, as if he didn't want to think about it.

"I know what *can't* make me happy," he said. "I can't be happy with an existence that's a lie—the sort of life I grew up in, where everything seemed fine, where we looked just like everybody else. But something underneath was so rotten my brother killed himself the first time he made a mistake."

"But not all normal lives are rotten beneath the surface."

"Maybe not, but I never want to be so deluded that a bit of bad news could kill me." He stood, extended a hand to pull Holly to her feet. "In this world, you go after what you want. If you don't get it, you cut your losses. No hard feelings to chase you to your grave."

"Is that how you feel about the guy who called in your brother's loan? No hard feelings?"

A hunted expression crossed Jared's face, then it turned arctic. "Let's get back." He turned and walked away from her.

CHAPTER TEN

IT DIDN'T TAKE A rocket scientist to figure out that Jared's parents were falling in love with Holly. Wasn't she the kind of woman any parent would dream of for their son? Pretty, smart, polite and deferential—in complete contrast to her attitude to Jared. And worst of all, she thrived on the cozy domesticity that had Jared pacing in front of the living room windows like a caged tiger.

Jared had brought women home before, partly to relieve his boredom, partly to reassure his parents and their neighbors, who inquired after him all the time. He was straight, he had a life. And Mary Jo, Helena, Cecie, whoever, was the proof. But he'd always taken care not to get his parents' hopes up. None of the others had been daughter-in-law material. Attractive, sure, but they were lucky to have enough cells to make one brain between them. They were more likely to smirk and say, "This is so cute," to Mom's pot roast than they were to attack it with the gusto that Holly applied to everything she ate. They certainly wouldn't have helped clear away after dinner, showed genuine interest in Dad's stamp collection or taken crochet lessons from Mom.

He didn't date dorky women.

So how his mother could be casting speculative looks

from him to Holly whenever she thought Jared wasn't looking was beyond him.

Yes, he'd felt…close to Holly after he told her about Greg when they'd walked together on Saturday afternoon. But that was because she'd caught him at a weak moment. After that, he'd kept things strictly impersonal, Jared assured himself as he stood in the kitchen making coffee on Monday.

Holly was taking a walk outside—he could see her now, through the slats of the wooden blinds above the sink, talking to his father in the garden. No doubt Dad was boring her with the story of his prize-winning camellia. And no doubt Holly wouldn't be bored.

"She's a lovely girl," Beth said behind him.

Jared jumped, slopping hot coffee over his hand. "Ow." He glared at his mother as he turned the faucet on and stuck his hand under the cold water. "Now look what you made me do."

"I must admit, when Holly first arrived, I wasn't sure what to make of her. Those clothes she wears…"

Jared couldn't help grinning as he peered through the blinds to check out, for only about the fiftieth time today, Holly's extremely short denim cutoffs and her bright green, midriff-baring tank top.

"I guess I'm getting used to the clothes," his mother said. "Underneath them is the sweetest, kindest girl."

Jared stifled a snort. Underneath those clothes was some of the sexiest lingerie this side of the Rockies.

Beth took a deep breath, "I know you say this is only a working relationship, dear—"

"That's right," he said coldly to forestall the inevitable "but."

"But—" *so much for that idea* "—I get the impression you like her."

"I like her," he said, and realized it was true. "But that's all." Except he wasn't so sure about the veracity of that. He considered telling his mother Holly was an FBI fraud suspect—that would put an instant end to this love affair between his accountant and his ultraconservative parents—but reluctantly dismissed the idea. "We have to work pretty closely, so it helps to like her. But she's not my type. I don't want to have sex with her."

He'd been deliberately crude, knowing it would deter Mom from pursuing the subject. Pink rose in Beth's cheeks, telling him he'd succeeded.

"I don't want to have sex with you, either," Holly said from the doorway. She walked into the room, hips swinging with exaggerated casualness, but her gray eyes smoldering. "Now that we're both clear on that," she said sweetly, "can I have my coffee?"

Oh, hell.

Beth gave him an amused smile—*get yourself out of this one, son*—and left the room with a murmured excuse.

Jared decided not to hand the mug over to Holly yet, just in case the contents ended up thrown back in his face. He moved to stand between her and the cups. "I'm sorry," he said. "Mom was in matchmaker mode and I said the first thing I thought of to shut her up. I knew she wouldn't want to hear about my sex life."

"No need to apologize." Holly's ability to keep her voice so pleasant while her eyes hardened to slate would have terrified a lesser man. "You said what you meant. I appreciate honesty, as you know."

"That's not what I meant at all."

"You mean, you *do* want to sleep with me?"

If someone could just hand him a shovel, maybe he'd dig this hole even deeper. "I've never thought about it." But now that she mentioned it, he was shocked at the pictures that flashed through his mind. He stared at her, aghast.

"Good," she said calmly. "And don't start thinking about it, either. Because I meant it when I said I don't want to sleep with you."

He snickered, and she gave a little exclamation of outrage. "Are you saying you don't believe me?" she demanded.

"That's exactly what I'm saying." No way did he believe the awareness between them was all on his side. He'd seen her stiffen at his touch, seen the flare of panicked excitement in her eyes. He knew the response of her mouth to his.

"You're despicable."

Holly getting all hot under the collar was a sight a man just had to take a moment to enjoy. Not that her green top had a collar—the heaving of her bosom was all too visible. Jared folded his arms and smirked, which enraged her all the more, as he knew it would. Her eyes sparked and her luscious mouth quivered with fury.

"I believed *you* when you said you didn't want to sleep with me," she sputtered.

"I lied."

"Well, I didn't." And when he laughed she added, "You know I don't lie."

"True," he said thoughtfully. "You wouldn't lie intentionally. But if you didn't *know* you wanted to sleep with me…" He advanced on her, and she backed away in alarm.

Until she reached the stove and could back no farther.

"You really should make an informed decision," he said smoothly, imprisoning her against the stove with one hand on either side of her.

"Don't you dare." A stupid thing to say to a man who relished doing what he was told not to. All Holly had to do was to turn her head away, to get her mouth out of his path…. But for the life of her she couldn't.

She knew he was a good kisser, but she hadn't expected the scorching pressure of his lips to part her own without even a second's consideration. This was no experimental kiss, this was full-on making out. At the first thrust of his tongue, something inside her melted into heated liquid. She gasped, and the hands she'd put up to ward him off clutched his shoulders in the interests of keeping her on her feet.

Then Jared's hands moved to the bare skin of Holly's waist and his touch made her jerk, the movement bringing her right up against the solid wall of his chest.

His low growl told her just how much he liked having her there and he deepened the kiss, sending impulses out to every nerve ending until she tingled all over. He cupped her bottom with one hand, pulling her against his hardness, reminding her of the question that had started this kiss.

Holly tore her mouth from his, gave him a shove that, catching him unawares, sent him backward a pace or two.

"No," she almost shouted. "I do *not* want to sleep with you."

The heat in his eyes turned from passion to anger, and for a moment she feared—hoped?—he would take her in his arms again and make her retract the words.

Instead he laughed softly. "Liar." Nonchalant, he picked up a mug of coffee, then left the kitchen.

KISSING HOLLY AGAIN had been a big mistake, Jared told himself as he forced his tread on the stairs into a measured pace, rather than the full-scale retreat he felt like making.

He headed into the office and sat down, planning to be immersed in his work before Holly got there.

Jared wasn't sure exactly how today's kiss had ended up having such a powerful effect on him. Especially right after his mother had been singing Holly's praises. That ought to have been a turn-off. He cursed as he burned his mouth on the hot coffee, and put the cup down on the desk. He felt dazed, certain of nothing except that he could've gone a lot further a couple of minutes ago. In his parents' kitchen!

It wouldn't happen again. He didn't doubt his own ability to pull back. He never had any trouble resisting a woman who wasn't suitable, no matter how attractive she was. But there was no conceit in acknowledging to himself that the strength of Holly's response meant she'd enjoyed the kiss. A lot. And if she'd enjoyed it, she would want to do it again. Women always did, in Jared's experience.

Normally that was a good thing, but in this case it

would be bad. For both of them. Maybe he needed to behave even worse toward her—be ruder, harsher. But Holly was such an ornery creature, it was hard to predict which way she'd…

Hold it.

As with all his best ideas, the solution was brilliant in its simplicity.

All Jared had to do was to convince Holly he was desperate for her, and she'd run a mile.

HOLLY SAT OUT in the yard with her coffee, determined not to go upstairs until she was good and ready. She knew why he'd done it. Because she'd told him not to. Why else would a reputed playboy like Jared, who could get any woman he wanted, kiss her?

Okay, maybe there was one other reason. She was the only woman, apart from his mother, within kissing distance, and he doubtless had withdrawal symptoms from his active social life. But the main reason was, she'd told him not to.

Which meant he would do it again.

She'd done herself a disservice by telling him she still didn't want him after that kiss, that mind-blowing kiss. He'd be all over her from now on, unsettling her, touching her with those casual but unmistakably intentional caresses, stealing kisses.…

Holly shifted on the hard discomfort of the wrought-iron love seat that overlooked Edward's rose garden. She fanned her face with her hands, consumed by a heat that had nothing to do with the afternoon sun beating down on her. What kind of jerk forced himself on a woman who told him she didn't want him, anyway? Wouldn't you think—?

"Aha!"

Edward lifted his head from the vegetable patch he was weeding at the side of the house. She waved and he turned back to his work, letting her nurse her brilliant idea in solitude.

It was so obvious and so right. If Jared had kissed her because she'd told him not to, all she had to do was to pretend she wanted him, and she'd take all the fun out of it for him. And voilà. End of unwelcome attention.

Briefly, Holly considered the possibility that Jared might want a dalliance with her, and that if she appeared willing she might land herself in more trouble. She dismissed the thought. He might be unethical, impulsive and arrogant, but Jared was a professional, and he really did want to focus on this deal they were working on. And he'd been telling the truth when he said Holly wasn't his type. He'd be relieved not to have to prove her attraction to him.

THE DUTY OFFICER at the FBI's Seattle field office phoned through to Crook just before three on Tuesday afternoon.

"There's a Maggie Stephens here to see you."

Simon's heart actually kicked in his chest.

He put a hand to it, then, catching Slater's curious glance, made a show of straightening his tie.

She was probably here to lay a complaint against him. Or to spin some story that would get him off her daughter's trail.

But he couldn't imagine Maggie in the sterile environment of one of the FBI rooms, so he picked up his wallet and went to meet her.

She was standing up against the chair that he knew the duty officer would have invited her to sit in, way out of her comfort zone. Her eyes lit when she saw him.

"Hello...Bert."

By now he'd figured out the rules of Maggie's name game. She always started off with a name she somehow knew he hated, like Bert or Eugene. Then she'd work her way through a few okay-but-no-thanks offerings— maybe Raymond or Lewis. Then just when he was about to give up, she'd throw him a crumb of cool. Ethan or Joseph or Brad. Just enough to make him feel there were...possibilities. That she saw him as a man.

"Good afternoon, ma'am." He addressed her formally, in the hope it would discourage her from playing her game in this public environment.

"Can we talk, Ralph?"

Crook felt the quizzical glance of the duty officer boring into his shoulder blades. The urge to get away from the office intensified. "Let's grab a coffee."

When they were out on Third Avenue she said, "I don't drink coffee, but I know a place that does good tea."

He walked alongside her, neither of them talking for several blocks, until Maggie turned into an alleyway between two buildings. A green awning gave the only indication that a café lurked down there.

The Aromatic Leaf Tea House wasn't a place Simon had been before. The clientele were more student and arty than professional. But he accepted Maggie's recommendation that he share a pot of ginger tea with her.

"You in Seattle for long?" he asked to relieve the awkward silence that fell after they'd ordered.

"I just arrived," she said, "and I'm going back tomorrow. A friend offered me a ride."

"A friend?" He feigned casualness.

She grinned. "A girlfriend who's kind enough to travel off-interstate. She invited me to drive up with her so I could visit Holly."

"But Holly's out of town."

She gave him a slow smile. "I know."

"Then why—? Oh." Puzzlement gave way to surprise, then pleasure, which Crook suspected translated to a goofy grin plastered all over his face. When she nodded confirmation that he'd read her correctly, Crook gulped. What did she want from him? She couldn't possibly be interested in him *that* way.

Just like he couldn't possibly be interested in her that way. Not when he was investigating her daughter. Of course, if Maggie did want to spend time with him…Crook's boss would kill him if he didn't take advantage of that.

"Have dinner with me tonight."

CHAPTER ELEVEN

MAGGIE FIGURED CROOK had justified inviting her to dinner on the basis it was work. In his mind, it probably didn't count.

That wasn't good enough. She'd put herself on the line coming to Seattle just to see him. She could understand Crook's hesitation, but it was time he admitted this was personal.

"You know, James," she said, "it's been a long time since I dated. How about you?"

His mouth curved into a reluctant, lopsided smile. "I haven't dated in ten years," he said. "I mean, I've tried, but I'm not good at it."

"And you're not about to start now?"

He nodded and his shoulders relaxed. But Maggie wasn't letting him off the hook that easily.

"You can call this dinner what you like," she said. "But I'm calling it a date. Even though—" she voiced the thought for both of them "—it seems unlikely that you and I have much in common."

He tightened his grip on the fine china teacup, and his words came out tight with frustration. "But I can't help liking you."

The simple statement resonated in a place long since

shut up inside her, and Maggie's next words caught in her throat.

Like Crook, she'd tried to date over the years. But the men who asked her out were either attracted to her figure and saw overlooking her peculiarities as the price to pay for a bedroom romp, or else they were activists who thought casual sex a sign of political unity. She didn't meet men who just liked her.

"I smoked a joint on the drive up here," she confessed.

That wiped the smile off his face. "You *what?*"

"I don't do it often these days. But I was nervous, and my friend offered me one and I accepted."

"Did you have any of that stuff on you when you were in my car?" He sounded faint.

"No."

Crook ran a hand over his face. "Why are you telling me this?"

"I want you to know I'm being honest with you," Maggie said. "I like this…thing, this game we have between us, but when it comes to something serious, I'll be honest with you."

"Is this about Holly?" he demanded. "Is she why you came to see me?"

"I wanted to see you," she said. "That's separate from Holly. But now I'm here, I need to talk about her."

"Then talk."

One thing about Crook, he genuinely did listen to her. Which meant he was Maggie's best shot at helping her daughter. "I don't have any proof Holly didn't do it," she said. "And I'll bet every mother tells you her kid is innocent."

"Most of them," he agreed.

"But you need to understand how deeply ingrained Holly's honesty is. I swear, she hasn't had so much as a parking ticket her whole life. She thinks overstaying on a parking meter is stealing. There's no way she would steal from people who trust her."

Crook knew Maggie believed what she was telling him. He was inclined to believe it himself. But on what basis? That every time her lips moved he thought about kissing them? That he wanted her to stop talking about Holly and start flirting with him again? "Let's assume you're right," he said. "But even the most honest person in the world will steal if she's pushed hard enough, just like a mother might murder to save her child. It all depends what's at stake, what matters most."

"That proves my point," Maggie said. "Holly's good name means everything to her. She would never risk that. I know you can't drop the charges because I think my daughter's innocent, but please, Crook, don't assume she's guilty."

"I wouldn't…" he began, then stopped. He had assumed just that when he'd first met Holly.

"What do your instincts tell you?" Maggie demanded.

Crook flinched. "I don't work on instinct. I work on evidence."

"You don't have enough evidence to convict Holly."

"We don't have any evidence against anyone else."

"Then find it," Maggie snapped. "Can't you find this Dave Fletcher? Holly says you're not even looking for him."

"Actually, we are," Crook said. "But that's none of Holly's business."

Maggie nodded. "That's a start. Thank you."

"I'm not doing it for you." Though the truth was, since he'd stayed at Maggie's place he'd been hounding Slater to hurry up and find Fletcher. "Maggie," he said, "I accept what you've told me about your daughter—that character stuff really is helpful. Believe me, it will have some bearing on my investigation." If he stayed on it. Maybe he should just enjoy his dinner date with Maggie and tell Pierce he wanted off the case.

She relaxed for the first time since they'd started talking about Holly. "Okay, subject closed," she said. "Now you get to tell me more about you."

The lightning-quick change of topic caught him off guard. "What do you want to know?"

"First up, are you married?" Maggie almost laughed out loud at the look on Crook's face. She hadn't for a moment thought he was married. He had a certain stiff-necked honor that indicated he wasn't the adulterous kind. But it always paid to ask.

"Sally, my wife, died ten years ago," he said. "She got skin cancer. She had one of those moles."

"A melanoma."

"Yeah. On the back of her neck. She wore her hair loose, so I didn't notice it until it was about the size of a quarter."

"Couldn't they cut it out?"

"They did, but the cancer had already spread. Sally had all the treatment, everything they could offer, no matter how bad it made her feel." Simon shook his head. "I was so sure she'd be all right. I promised her it would be okay."

His arrogance at the time seemed breathtaking. Had he thought he was God, that he could promise his wife a cure for cancer?

No, not God. But he'd assumed the instincts he relied on every day in the field somehow applied in the realm of medicine. He'd been as certain of Sally's survival as he'd ever been of anything. As certain as he was of his attraction to the totally unsuitable woman sitting opposite him now.

"You had a good marriage," Maggie said.

"Sally was the best," he said quietly. "I'm lucky we had the time we did."

"She was lucky, too. No wonder you haven't dated much. Your marriage sounds like a hard act to follow."

"I loved being married, and when Sally died I thought I'd want to marry again eventually," Simon said. "I still miss her, but that's not what's stopped me finding someone else. It just isn't that easy."

"I don't want to get married again," Maggie told him. "I need you to know where I'm coming from."

He nodded. "So, dinner tonight?"

"Sure." Maggie kept her agreement casual, but the stirring inside her was a far more serious matter. She cast around for another topic of conversation, something less personal. "How long have you worked for the FBI?"

"Nearly twenty-five years. I retire in a couple of months."

"Retire? Aren't you too young for that?"

"I'm fifty," he said. "The Bureau has mandatory retirement at fifty-seven, but I qualify for my pension now, so I thought I'd go early…. I haven't enjoyed my job much the past few years."

"But what will you do?"

Even as he told her, he wished he'd planned something more exciting for the rest of his life. Something that would intrigue a woman like Maggie.

"I put a down payment on a condo in Florida. My brother and his wife live there. We're close and…I'd like to be near them."

"You're too young to move to Florida," she protested.

Maggie Stephens, Crook figured, would be too young for Florida when she was ninety. "It has a great climate," he mumbled, unable to argue with her. Unable, almost, to remember why he'd ever wanted to go to Florida in the first place.

"So you'll, what, sit by the pool all day? Play golf?"

"You make it sound like a death sentence. I see it as a new beginning."

"The beginning of the end."

"No. I want something different from life, Maggie. I haven't met anyone I want to marry, but I want to be near people I love. That makes it Florida or Florida. And though I won't be working, I intend to be busy. I'm going back to college to study photography."

"Photography?" She smiled, and he felt he'd redeemed himself. "That's like art."

"Not the stuff I want to do," he said. "I'm thinking technical photography—the kind of thing we use in law enforcement. Crime scene pictures, photos of fire damage…" His cell phone rang and he answered it. "Hello, Slater."

Slater was the younger agent who had also visited her. Crook cursed under his breath, and she looked sharply at him—he wasn't the cursing type. Maggie waited, a chill seeping through her bones.

He switched the phone off. "There's been a development in Holly's case."

She knew better than to ask him for privileged information. "Will you go see her?"

Crook nodded. "I'll drive out to Kechowa." He paused. "Maggie, I'd better take a rain check on dinner."

That's when she knew the news was really bad.

HOLLY DIDN'T LOOK UP when Jared arrived in their makeshift office on Wednesday morning, the day after he'd kissed her so thoroughly in the kitchen. Happy not to make small talk, Jared immersed himself in his work.

"Um…Jared?" she said a few minutes later.

"What's wrong?"

She gave him a brilliant smile and leaned across the desk to pass him a spreadsheet.

He caught a glimpse of the creamy swell of a breast edged with hot-pink lace beneath her shirt and averted his eyes, trying not to recall the exact details of that particular item of lingerie.

He sat back in his chair, forcing his gaze up to her face, but carefully avoiding her lips. "Did you have a question?" he asked, suddenly dry-mouthed.

"The figure I've circled, what does it refer to?"

He scanned the page. "It's…uh…"

"Shall I show you which one I mean?" She leaned across the desk again.

"No," he snapped. Should he point out she'd left too many buttons undone on that blouse? He decided against it. She'd probably accuse him of sexual harassment. "I've found it."

He gave her the answer she needed, only to find she had another question. And when he handed the spreadsheet back to her, she walked around and perched on his side of the desk to ask something else. For a second, he entertained the crazy notion that she was coming on to him, sitting here like this with her short navy-blue skirt riding up her thighs so that if he reached out, like so…

Just in time, he pulled his hand back. He shoved his chair away from the desk, putting a good three feet between them. "I'll go make us coffee," he said, and bolted from the room.

In the kitchen, he almost convinced himself that anything provocative was the product of his imagination. On the other hand, what if his theory had been right? That now she'd had a taste of him she wanted more? Jared was taken aback to think that Holly was just like other women. But if he was right, now was the perfect time to put his plan into action—to scare her off with his attentions. Yet he was strangely reluctant to take that step.

Thankfully, when he arrived upstairs with two mugs of coffee, Holly was back on her side of the desk. He deposited his cup, then handed hers over.

"Thanks." As she took it from him, her fingers

brushed his, quite deliberately, he was sure. He couldn't let go of the mug fast enough, and slopped hot coffee over his thumb for the second time in two days.

He didn't make a sound, but she must have seen him wince.

"Are you okay?" Holly put her cup on the desk and grabbed his hand. She pulled a tissue from the box in front of her and wiped Jared's thumb. He gritted his teeth and waited for her to finish. Willed his body not to respond to her touch, to her worried, soothing noises.

But he hadn't prepared himself for her to lift his hand to her mouth and plant a gentle kiss on his thumb. He gave a strangled sound and tried, not very hard, to pull away.

"Just making it better," she said softly and, as if to prove her point, did it again. For a moment he couldn't remember any injury. He certainly felt no pain, though he didn't recall any of his mother's kisses having such a powerful analgesic effect during his childhood.

Just as he was about to tell her he was fine and retrieve his hand, she nipped the pad of his thumb between her teeth, and desire swept through him like a brushfire, burning reason in its path. She'd asked for it.

He hauled her closer and joined his lips to hers with a ferocity designed to terrify her.

Holly's abandon was even greater than yesterday's, as she welcomed his entry into her mouth, burying her fingers in his hair to pull him closer, her body straining against him.

Her seductive warmth enveloped him, and he wanted more. He tugged her shirt out of her waistband and with his fingers traced circles on the bare, satin skin of her back, eliciting a shuddery groan from her.

He'd never felt anything like it.

His hand moved for the clasp of her bra. He fiddled with it, for once in his life too crazed to manage it easily. She whimpered with impatience, and the sound brought Jared back to reality.

He pushed her away—the movement too abrupt for courtesy or dignity—and moved across the room. "Yesterday you said you didn't want to do that." His voice croaked as he ran a hand through his hair, disheveled by her hands.

"You said I was lying." Her face was aflame as she tucked her shirt in.

"We can't do this, Holly." Jared paced the office to avoid meeting her eyes. Boy, had he read her wrong on this one. He had to douse this right now. "You were right, this is business, and there are some things you don't mix with business. Just because there's an attraction, we don't need to act on it. We can be sensible about this." Was this him talking? Jared Seize-the-Day Harding?

"If that's what you want," she said with a meekness that might have made him suspicious if he hadn't still been trying to clear his head.

"Definitely," he said. "Are we agreed?"

"Agreed."

He thought about shaking her hand to seal the deal, but that might be asking for trouble. He'd achieved what he wanted, even if it hadn't exactly gone down the way he'd planned. Jared nodded curtly, let out a long breath and sat at his computer.

Holly did the same, but she stared unseeing at her screen. She felt as if she'd played with fire and narrowly escaped an inferno. Right up until he'd taken her in his arms, she'd been in control. But when his lips claimed hers, she'd lost all memory of why she was doing this and given herself up to the longing that engulfed her.

Of course, she would have pulled back in the end. Just like yesterday.

Oh, yeah? When, exactly? She shook off the thought. It didn't matter now. While she wasn't usually an advocate of the end justifying the means—that was more Jared's philosophy—she'd succeeded in terrifying him into a professional relationship. Round One to her.

Safe on her side of the desk, she allowed herself a small, triumphant smile.

CHAPTER TWELVE

THE SOUND OF A CAR pulling into the Hardings' driveway on Friday morning was so unusual that both Jared and Holly glanced out the window. Holly groaned at the sight of the man scrambling out of a middle-aged Ford Mustang.

Jared pulled the reports that had arrived by overnight courier from the Harding Corporation office into an almost orderly pile. "Looks like your friend from the FBI."

"Maybe it's good news," Holly said hopefully as they walked down the stairs. "Maybe they've found the money."

Beth had admitted Special Agent Crook, now waiting for them in the hallway below. He must have heard that comment, because he rolled his eyes in that annoying way he had, as if Holly might have said it just for his benefit.

She introduced Crook to Jared, who guided them into the dining room.

"There's no need for you to stay, Mr. Harding," Crook said as he sat.

"No problem," Jared returned pleasantly. "Holly would like me here."

At the agent's questioning glance, she nodded. "Did you find Dave?" Holly asked.

"It would appear that way."

The answer was too obscure for Holly, but Jared picked up on the agent's implication right away. "Fletcher's dead."

When Crook nodded, Holly made a strangled protest.

"The car Fletcher rented in Mexico was found burned out on the edge of the jungle. The Mexican police found his wallet under the driver's seat…and human remains in the back of the car."

Jared frowned. "Why in the back?"

"He may have been killed elsewhere and driven to the site where the car was set alight."

Holly found her voice. "Why would someone kill Dave? Do you think he had the money on him?"

Crook shook his head. "Unlikely." He straightened in his chair and looked Holly in the eye. "Ms. Stephens, where were you on the weekend of August seventh and eighth?"

That was almost two weeks ago. Jared had kissed her that Friday evening, and she'd forbidden him to come back until Sunday night.

Jared spoke first. "She was in the apartment next to mine all weekend. We were working on a major deal."

He hadn't exactly lied, but he was implying he'd been there with her. Crook, however, was alert to any evasion. "Did you actually see Ms. Stephens over the course of the weekend, sir?"

Jared scowled. "No."

Holly wasn't sure whether to be relieved or disappointed that he'd told the truth. "I was there all weekend," she said. "I certainly wasn't in Mexico. You'll know that if you talk to Immigration or the airlines."

Crook sighed with what almost seemed genuine regret. "It's not that simple. If you're planning to kill a guy, you're not going to fly under your own name. As I'm sure you know, the border with Mexico is rife with illicit traffic."

"What makes you think Holly was involved?" Jared demanded. "Fletcher could have been in any kind of trouble. We still don't know why he took the money."

Holly decided now wasn't a good time to suggest Dave might be innocent. Besides, she hadn't believed it herself for some time.

For once, Crook didn't insist that Holly had taken the money. No, it was far worse than that. "Fletcher was staying in a village nearby. He spent some time in the local bar. Witnesses say he had a loud argument about money with a woman who arrived to see him." Crook fixed an unblinking stare on Holly. "A woman whose description matches yours."

There was a minute's silence while Holly and Jared digested the information. Crook didn't seem in any hurry to break it.

"No one saw me that weekend," Holly finally said. "I didn't leave the apartment. I didn't make any phone calls." How she wished now she hadn't refused to meet with Jared all weekend.

"You don't have any evidence linking Holly to Fletcher's death," Jared said.

"Not beyond the assertion of witnesses that Fletcher

argued with a woman who looks like Ms. Stephens,"
Crook agreed. "But that's enough for me to take her
into custody for questioning. We could keep her in a cell
for a couple of days while we find that evidence. If it
exists."

Only that last qualifier kept Holly from moaning. It
didn't sound as if Crook was convinced she was guilty.

"Let me tell you the theory my colleague, Agent
Slater, has," Crook said conversationally. "Slater has
great instincts—he's usually right."

Jared's eyes narrowed. "Go ahead."

The two men spoke as if Holly wasn't there.

"Slater reckons Fletcher and Ms. Stephens were in on
this together. Fletcher took the money and got out to
Mexico. Ms. Stephens planned to follow him there. But
Fletcher double-crossed her, tipping off the FBI about
the theft. If we hadn't had that mystery call, it might not
have been discovered for weeks, giving them plenty of
time to set up a new life in the Bahamas or wherever."

Crook sat back, his finger splayed on the table.
"When she realized what Fletcher had done, she knew
it was too risky to run. She stayed put and hoped a lack
of evidence meant she wouldn't be convicted. But she
had to deal with Fletcher and secure the money. So she
flew down to Mexico on a fake passport, met up with
Fletcher and killed him. Probably shot him—"

"I don't know how to use a gun," Holly protested.

"—then she drove into the jungle, torched the car and
flew home, ready to start work on Monday."

"Sunday night. Jared and I met on Sunday night…
Not that I flew back in from Mexico," she added hastily.

"Gee, and I thought that was a confession," Crook said.

"What do you think of your colleague's theory?" Jared asked.

Crook rubbed his chin. "Slater does have a talent for understanding the devious criminal mind, and he's not often wrong. But on balance, I think he's wrong this time."

"Why?" Holly asked.

Jared groaned. "Don't push your luck, Holly."

"Some people don't have it in them to commit a crime," Crook said. "You're lucky to have a very convincing character witness."

"I am?" Holly had no clue whom he meant.

Crook looked annoyed. "Your mother."

Mom! Holly's jaw dropped and she quickly shut her mouth. Jared had been right about there being something personal between Mom and the FBI agent.

"Who would know Holly better than her own mother?" Jared said smoothly.

"I'm not saying you didn't do it," Crook warned her. "I'm saying the evidence to date doesn't convince me that you did. You don't have an alibi for that weekend, and we'll be searching for more evidence. Chances are I'll be back with more questions."

"But for now, you're finished," Jared suggested helpfully.

Crook's glare was baleful. "For now."

The FBI agent saw himself out. When he'd gone, Holly buried her face in her hands. Jared's fingers found the nape of her neck beneath her hair, rubbed it in a way that was reassuring, soothing rather than erotic.

The door from the kitchen opened and Beth entered the dining room bearing a tray of cookies and coffee. She looked around, bewildered. "Has your guest left already?"

Beth was too polite to ask why the FBI had visited her house, Holly knew. But she felt bad hiding the truth from Jared's parents when her problems had encroached upon their peaceful home. "He decided not to arrest me for murder, I guess," she said with a shaky laugh.

She felt Jared start next to her. "Arrest you?" Beth said. "Goodness, dear, why would he do that?"

"Um...I should warn you, Beth, he may be coming back. So I'll understand if you don't want me here, if you're worried I might give you and Edward a bad name."

Edward appeared in the doorway, stripping off his gardening gloves. "Do I smell coffee? And what's this about a bad name?"

Holly turned to Jared. "I'd better tell them the whole story."

Jared shut his eyes, gave her a do-what-you-want wave, knowing nothing he said would make any difference. Knowing his mother would not doubt Holly's innocence for a moment. Knowing that, in Mom's eyes, she would attain martyr status, and Mom would love her all the more for it.

Holly talked at length about what had happened, her words punctuated with cries from Beth and the occasional grunt from Edward. When she'd finished, she sat back and waited.

"My dear." When Beth reached across the table and took Holly's hand in both her own, Jared knew he'd guessed right. "That's simply awful. You must stay here as long as you need to—mustn't she, Edward?"

Jared leaned back, arms folded, and waited for his father to pour cold water on Mom's excessive offer. Dad would hate it if word got around they were harboring a suspected fraudster, let alone a murderer. Jared didn't want Holly's feelings hurt, but it was time someone calmed Mom down. He looked to his father expectantly.

"Quite right," Edward said. He cleared his throat and added gruffly, "And if they want to arrest anyone, well, they'll have to get past me first."

Jared groaned. His parents and Holly ignored him as hugs were exchanged, tears wiped, noses blown.

BACK UPSTAIRS in the office, Jared perched on the edge of the desk and pulled out his cell phone. "With Dave dead, I might as well call off Colonel Briggs."

"Who?"

"The private investigator I've had looking for Fletcher."

"You've had a— Why?" Holly sat forward in her seat and shot him an accusing look.

"Let's just say I didn't have a lot of faith in the FBI's ability to look farther than the end of its nose."

"But the FBI found him," Holly pointed out.

"Yeah, well, even they get lucky sometimes." Jared turned away and dialed the number before she could castigate him for hiring a detective without consulting her.

"M'boy." The Colonel had obviously recognized Jared's number. "I was just about to call you myself. Great minds, et cetera."

"Thanks, Colonel, but your services are no longer required. Dave Fletcher's turned up dead."

"Dead?" For the first time in Jared's memory, the Colonel sounded flummoxed. "He looks perfectly healthy from where I'm standing."

"What are you talking about?"

"Your man Fletcher is sitting not fifty feet away from me. Unless dead men drink coffee, he's very much alive."

"Are you certain?" Jared struggled to regroup.

"Absolutely. He's calling himself David Jenkins and he's got gray hair and a mustache, but there's no doubt it's your man."

"Jared, what's happening?" Holly half whispered.

He put a hand over the phone. "Dave's alive, the Colonel found him." He addressed the investigator again. "Where are you, Colonel?"

"Auckland, New Zealand."

"Can you keep an eye on him until I get there?" Jared discussed the details with the Colonel, then ended the call.

"I don't believe it." Holly's voice shook with mingled relief and anger. "Where is Dave? Can I talk to him?"

"He's not exactly in downtown Kechowa," Jared said. "He's in New Zealand. We'll fly down on Monday and see for ourselves."

"We're not going anywhere," Holly said. "I'll call Agent Crook, and he can have Interpol arrest Dave."

"Good luck with that."

Holly ignored Jared's skepticism as she dialed Crook from her cell phone.

The skepticism became an outright smirk when

Crook made her repeat everything she said at least twice. She swiveled her chair so her back was to Jared.

"Colonel Briggs says it's definitely Dave," she told the FBI agent, exasperated. "Can't you have someone take him in for questioning?"

"Look, Ms. Stephens." Crook sounded every bit as irritated as she felt. "I have a dead man here with plenty of evidence to suggest he's Dave Fletcher. You have a guy who doesn't look like Fletcher, doesn't call himself Fletcher, in a country where we have no record of Fletcher going, who's been identified by some geriatric P.I., who may not know one end of a criminal from the other."

"All I'm suggesting is that you ask the guy some questions."

"I'll pass your information to my colleague, Agent Slater," Crook said. "He can take it from there."

Holly couldn't budge him from that position, couldn't even get him to agree contacting the New Zealand police was a top priority. She switched the phone off and tossed it onto the desk where it clattered among her papers.

"I assume Crook is going to drop everything and fly to New Zealand?" Jared asked.

She sent him a quelling look. "He wasn't happy about your hiring the Colonel to find Dave. He's going to ask his colleague to follow up."

"Wow, when you say jump, those guys jump."

She glared at him, but couldn't hold back a smile. "Yeah, I really showed him who's boss."

"Even if Crook's colleague gets right on it," Jared said, "Fletcher's probably a New Zealand citizen, if his mom was born there. It may not be easy to extradite him."

Holly slumped back in her chair.

"If we want him caught," Jared said, "we'll have to go get him."

She blinked. "You've been watching too many movies. How are *we* going to get him?"

She had him there. Jared was making this up as he went along.

But she didn't wait for him to answer. "Anyway, this has nothing to do with you. I should go down there and talk to Dave, convince him to give the money back."

Jared snorted. "Lady, with your diplomatic skills you've got about as much chance of that as you have of convincing the NRA to support a firearms ban. Don't forget, I'm up for half a million dollars if you don't turn up for your trial, and if you think I'm going to let you loose on Fletcher's trail when there's every chance you'll end up dead…"

"I will not!"

"Somebody already did," he pointed out. "I'm coming with you to protect my investment. The court didn't make you surrender your passport, did they?"

She shook her head. "I don't need you," she said stubbornly.

Jared groaned. She would argue the point for eternity. Unless he could throw her off balance.

He leaned across the desk and captured her chin between his thumb and forefinger. The surprise that parted her lips allowed him to take her mouth, to sample again the heated pleasure of her kiss.

When it had gone on long enough that any other woman would be putty in his hands, Jared pulled back.

Holly touched her lips, then rubbed at them. "Can't we go before Monday?" She resumed their conversation as if there had been no interruption. Only now, Jared noted with glee, she had accepted that he was going with her. "Why not tomorrow? What if Dave disappears?"

Jared kept his voice even, not willing to risk setting off her defenses. "I have to be in Kechowa this weekend. Family stuff. Dave won't get away with the Colonel watching him."

"Do you think they'll let me leave," Holly said in sudden alarm, "now that I'm a murder suspect?"

"You were bailed on fraud charges, not murder." He soothed her with magnanimous protectiveness. "You can go anywhere you like. Crook's just fishing at the moment—I doubt you're officially a murder suspect."

"But what if he comes back? He'll expect to find me here."

Jared tsked, done with the protective thing. "Then he'll be disappointed, won't he?"

ON SUNDAY MORNING an uncommon level of activity drew Holly to the kitchen earlier than she might otherwise have gotten up. They were all there, the Harding family, eating breakfast in a silence underpinned by tension.

But Beth gave her usual welcoming smile. "Morning, dear. I was going to bring you up a cup of coffee and ask if you'd like to come with us this morning."

"Come with you?" Holly registered Jared's surprise, saw him turn to his father, saw Edward's curt nod.

"To church," Beth said. Beth and Edward were

regulars at the First Kechowa Church on Main Street, Holly had learned. Last Sunday, Holly and Jared had stayed home working. Today, Jared wore a crisply laundered white shirt and a tie, although he still looked completely untamed.

"It's a special day for us," Beth said. "The anniversary of Greg's death. He died on the last Sunday in August twenty-one years ago. Jared always comes home to join us in remembering Greg and visiting his grave afterward."

"I...thank you for asking me." Holly struggled to get the words out past the lump in her throat. "I'd be honored to come." She looked down at her clothes—Summer's cutoffs and an off-the-shoulder T-shirt. "I'd better get changed or they won't let me in."

Beth pushed a cup of coffee into her hands. "The service is at nine. I'll get your breakfast while you change."

The problem was, nothing in her sister's wardrobe was suitable for a memorial service and Holly had left her navy suit in Seattle. She was still staring at the meager offerings spread out on the bed when Jared rapped on the door.

He stuck his head around without waiting for her to invite him in. "Hurry up, you've only got five minutes to eat."

"Look," she wailed. "How can I wear any of this stuff?"

She gathered up an armful of the skimpy, flirty clothes in every color of the rainbow, then tossed them back onto the bed. "Nothing here is even remotely solemn."

"Mom and Dad are used to your clothes. They won't expect you to appear in something ultraconservative."

"But I feel bad about dressing like this today."

"Don't," he said, and his abruptness made her look up. "It's what's on the inside that counts, not your appearance."

Resentment glinted in his eyes. Holly didn't have time to go there. She pressed her lips together and turned away. "I'll be down in two minutes."

True to her word, as Jared had known she would be, she appeared in the kitchen in a short black skirt and white T-shirt, with a baby-pink jean jacket slung over her shoulder. With her hair caught back in a headband and a light touch of makeup, she at least looked neat and modest, if not the conservative woman she was.

Which didn't abate his anger one bit.

Childishly, he kept a stiff distance between them as they drove to the church, and even in the crowded pew near the front of the church. This had gone too far. His folks should not have invited Holly to the service without consulting him. And if they had consulted him, he'd have said a definite no.

Every year he came back to Kechowa for this pointless ceremony. *He* certainly didn't need it to keep Greg alive in his memory. Jared was planning a more concrete memorial—the ruin of Keith Transom. He doubted his parents needed the annual ritual, either.

He accepted the unwelcome knowledge that they probably saw it as a means of getting him back home. He ducked out of Thanksgiving and Christmas whenever he could come up with a convincing excuse, but he wouldn't dare refuse to be here this week.

Most years, he brought a woman with him. Ostensibly his girlfriend, someone he couldn't bear to leave, even for a few days. But in reality, a convenient buffer between him and his parents and the conversations they might want to start. By unspoken agreement, he never invited the girlfriend to the church or to visit the grave. But she ate the special dinner, Greg's favorite—she could hardly be excluded from that. And that's when he needed her presence, whoever she was. Mealtime was the greatest risk of opening it all up again.

It hadn't occurred to him his parents would invite Holly to join them at church. Even worse than this break from tradition was that it seemed...right, having her here. Somehow, her pink-and-black presence made the pastor's advice about the importance of family as God had designed it more meaningful and yet at the same time distracted him from the gloomy purpose of the occasion.

What Jared wanted was to sit here in furious contemplation of the waste of his brother's death, to be filled with righteous indignation, which would fuel his vendetta against Transom. And to leave convinced he'd fulfilled his obligation to his parents for another year.

But today, he sat here mourning the loss of the ideal family he'd thought they had until that day twenty-one years ago. Except it was only an illusion he'd lost. The ideal had never existed. Which made the unfamiliar ache in his chest impossible to understand.

Jared lived strictly in the realm of the possible.

He let his shoulders relax only after the service ended and they had filed out into the sunshine. His parents were surrounded by well-wishers, alerted, no doubt, by

Jared's presence to the fact that today was the anniversary. He and Holly stood some distance apart from the throng.

"You didn't want me to come today," she said. "I'm sorry. I didn't realize until we were in the church. You should have said earlier."

He shrugged. "Doesn't matter now."

"I'll take a cab home," she said, looking around as if a taxi might materialize in quiet, downtown Kechowa on a Sunday. "I won't come with you to the grave."

"I told you, it doesn't matter now." And he'd have his parents to answer to if she disappeared. It was hard enough talking to them today without arguing about Holly.

"But if you don't—"

"Just shut up and come," he snapped.

So she did.

The grave was simple, well-tended. Holly brushed tears away so she could read the inscription: *Gregory Edward Harding, Beloved son of Edward and Elizabeth, Brother of Jared. Forgive us our weakness.*

Forgive us our weakness? Holly didn't like to disturb the silence that had fallen over the group by asking the meaning of the inscription. Beth knelt on a cushion to pull weeds from among the tulips that bordered the grave. Edward squatted next to her, focusing intently on the movements of his wife's hands. Though no words were exchanged, Holly sensed they were in accord.

Not so Jared.

The younger son—it was hard to think of him as ever having come second to anyone—stood aloof, lost in his thoughts. Holly saw past his set expression to the moisture in his eyes. She almost wished she hadn't come, hadn't ruined this day for Jared. Yet she was sure that in some way her presence was making it easier for the whole family.

When Beth had finished, his parents stood and said a prayer. Holly joined in the amens, and knew a sense of peace as they walked back to the car.

When they got home, Jared headed toward the woods at the back of the house. "I'm going for a walk," he said over his shoulder. Then, to her surprise, he added, "Come with me, Holly?"

She caught him up on the edge of the wood and they walked side by side into the gloom, the sun fading behind them with each step, until only the beams strong enough to make it through the trees provided a dappled illumination.

"I was rude to you earlier," Jared said.

It was not by anyone's definition an apology. Holly figured he was acknowledging he'd done wrong, but that he didn't regret it. She appreciated his honesty.

"It's okay, I'm used to it," she said, and he grinned.

"Ouch. Don't you ever make allowances for a guy having a bad day?"

"I certainly do," she retorted. "Why do you think I didn't quit?"

He laughed out loud, and the sound lifted her spirits. Jared took her hand, and although she felt the familiar flood of awareness, she knew it was companionship he had in mind.

"Thanks for being so good about today," he said. "It can't have been easy for you."

Holly was at a loss how to answer that. Yes, it had been difficult to see the distress suffered by the older couple she'd become so fond of. Difficult, too, knowing Jared didn't want her there, that he also suffered and that her presence couldn't alleviate his torment. But at the same time she'd known a sense of belonging unlike anything she'd experienced. She couldn't regret that.

But if she tried to put it in words it would sound at the very least intrusive and at worst voyeuristic, as if she were feeding off their pain. So she squeezed his hand but said nothing.

"What did those words mean on Greg's tombstone— forgive us our weakness?" she asked.

Jared stopped in his tracks. "I don't know," he said in surprise. "In all these years I don't think I ever actually noticed them. I guess I've always been busy with my own thoughts, and trying to keep out of Mom and Dad's way when we're there."

"Maybe I'll ask Beth."

"No, don't." He started walking again, faster this time, pulling her along with him. "Tonight we have a meal in memory of Greg, and it's difficult to find a topic of conversation that doesn't lead to an argument. I'd rather we didn't talk about the gravestone."

"Okay, no problem."

He slowed his pace again and they wended their way in a wide circle through the woods and back to the house.

DINNER WAS CORN BREAD, Virginia ham and potato salad, followed by blueberry pie and vanilla ice cream.

Holly held a hand to the level of her chin to

indicate just how full up she was as she laughingly refused a second helping of pie. "That was wonderful, Beth."

"Greg always loved it, too." There was calm acceptance and pleasure in the older woman's voice. No edge of pain. "We should eat it more often."

"No reason why not," Jared said, and the sarcasm in his tone prompted Holly to look at him. "Saving it for once a year isn't going to bring Greg back."

"Nothing could bring him back. Your mother and I always accepted that." Edward spoke quietly, but with a strength that dared Jared to argue with him.

As if Jared would turn down a dare.

"It wasn't a matter of bringing him back, it was about not letting that jerk get away with it."

Holly suspected this was the exact argument Jared wanted to avoid. It seemed the Hardings were drawn to it like moths to a flame, unable to resist the warmth it provided. She wriggled in her seat, sure none of them could want her here, but unwilling to remind them of her presence by getting up to leave.

"Suing Keith Transom would have made it harder for us to deal with Greg's death, not easier." Beth's tone was pleading.

Keith Transom. Dave Fletcher's client, the man who'd filed a lawsuit against her. Was Transom the man who had called in Greg Harding's loans?

She turned to Jared. "Why didn't you tell me—"

"Stay out of this," he ordered. "Transom might have learned that cheating a man out of his business was wrong, Mom. He might at least have regretted what he did."

Edward took his wife's hand. "Son, you had every right to be mad at me and your mother back then. You were only a kid, and you felt we'd let you down. We were coping the best we could, and I don't doubt that in some ways we failed you. We're sorry."

Holly could tell from the drop of Jared's jaw that the familiar argument had taken a new turn.

"What's brought on this sudden contrition?" he demanded.

"We're scared we'll lose you, too." Beth's voice was clogged with unshed tears.

"What?" Jared stared at them. "I wouldn't kill myself."

Beth winced. "That's not what I mean. Sometimes I'm afraid we've already lost you. You were so angry back then, and you still are." She turned to Holly—so, they hadn't forgotten she was there. "When we told Jared we weren't prepared to sue Keith Transom, he laid a complaint with the police. He demanded they charge the man with inciting to commit suicide."

Holly could just imagine an enraged fourteen-year-old storming in and making demands. She could equally imagine the police response. "They wouldn't do it."

"Idiots," Jared said, his frustration still palpable after all these years. "They said there was insufficient evidence. But as soon as I stole something from the drugstore, they were on me like a ton of bricks. Their priorities were completely screwed up."

Holly could contain herself no longer. "Why didn't you tell me Transom was the one?"

He eyed her coldly. "You didn't need to know."

Holly ignored the puzzled glances of his parents. "It

doesn't make sense. When you told me about Greg, you avoided all mention of Transom's name."

"Then it was my mistake for telling you anything at all," he growled, waving a hand to silence Beth's protest. "I don't owe you one word more."

Holly's anger burned even hotter than her hurt. "I'm sorry you had a moment's weakness and told me about your brother. But I expect you to be honest with me, and if the only reason you decided to help me with my court case was because you hate Keith Transom, then I—"

Jared made violin-playing gestures with his hands. "Why I do what I do is none of your business. Yeah, maybe I thought that because my family—" he glared at his parents "—didn't do anything to stop Transom way back then, it was partly our fault that he's still out there playing his dirty tricks. Maybe I thought I owed you."

Holly pushed her chair back and jumped to her feet. "You don't owe me anything but the money you're paying me to work for you and the honesty you promised me when I took the job. So far I've seen precious little of either. You can forget about going after Dave with me. I don't want your help. I'm going on my own." She stormed from the room.

"The hell you are." Jared was on his feet, striding after her. "I'm paying her airfare and what I say goes."

Beth and Edward were left sitting in sudden blissful silence. Beth smiled tentatively. "That went well," she said.

And then the two of them were guffawing in helpless laughter amid the remains of the blueberry pie.

CHAPTER THIRTEEN

HE'D MADE A BIG MISTAKE. In his insistence on accompanying Holly—who still wasn't speaking to him after their argument yesterday—and in his determination to get the better of Transom, Jared had overlooked one major issue.

He hated to fly. Seriously hated it.

It wasn't fear. It was the same reason he avoided taxis and flatly refused to get on a boat. Motion sickness.

It was the most ridiculous, feeble ailment for a grown man to suffer. And it was utterly disabling. He took pills, drank ginger ale, wore acupressure wrist bands, did everything any quack had ever recommended to handle his condition. And failed.

"What's wrong?" Holly asked when his pace slowed as they approached the terminal at Sea-Tac Airport. Her first words to him since last night.

Should he tell her? Or should he let her figure it out when she saw him barfing into the paper bag?

"Nothing." Oh, yeah, macho to the last.

By the time they were in their first-class seats, Jared next to the aisle so he could make a dash for the lavatory, a fine sheen of sweat had broken out on his forehead.

Holly ordered champagne for her pre-takeoff drink. Jared ordered ginger ale. "Here's to a successful trip," she said, suddenly convivial.

He raised his glass. *Here's to surviving it.*

Holly busied herself fastening her seat belt. When she was done, she looked expectantly at Jared.

"What?" he asked.

She nodded toward his lap. "You need to buckle up."

He always delayed putting his belt on. Being strapped in somehow brought the nausea on quicker. "Who says?" he demanded. "The Control Freak of the Year?"

She clucked. "That sign right above your head. FAA regulations. Fifty years of airline best practice. And I'm sure I can get the flight crew to confirm—"

"All right, all right." He buckled the seat belt and scowled at her. "Happy now?" He shut his eyes.

"Something's wrong, isn't it?"

If she continued to badger him, he wouldn't last five minutes. He had to scare her back into her corner. Though it required a massive effort, he leaned over and favored her with his most intimate smile. The one with the bedroom eyes.

"Yes, something's wrong," he murmured, as he leaned closer still. "I can't stop thinking about how much I want you in my bed."

Damn! He'd been lying, but somehow a jolt of excitement coursed through him, alerting all his senses. *Down, boy.* He shifted in his seat as he waited for his words to have the desired effect on Holly—to turn the concern in her gaze to discomfort, then panic.

For a moment he thought it had worked. She jerked

back as if she'd had an electric shock. Then she leaned into him, so close he could see the blue flecks in her gray eyes. The slow blink of her long lashes was, bizarrely, the most erotic thing he'd ever seen, even more erotic than the glide of her tongue over her bottom lip before she spoke.

"I say we join the mile-high club," she whispered, not as quietly as she should have.

Jared almost groaned. While he would never, ever join the mile-high club—his motion sickness guaranteed that—the suggestion resonated in the most disturbing way. Then Holly added, "As soon as the seat belt sign is switched off, of course."

He didn't know what she was playing at, but she hadn't meant what she said. Which wasn't the relief it should have been.

"I'm tired," he stated. "I'm going to sleep." He downed his ginger ale and leaned back.

A few minutes later, he heard the flight attendant removing their glasses and instructing Holly to tighten her seat belt.

"It's as tight as it will go," Holly said crossly.

Jared couldn't resist. He sat up and addressed the attendant. "I've been trying to get her to tighten that thing ever since we got on board," he confided. "But she thinks there's one law for her and one for everyone else. I'll bet people like that make your job harder."

The woman gave him an appreciative smile. "Thank you for your help, sir." Holly made a gagging sound, and Jared fought the urge to laugh, a welcome change from the urge to throw up.

The plane began its taxi down the runway and Jared tightened his grip on the armrest as he tried to sleep. The takeoff was relatively smooth, and he exhaled deeply.

He felt two cool, feminine hands lift his left hand from the armrest. He opened his eyes. "What are you doing?"

Holly had twisted to face him in her seat. "I understand, baby," she whispered, her tone half-flirty, half-tender.

"I don't," he whispered back.

"You're afraid of flying."

"I am not." He tried to disentangle his hand, but she held it fast.

"It's nothing to be ashamed of. Around twenty percent of the population experiences a phobia to a significant extent. My mom is afraid of speed. Yours is just a more severe case than most."

"I am *not* afraid of flying."

"Denying it won't help. You can't overcome your fears until you confront them. There are courses you can take—"

To Jared's relief, the seat belt sign turned off. He scrambled out of his seat and headed for the lavatory.

"—and hypnosis works for some people…"

When he got back, feeling marginally better, Holly started in again. "Stop thinking about the fact that we're thirty thousand feet up in the air with nowhere to go but down."

If he really was scared of flying she'd have him paralyzed with fear.

"Holly," he said, "I am not afraid of flying, and that's the truth."

"Then what's wrong, baby?"

She wasn't going to let him rest until he'd told her, and he had to put an end to this "baby" business. "I suffer from motion sickness," he said, wishing there was a more impressive name for it. Something Greek or Latin.

For a bare moment Holly looked sympathetic. Then she laughed. "Does this mean you'll leave me alone? I don't have to pretend I'm hot for you?"

"You *are* hot for me," he said. Then he realized what she'd said. "What do you mean, pretend?"

She blew out an impatient breath. "I've been acting like I want you so you'll back off."

Jared's nausea receded under a tidal wave of outrage. "*I'm* the one who's been pretending I want you. You can't keep your hands off me."

She waggled her hands in front of his face. "Look, no hands. Face it, Jared, nothing scares you more than a woman who wants you too much. It was a brilliant strategy on my part."

"That strategy was mine."

"If I'd known all it took to cut your libido down to size was to put you on a plane," she said, "I'd have done it ages ago."

He grinned reluctantly.

"Is it the same in a car?" she asked.

"Cars, buses, trains, planes, you name it. Any time I'm not driving." He waved away the stewardess who wanted to take his lunch order. Holly, in contrast, appeared intent on working her way right through the menu.

"You don't mind if I eat in front of you, do you?" She'd caught his pained look.

He shook his head. "I'll be asleep." He shut his eyes to prove it.

But Holly had other plans. "I've had a great idea about the Greerson family."

Jared was about to tell her he didn't want to hear another word about her sympathy for Wireless World's owners when the plane hit a patch of turbulence. As the aircraft lurched and shook, it was all he could do to keep from throwing up. But Holly, the heartless witch, used his agony as a chance to expound her social-worker accounting theories.

And Jared, afraid that if he opened his mouth he'd see his breakfast again, had to sit and listen in silence.

THEY CHANGED PLANES in L.A., boarding an Air New Zealand flight for Auckland. Jared went straight to sleep. It was two hours before a pocket of turbulence woke him. Holly was eating her dinner. Watching her butter a bread roll with meticulous precision, he was struck again by the contrast between her usual careful restraint and the abandon that, whatever she might claim about it being a pretence, overtook her when she was in his arms.

Which one was the real Holly?

"What are you going to do when this is over?" he asked. Silence. "Don't tell me Ms. Control Freak hasn't thought about it. I wouldn't believe you."

"Things have changed," she muttered evasively.

"Distract me from my suffering."

She gave him a sharp look but then appeared to reconsider. "I guess it might help to tell someone like you."

He grinned and, blessedly, the nausea receded. "Remind me what 'someone like me' means?"

"Someone who's succeeded without an overarching goal to drive what he does. If you can wing it and survive, why can't I?"

"You don't think I have an overarching goal?"

Momentarily, he'd dumbfounded her. "Do you?" she demanded.

"Everyone has an overarching goal, even if it's only to retire in comfort after forty years at the office."

She laughed. "I don't think that's you. Stop avoiding the question. Is there a purpose to what you're doing?"

"All life has purpose," he said sanctimoniously. She slapped the back of his hand on the armrest between them. "Ouch."

"Okay," she said, "but tell me this. If you don't achieve it, what will you do?"

He had a second's terrifying glimpse of a yawning chasm of futility. If he didn't defeat Transom, what next? And even if he did win, what lay ahead? Clamminess gripped him, and with it the nausea returned.

Holly's hand closed over his. "You've gone pale," she said. "Are you feeling bad again?"

With one slight movement he turned his hand over and clasped her fingers tightly. "Help me, Holly," he said, barely certain what he was asking her.

She took it as a request to provide distraction.

"You can give me some advice," she said. "My previous five-year plan was to get Summer and River through college and then find my father."

Jared tightened his grip on her hand, aware that despite her apparent self-sufficiency, her plan had depended entirely on the cooperation of others, who'd let her down.

"But now the kids have dropped out, and I can't even think about looking for Dad unless I'm vindicated. Even then," she added morosely, "mud sticks. Some people will refuse to believe I'm innocent. Who's to say my father won't be one of them?"

"He can't be that stupid, with you for a daughter," Jared said gruffly.

She blinked at the unexpected compliment. "The thing is," she said slowly, as if she was figuring this out as she went along, "I can't build my life around something so uncertain. And even if I do see him and everything's okay, I can't go back to being eight years old. I still have to find a way forward on my own."

It sounded lonely, but Jared knew what she meant. Relying on others for fulfillment would doom her to disappointment.

Like I'm doing with Transom. He brushed the thought aside. "What are your options?"

"Rebuild my business—alone. But it could take years with this scandal behind me. Or I could take a corporate job, or move into an existing larger partnership."

"I'm not sure you'd get on too well in an environment where you're not the top of the tree," he said frankly.

She grinned. "So you noticed my abrasive personal style."

"Any more abrasive and you'd be sandpaper," he agreed, and enjoyed her squeal of outraged amusement.

After a pause, she said, "Jared, you know that I say what I mean, and that I appreciate honesty in others."

Her sudden seriousness, coupled with the use of the word honesty, put him on guard. She bore all the signs of a woman about to get heavy. He disentangled his hand from hers and grunted noncommittally.

"I know you like my work, and I've found working with you to be challenging and enjoyable—mostly." She bit her lip, and he wondered if she rated the kisses as enjoyable. "When my name's been cleared, I'd like to work for you in an official capacity. It would help me get back on my feet, and there are chief executives out there who'll follow your lead in giving me work."

His boldness of vision teamed with Holly's creativity and technical skill... It could work, no doubt about it.

But once Holly knew what he was doing to Transom, her offer would be off the table. Permanently. For a scant half second Jared wished he didn't have to pursue Transom, wished this deal could be exactly what he'd told Holly it was.

But even if it had been aboveboard, how long would it be before he messed up their working relationship by throwing her onto the boardroom table and making love to her?

He gave it two weeks, max.

He shook his head. "It's not a good idea, Holly."

CHAPTER FOURTEEN

HURT FLASHED IN Holly's eyes and her knuckles whitened where her hands were clasped in her lap, but she gave a stiff nod.

"It's not about your work, you know that," Jared said.

"Just my sandpaper personality, huh?" The lightness of her tone didn't fool him.

"Holly, please." This was the kind of situation Jared hated—where something was his fault but he had no intention of fixing it. As the plane lurched into an air pocket and brought his stomach into his mouth, he clenched his teeth tight and shut his eyes.

A huffing sound from the next seat told him Holly saw it as an evasion tactic. He felt too ill to care.

NEAR THE END of the flight, when it was calmer and Jared was feeling just about okay, Holly said, "We haven't discussed what we're going to do when we get to New Zealand."

"That's because I haven't thought about it," Jared said.

"You've figured out that Dave isn't likely to just hand over the money. You must have a plan."

"I'm a seat-of-the-pants kind of guy."

Holly waved a hand to indicate the aircraft. "I don't

imagine you took time away from work and spent all this money with no idea of how we're going to get what we want."

Okay, she was right. But Jared knew she'd hate his idea, so he'd avoided mentioning it. Now, he was too ill to invent a plausible lie. "The Colonel has some pills."

"Pills?"

"We feed them to Dave, they put him in a semitranquilized state. He can walk, answer basic questions, but he can't escape. We take him back with us on the next flight we can get." Which meant more flying. He shut his eyes.

"Are you crazy?" Her words reverberated in his head. "Jared, that's kidnapping. He's going to report what happened and we'll find ourselves up on charges far worse than fraud."

Jared intended to scare Dave into not revealing how he'd been returned to Seattle, but now wasn't the time to tell Holly that. He dismissed her arguments with a tired wave.

"No," she said firmly. "We are not drugging and kidnapping Dave." When she put it that way, it didn't sound like a great idea.

"Then what do you suggest?"

"I don't know, but it's got to be legal."

She did that thing of taking his hand in hers again, chafing it anxiously. "I want you to promise me, Jared. Whatever we do will be one hundred percent legit."

He groaned as the plane hit another patch of turbulence and lurched down then up again. Holly took the groan as reluctance to accept her stipulation and shook his arm. "Promise."

If there was any chance she would let go of him, stop rocking him back and forth, he'd promise her his soul. "Promise," he choked out, and sank into sleep the second she released him.

"New Zealand?" Special Agent Simon Crook clamped down on the pen between his teeth as he spoke into the phone, muffling his next words. "When did she leave?"

Beth Harding sounded flustered. "They both left— Jared went with Holly. They drove back to Seattle on Monday morning to catch a plane."

Yesterday. If Holly Stephens was intent on doing a runner, she could have well and truly vanished by now. And Harding had posted her bail—that he'd gone, too, couldn't be a good sign. Crook should have figured there was something between Holly and Jared when Harding put up all that money.

He cursed himself for not asking the court to have Holly surrender her passport.

He hung up on Mrs. Harding and put a call in to U.S. Immigration, which confirmed Holly's flight details. That made Crook feel marginally better. At least she wasn't trying to hide her trail by using a false passport.

What next, dammit?

He could phone Maggie Stephens and see if she knew where Holly expected to find Fletcher, although it was unlikely Holly would have confided in her mother. But Crook was acutely aware it had been a week since their aborted dinner date.

He picked up the phone, then put it down again.

Before he spoke to Maggie he had to decide once and for all whether he suspected her of any involvement in the crime.

He kicked his chair back from the desk and swiveled away from the phone. Across the open-plan office he saw Slater talking to Pierce. They looked cozy. He ignored his resentment. It didn't matter.

I don't believe Maggie is involved. Huh. He really *didn't* think she was involved.

Now he had to decide whether the fact that he'd become friendly with the mother of a suspect was interfering with his judgment. Because when he saw her again, he'd be tempted to become even friendlier.

About fifteen years ago, when the son of good friends of his and Sally's had gotten into trouble, Crook had been assigned the case. He'd talked to his boss—not Pierce back then—and they'd agreed he could be trusted to pull out if he felt his integrity might be compromised. Crook had told his friends he would never mention the case to them. That had worked for the three months the investigation dragged out. Until Crook arrested their son, and the kid went to jail for a year. After that, the friendship hadn't been quite the same.

Crook grimaced. At least he knew he could do his job without compromise. So what was the difference between that situation and this one?

Back then, he'd cleared his involvement with his boss.

Crook scanned the office again. Pierce and Slater were still chatting. He sighed, got to his feet. Might as well give them something to chuckle about.

IT TOOK SEVERAL MINUTES for the trailer park owner to bring Maggie to the phone. Minutes during which Crook rephrased what he was about to say several times. When she finally came on the line, he said, "Maggie, it's—" he remembered he was meant to be anonymous "—me."

"Adam," she said warmly.

It took Simon a moment to realize that she knew exactly who he was and that her enthusiasm was intended for him. That put a smile on his face, until he remembered the reason for his call. "It's about Holly," he said. "She flew to New Zealand yesterday with Jared Harding."

"Jared Harding?"

"Her boss."

"Oh, yes, the guy at the courthouse. Why did she do that?"

"She thinks Dave Fletcher is there. I thought maybe she'd told you her plans?"

"No." He could almost hear Maggie's mind working. "Why would she go after Dave herself? Why wouldn't she tell you where he was?"

This was the part Simon wasn't looking forward to. "Uh, she did say there'd been a sighting of a man who might be Fletcher. But we just flew a body back from Mexico that we're pretty sure is him. We're working to ID it now. I told Holly that Slater would follow up on the New Zealand thing."

"And did he?"

Crook had learned the dislike between Slater and Maggie went both ways. Right now, he didn't much like Slater himself. "Not as far as I know."

"Obviously, Holly didn't trust the FBI to follow up

so she's doing the job herself," Maggie said proudly, as if her daughter's refusal to trust the authorities was proof of some mother-daughter bond.

Crook sighed. "I'm going to have to search her condo again, see if we can find anything that might tell us where she's gone."

"I need to be there," Maggie said. "Someone must represent Holly's interests."

"Not legally, they don't have to. I'll get a warrant."

"I'm not talking about legally. Please, Crook, I want to find Holly as much as you do, and I know there's an innocent explanation. If I get a bus this afternoon, I'll be in Seattle tonight and you can do the search in the morning."

"The bus takes the interstate," he reminded her.

"I know," she said quietly.

Simon took a deep breath. He might have just talked to Pierce and got his boss's reluctant concession, but this was still a step he couldn't take lightly, for reasons entirely unrelated to his professional integrity. "I'll come fetch you. I can be there by lunchtime and we'll be in Seattle by late afternoon. I want to do that search today."

There was a long silence. At last, in a strangled voice, Maggie said, "Thank you."

AT FOUR O'CLOCK Crook opened the door of Holly's condo, using the key the FBI had commandeered from her, and stepped inside, Maggie close behind. When she hesitated in the small foyer and looked around her, Simon realized she'd never been here before.

He got straight to work, his anger toward Holly driving him to comb her possessions with new energy.

Maggie watched him for a few minutes, then said, "Can I help?"

He shook his head. "I have to do it." Though already he had a feeling he was wasting his time. An hour later, he was certain of it. The only link between Holly and New Zealand was the World Atlas he found in her bookcase.

"What now?" Maggie asked.

"It's still a possibility that Holly and Fletcher were in this together. He double-crossed her, and now she's returning the favor. She may still know where the money is." He grimaced. "I'm going to have to put out an alert for them, get the New Zealand police looking for—"

"No! Think about it. If Holly was up to no good she'd be a lot more secretive about it. You'd have no idea where she is. Listen to your instincts."

If only he could. Simon sighed. "Maggie, I'm sorry, I don't work that way."

"What do you mean?"

He sat on Holly's couch—rather more luxuriously stuffed than her mother's—and Maggie sat next to him, facing him. "When Sally died, it really shook me up. Not just because I missed her, but because I'd been so convinced she'd survive."

"That was hope," Maggie said. "You wanted her to live."

"Maybe." He spread his hands in front of him and for the first time he could remember didn't think his left hand looked odd without the gold band he'd removed five years ago. "But one of the things that made me a good agent when I started out was my strong instincts. And they got better as time went on. I could trust them even when the evidence pointed in the opposite direction.

"After Sal's death, it wasn't just that I didn't trust my instincts—I didn't *have* any instincts anymore. If it wasn't in front of me in black and white, I couldn't see it. I had to give up undercover work. I'd lost the knack." He took Maggie's hands in his, caressed them with his thumbs. "So when you tell me to trust my instincts about Holly…" To his surprise, Maggie was smiling.

She squeezed his hands. "What do you call this, then, Special Agent Crook? You and me?"

He looked down at her long fingers, knew he wanted to feel them all over his body. "I call it madness."

"Uh-uh." Maggie shook her head. "You're not crazy. I might be, but you're definitely sane. What you've got going here is a full-blown case of gut instinct. All the evidence suggests you and I would have nothing in common, that we wouldn't even like each other. But your intuition tells you to like me."

Simon wasn't sure his randy hormones counted as intuition. But he liked the thought of it. "Your logic is totally screwed up," he said. "I told my boss today that my relationship with you has gone beyond professional."

She stilled. "What did he say?"

Crook rubbed his chin. "The word idiot came up, along with crazy. But I told him this wasn't open to negotiation. That if he didn't trust me to identify a conflict of interest, I'd quit now."

"Wow."

He shrugged. "It wasn't that impressive. Pierce has been involved in a couple of unfair dismissal cases. He didn't want me complaining to HR." Besides, Pierce was a pragmatist. He was probably still thinking Crook might find some kind of evidence against Holly if he hung around Maggie.

Simon tugged her an inch or two closer across the couch. In an instant, he was painfully aware of the firm, soft flesh beneath his fingers, the laughter and concern in her green eyes, the intake of breath that caused her breasts to swell against him. He couldn't live another instant without kissing her.

He pulled her against him and captured her lips with his, kissing her hard. Her "oomph" told him she hadn't expected such a bold approach. The excitement went straight to his head and he plunged in, kissing her harder, until he realized she was twisting her head.

He stopped instantly, mortified, dragged his mouth from hers. "I'm sorry," he blurted. "I should never have—"

"Easy, boy." Her voice was gentle, and she touched a hand to his cheek. A chuckle escaped her. "Where's the fire?"

"I don't know, I…" Simon stuttered to a stop.

"I'm out of practice with this stuff. Let's go a little slower." As if to spell it out to him, she put her arms around his neck and oh-so-slowly pulled his head down to hers. He was too surprised to move, which made it easy for her lips to brush against his in a gentle caress. She kissed the corner of his mouth, then moved to the center. Gradually, the pressure of her mouth increased as he responded, and at last he felt the tip of her tongue flirting against his lower lip.

Cautiously, he parted his lips. The subsequent melding of their mouths was nothing like his frenzied attack—a small part of his brain told him he was going to feel like a complete jerk later. Her curious, teasing exploration had him more aroused than he could ever remember being.

Crook realized he'd been holding his breath, and he expelled it in a groan. He released his too-tight grip on Maggie's upper arms and did what he'd been longing to since the moment he'd first seen her—buried his hands in that magnificent hair. She squirmed closer to him and leaned back until they were practically lying on the couch, and her kiss deepened.

It seemed an eternity before they finally surfaced.

Maggie shook her head briskly. "Wow, Ernest," she said, "that was quite a surprise."

"It was a good surprise," he said. "For me. A very good one. Now that we've, uh, done that, I think you should know my name. It's—"

"Don't tell me."

He looked at her helplessly. "Maggie, this is crazy."

"It's not crazy." She wriggled from his embrace, sat up straight. "You know the old fairy story *Rumpelstiltskin?*"

He strained to recall it. "Some woman has to guess this weird little guy's name."

She pulled a plump cushion into her lap, and fingered its piped edges. "Or he'll take her baby away. Like you want to take Holly."

"I'm not going to drop the charges against her if you guess my name right."

She clucked as if *he* was the weird one here. "There's nothing I can do to help Holly. Do you know how hard that is for a mother?"

He shook his head. He and Sally had tried for a baby, but it had never happened for them.

"Sometimes I tell myself that if I paint a certain picture, someone will buy it," Maggie explained. "If I drink three cups of peppermint tea, Summer will pass her driving test. If I guess your name—"

"Holly will be okay," he finished for her. "You do know there's no logic to this."

Her hands gripped the cushion. "Please, John, allow me the illusion of some control."

"John," he protested.

"As in John Wayne. A fine man."

Simon harrumphed. "A bit old, isn't he?"

"Actually, he's dead," Maggie said apologetically.

Crook rolled his eyes. Still, why not let her have her way? However uncomfortable he might be making out with a woman who didn't know his name.

"Please, Crook," Maggie said, serious again. "Listen to your instincts about Holly. I know you have them. What do they tell you?"

They told him Holly was innocent.

Well, he would think that, wouldn't he? He wanted Maggie, so he wanted things to work out for her daughter.

"I don't know," he said.

"You're not sure Holly's guilty?"

"I guess."

"Then give her the benefit of the doubt," Maggie said. "She may even be helping you."

"The FBI doesn't like people interfering with an investigation."

"Please, Crook. I know I'm right."

"Okay," he said. "I'll go with my gut, and leave her be for now. But I can't speak for Slater, or anyone else on the case."

"Thank you." Maggie kissed him on the cheek. "Crook, will you drive me back to Marionville and stay the night?"

He tamped down a wild hope. "You mean, in the kids' room, right?"

Her grin was sheepish. "Yeah. I like you, but it's been a long time since I trusted a man with more than a kiss."

They stood, and Crook straightened the cushions, bringing the couch back into line with the rest of Holly's immaculate living room. He'd progressed from flirting with a suspect's mother to making out with her on the suspect's couch. Man, he was in deep. Suddenly reckless, he said, "Maybe I could hang around at your place all day tomorrow. It'll give us some more time together."

She nodded. "Can you get a day off at such short notice?"

Crook was absurdly pleased she hadn't suggested he fake an illness. "No problem. My boss is begging me to use up some of my leave. But, Maggie, I'm only driving you back on one condition."

"What's that?" She preceded him out the door, waiting while he locked up.

"From now on we don't talk about Holly. Ever. Whatever I do about tracking her down in New Zealand will be nothing to do with you." In fact, he'd already made up his mind to wait and see awhile, but that could change any time. "You need to accept that I might put out an alert for her, and that if I decide she's guilty I'll do my best to put her away."

Her expression was somber. "I know."

CHAPTER FIFTEEN

WHEN THEY LANDED IN Auckland, Jared phoned Colonel Briggs, who was still staking out Dave's current location, to get the address. Holly wanted to go directly there. Even with the Colonel watching, she didn't want to risk that Dave might move on when they were so close. Jared agreed, though it meant adding car sickness fueled by the cigarette-smoke-infested taxi to his woes.

Holly's several attempts to pronounce their destination—Karangahape Road—were mercifully foreshortened when the taxi driver told her the locals called it K Road. The hotels and department stores at the start of K Road gave way to strip clubs and sex shops as they progressed its length. The taxi stopped outside a travel agency offering tours to Bangkok that obviously focused more on the attractions of very young Thai women than on the culture. The travel agency was closed.

"This is the place," the man said cheerfully. "You might want to try upstairs."

Jared paid him while Holly clambered from the car. She steadied herself with a hand on the trunk, her knees suddenly weak. Then Jared was beside her, warily, scanning their surroundings. "Time for action."

Holly looked dubiously at the scarred red door, which

presumably led to an apartment above the travel agency. "I appreciate you giving me a chance to do this my way."

"I was too sick to argue with you," he pointed out. "Asking Fletcher nicely to give the money back is the dumbest idea I ever heard."

"Dave did something stupid, but he's not a bad guy at heart."

Jared lost his patience. "We'll soon find out. Why don't you go on in? Unless you're afraid?"

She stiffened. "Of course not." Having Jared along would have made it a lot easier, but they'd agreed his presence should remain a secret for now, an ace up their sleeve. And hadn't he made it plain on the flight that Holly would have to get used to being on her own again? She lifted her chin. "If I'm not out in an hour, come find me."

Jared leaned against the window of a strip club, where he was sure he wouldn't be visible to anyone upstairs. Holly walked to the door. Her sister's skimpy clothes, unsuited to this winter's day, were no more outrageous than what some of the other women wore on this seedy street. Holly pressed the bell, and Jared held his breath.

The door opened, but he couldn't see if it was Fletcher himself in the doorway. There was a brief tussle as the occupant obviously tried to shut the door again, then Holly hurled herself inside and the door closed.

"HOW COULD YOU DO THIS to our business?" Holly shrieked the words as she raced up the narrow internal staircase on Dave's heels. So much for the reasonable approach she'd intended.

Dave, his hair dyed a startling gray, reached the landing and turned around so abruptly that she bumped into him. "I don't have to talk to you. Get out."

Holly pushed him into the living room, whose pollution-grimed windows admitted a dull winter light, illuminating the stains on the shabby carpet. There was no sign of the millions Dave had stolen. "I'm not leaving without the money."

He pulled a cigarette pack from his shirt pocket. He scowled at her as he lit up. "You'll be here a long time then. How did you find me?"

"What does it matter? I'm here now and I want that money back."

"Too bad."

"Dave, you've committed a serious felony." At last, she found sweet reason. "You can make things better by paying the money back. Maybe they won't send you to prison."

"They won't send me to prison because they don't know where I am." He held up a hand to forestall her. "You haven't told them, or they'd be here. I'm all set up to move on fast—as soon as you're out of here, so am I. They won't find me."

She looked around. Apart from the cell phone on top of the newspaper that was spread across the coffee table, he had little in the way of personal possessions. She saw a tattered maroon sofa and a dark-stained bookcase with rows of old hardcovers that looked as if they hadn't been read in decades.

Through an open doorway Holly glimpsed a dated kitchen, cabinets painted a dull orange. A lone upturned mug drained on the counter. "Is this why you did it? So you could live in a dump in a red-light district at the end of the earth? I hope it was worth it."

Dave grabbed at her and she yelped. "What the hell are you—"

He dragged off her jacket, the pink jean jacket she'd worn to church in Kechowa, and ran his hands over the pockets.

"I knew it." Triumphant, he pulled her voice-activated tape recorder out of the breast pocket. "You never go to an important meeting without this thing."

Holly watched it disappear into his pocket. Damn. Through gritted teeth she said, "The money."

"It's gone." He added with an infuriating smile, "Most of it."

"Gone? You spent it?"

"I invested it," he corrected her. "As you know, all investments involve risk. The higher the risk, the higher the potential return."

And the bigger the fall if things didn't work out. Holly steeled herself. "What was the investment?"

Dave scooped up his cell phone off the coffee table and moved to put it on the sideboard behind the sofa. "I had a surefire tip that the stocks in a power company were about to go through the roof—they were an acquisition target."

"Insider trading."

"Smart trading," Dave amended. "Through a series of offshore accounts that'll take the authorities some time to unravel, if they ever do. But the acquisition never happened, the company declared major losses and the stock price dropped like a stone a week later. There was no way I could sell, no way of getting the money back before you noticed it was missing."

Appalled, Holly sank into the room's single armchair. A sharp spring stabbed her backside through the thin cushion and she got up again quickly. "Stock market trading is a gamble even when you know what you're doing. Why would you even go into it? And why use our clients' money?"

Dave's mouth turned down in a sneer. "You were always so superior, always thinking you were better than I was. Every time I suggested a high-return investment for our clients' funds you refused. You had no imagination."

"I was looking after their money during a time of fiscal uncertainty," she said. "I would have been happy to consider something slightly higher risk when the market settled down."

Dave kicked at the sideboard. "You were always creaming off the best projects and giving me the stuff any new graduate could do."

Holly couldn't deny that. "It was my reputation that brought the good clients in, and they wanted me doing the work."

"If that stock hadn't gone sour, right now I'd be handing our clients a return on their money they never dreamed of. Plus taking a hefty commission for myself." He paused. "Actually I took part of the commission before I made the investment. Ten percent."

"Six hundred thousand dollars," Holly said slowly.

He shrugged. "Not worth going to prison for, but enough to start over. I'll have to find something else to do."

"Something other than stealing?" she asked. "Or something other than hiding out in a hovel, leaving me to take the rap for your crime."

"I knew you'd notice it missing right away," he said. "Setting the Feds on you gave me more time to get out. Anyway, you won't be found guilty. You're so squeaky-clean you'll be back in business in no time. The clients will get paid out by the insurers and I'll be a low priority on the Wanted list."

"The FBI thinks I killed you," Holly blurted.

She could tell that shook him. "What?"

"They found your rental car burned out in Mexico. With your wallet and your...remains. At least, what they think are your remains."

Dave frowned. "As soon as I got my fake passport I abandoned the car. I left my wallet with my ID in it."

"So the body isn't the woman you argued with?"

"What woman?" His puzzled expression cleared. "Oh, her. She was just a girl I met at the beach. An Australian tourist. Stupid cow wanted to borrow money for her airfare home."

"So you don't know whose body was in the car?"

"I just told you, didn't I?"

Satisfied Dave hadn't killed anyone, Holly turned to the next most important matter. "How did you get my PIN?"

"Easy. I concealed a video camera in the ceiling above your desk. It only took a day to catch you checking the bank account." Dave's voice cooled. "Now get out of here, Holly."

"Not until you agree to turn yourself in."

Dave sighed, opened a drawer in the sideboard he was leaning on, and casually pulled out a gun.

Holly's eyes widened, but she made no sound.

"I'm not going to kill you," he assured her. "I'll just injure you so you don't try to stop me leaving." He looked her up and down as if trying to decide where best to put a bullet into her. He aimed at her knee, steadied his gun hand with his other hand.

"You don't have to shoot me." Fear made her voice breathy. "I'll go."

"You'll go to the cops," Dave said.

He wouldn't believe her if she denied it. "Yes."

Dave thought for a moment, his gun still trained on Holly's knee. "I'm ready to leave," he said, more to himself than her. "I'll be out of here before the police arrive." He lowered the gun, looking just about as relieved as Holly was that he didn't have to shoot her. She could almost see his struggle to think of a next step.

"Get out now," he said. "Cross the street and head to the bus shelter on the other side. Sit there and don't move, don't speak to anyone, for thirty minutes. I'll be watching you from the window. If I see you talk to anyone…"

"But you're leaving," Holly said.

Dave's face darkened. "Don't get smart, Holly. You won't know exactly when I've left, I'll go out the back way. Just do as you're told for once."

Holly walked down the stairs and out of the apartment, praying Jared wouldn't rush to her side and demand to know what had happened. How far could a bullet from that gun travel? She kept her focus directly in front of her, rather than looking to the left, where she knew Jared was. She crossed right there, because walking down to the lights would have meant turning in the opposite direction from the bus shelter, and she didn't want Dave to think she was going against his orders.

She sat away from the other waiting people and looked across the road. She could see the windows of the apartment, and she thought she saw Dave looking out at her around the edge of the drapes.

Jared was watching her but thankfully making no move to cross the street toward her. He was leaning against the window of a strip club. At first glance the pose appeared indolent, but even from this distance Holly sensed the alertness coiled within him. He must have figured that sitting in the bus shelter wasn't her idea, and he was waiting to see what happened.

Holly wished desperately that she could signal him to go around the back of the building to catch Dave as he left. She shut her eyes and tried to send the thought to him. Then immediately opened them again. She didn't want Jared confronting a nervous, gun-toting Dave Fletcher. The terror inspired by the thought of a bullet entering Jared's firm, perfect male flesh exceeded any fears she had for herself.

Stay right where you are. Don't move. Whether he got her thoughts or not, he did as she wanted. Keeping one eye on the minute hand of her watch and one on Jared, Holly didn't notice the youth who approached her until his voice startled her.

"Excuse me, do you have the time?" He was maybe sixteen, a dark wisp of mustache gracing his upper lip.

Holly stared at him, terrified. What if Dave thought

this guy was working with her? She clamped her lips together and looked straight ahead.

"Hey, do you have the time?" Not so polite this time. How ironic if he stabbed her in a fit of bus-shelter rage. Still she said nothing. The boy cursed and moved along, and she heard him asking someone else.

When the longest half hour of her life was finished, Holly looked up at the window. No sign of Dave. She jumped to her feet and ran across K Road, ignoring the angry horn of a bus and the yell of a taxi driver.

Jared raced forward to meet her and hauled her onto the sidewalk. "Are you nuts, running out into the traffic?"

"He's gone, he got away. He said I couldn't move for thirty minutes. He had a gun." Holly babbled the words, clinging to Jared like a limpet.

When she finished, he pressed kisses into her hair. "It's okay," he soothed. "You're safe, my brave girl."

It was true. In the arms of one of the most dangerous men she'd ever met—she felt safe. She twisted out of Jared's hold. "Did you hear me? He got away."

Jared stayed infuriatingly calm. "We'll find him."

"How?"

"I've got the Colonel watching the back door. He'll follow Fletcher wherever he's going. I knew that for you to be jaywalking, something must be badly wrong. I figured I wasn't meant to approach you."

She gave thanks that she'd sent him such a clear message. But her foray into danger had solved nothing. "Dave's never going to give that money back."

"Didn't I tell you that?" Jared stuffed his hands into his pockets and stepped back from her. "We tried this your way, Holly, and now it's time for you to let me take over."

"But we're both—"

"No," he said. "From now on I'm responsible for getting Dave Fletcher. Do you understand?"

She understood, all right. He was asking her to hand over total control. Even now, when she'd barely escaped being shot, the thought terrified Holly. She frowned as she looked up at Jared, ready to argue that she knew Dave better than he did and it was her business, anyway.

Standing here on this sordid road, in this far-off country, in this fantastic mess she was in, Jared was solid, real. Holly let out the breath she'd been holding and nodded. "You're in charge."

DAVE FLETCHER was on an island called Waiheke in the middle of Auckland's Hauraki Gulf. It figured. It wasn't enough that Jared should have endured fifteen hours of flying. Now he had to get on a boat.

Holly, of course, noticed the tightness of his grip on the catamaran ferry's handrail. "You're feeling sick again?"

He nodded, unable to speak. She clucked impatiently and, mercifully, disappeared into the main cabin, leaving him and his heaving stomach in peace. The waters of the Waitemata Harbor sparkled in the early spring sunshine. With a fresh wind blowing in his face, Jared could almost appreciate the beauty of the scene.

The ferry trip took half an hour, then they disembarked on the wharf at Waiheke's tiny port, Matiatia.

The Colonel met them and drove them to an exclusive hotel at Palm Beach, where half a dozen guest suites sprawled down a foliage-encrusted hill overlooking white sands and an azure sea. Their suite was the bottommost, set halfway down the hill.

From its balcony the Colonel pointed out the house Dave had fled to, one of the many properties in the area available for vacation rentals, just fifty yards below and to the left of them.

Because of the steep terrain, the front of Dave's single-story dwelling was on poles, while the rear nestled into the hillside. The house had decking around two sides, which helped distract the eye from the fact that the side facing the beach was painted lilac, while the other side's white paint was flaking off.

When the Colonel departed, Holly looked around the suite. It was one room, big enough to hold a couch and a small dining table and chairs, as well as the king-size bed with its pale blue-and-green duvet and matching pillows. Behind a pair of folding doors she found a kitchenette where someone, presumably the Colonel, had stocked the refrigerator. Through a doorway behind the bed, she discovered a white-tiled bathroom with a shower big enough for two. She looked at Jared, who held a pair of binoculars trained on the house where Dave was hiding. "There's only one bed."

"You do surprise me."

She bristled at his laconic tone. "I'm not sharing a bed with you."

He kept his gaze fixed on whatever he could see through the binoculars. "Afraid you'll lose control and ravish me?"

"I do *not* lose control."

"Oh, yeah, I forgot." He turned to face her. "So you're afraid *I'll* lose control?" His tone was mild, but she wasn't fooled. Nor could she picture him losing control. Any "ravishing" Jared might undertake would be a deliberate, purposeful seduction...

"That's not the point," she said.

"Seems to me you don't have a point. We should have no trouble sharing a bed." Jared turned back to the window. "Not that we will be, anyway."

"We won't?"

"Nope. You and I will be taking two-hour shifts watching Fletcher through these binoculars. All night."

"It'll be dark," she reminded him sweetly. "We won't be able to see."

"Gee, I never thought of that. Maybe it'll help if we turn on this night sight." He fingered a button on the top of the binoculars.

She huffed. "You can turn on every light on the island if it means I don't have to sleep in the same bed as you."

HOLLY HAD RELUCTANTLY agreed not to leave their suite for the duration of their stay. The risk of being seen by Dave wasn't worth taking. In fact, as soon as they were sure they could get Dave back to the U.S.A., she would fly home, leaving Jared to do the dirty work. Until then, Jared could go out, and he would, just as soon as Dave made an appearance.

At six o'clock, halfway through Holly's first watch and just as she was thinking about turning on the binoculars' night sight, Dave walked out the back door of his cottage and down the uneven pathway to the road. Jared was out the door within seconds, and Holly saw him join the road about twenty yards behind Dave. Both men were in view for maybe half a minute, heading parallel to the beach away from the resort. Following Jared's instructions, she phoned the Colonel. If Dave went anywhere in a car, the older man would follow him.

FLETCHER'S DESTINATION turned out to be nowhere more exciting than the small café at the far end of the beach, a five-minute walk from the resort. Jared didn't go in after him. Instead he bought fish and chips from the takeout next door and ate them sitting on a bench that afforded a view of the café door but wasn't directly facing it.

So when Dave came out an hour later, he didn't see Jared in the near darkness. Jared trailed him back to his cottage, then called Holly from his cell phone to tell her he would head back to the café to find out what Dave had been up to.

The café had nothing to commend it except that it was the only one in the area. Jared took in the spindle-backed chairs of knotted pine at almost-matching tables, and decided in favor of a stool at the expanse of scuffed, water-ringed timber that could loosely be called a bar.

He ordered a beer from a man he guessed was the proprietor, and made idle conversation while the man poured the drink. Soon, he brought the talk around to the subject of visitors to Waiheke Island.

"You're the second American I've had in here tonight," the waiter said. "The other guy just left."

"A regular customer?"

"Not yet." The man grinned. "But we're the only café at Palm Beach and most people get lazy on vacation. They eat here every night. Can I get you some food?"

"I've eaten, thanks. But maybe tomorrow."

HOLLY TOOK HER two-hour shifts during the night without complaint. That Jared did the same was not a surprise— once the man committed to something, he stuck with it—but it still puzzled her that he was getting so involved. She could see why he wanted to help her beat the Transom lawsuit, but to have spent all that money finding Dave... She would pay him back, of course, but he hadn't made that a condition. And now to have flown all this way, feeling so sick, and to stay up half the night...

Holly didn't know anyone else who would do that for her.

The thought warmed her as she lay in bed, unable to sleep despite jet lag and having taken two shifts at the window. In the light of the half moon that shone through the ranch-slider, Jared's silhouette was a dark distraction from slumber.

He wore a T-shirt and boxer shorts. She'd seen him pull the shirt on when he got out of bed to relieve her. Lying in a bed that had recently held Jared—almost naked—made it very hard to sleep.

From the sudden heat that flushed her body, Holly knew her thoughts had gone too far in the wrong direction. And they weren't going to right themselves while she could see Jared's muscular shoulders and arms sculpted by the moonlight.

She slipped out of the bed and retrieved one of the terry robes from the back of the bathroom door. "Put this on," she said.

Jared stiffened, as if she'd startled him, but didn't turn from his scrutiny of the cottage below. "What is it?"

"Just a robe. You'll catch cold."

"You're not my mother." She might have predicted the dismissive words. But he shrugged into the robe, leaving it open so that now, up close, she could still see the taut outline of his torso, and if she lowered her gaze just a little—

"You should be asleep." The sharpness of his tone jerked her eyes back to his.

"I'm too tense," she said, and saw the flash of his teeth as he smiled. "I'll take your shift, if you like. There's no point both of us being awake."

"Uh-uh. You'll be a wreck tomorrow." He shifted along the couch toward her, then patted the space he'd vacated. "Sit here a minute."

She did, and was surprised when he handed her the binoculars. "But you said—"

"Keep an eye on Fletcher's place for me. You won't be able to sleep until you get rid of that tension." He put his hands on her shoulders and began to massage her with slow, firm, deliberate movements.

"What are you doing?"

His chuckle told her what a dumb question it was. Holly clapped the binoculars to her eyes and focused on Dave's cottage, on the shadows cast by the moonlight on the hillside below. On anything but her hyperawareness of Jared's fingers.

He pushed the straps of her soft cotton tank top aside, and only the fact that she was holding the binoculars stopped them slipping down her arms. With his thumbs he applied exquisite pressure to her shoulder blades. Holly leaned into his touch with a groan. "That feels so good."

He paused, then intensified the pressure, starting a chain reaction of sensation through Holly's body. She gasped, and immediately he eased off.

"Did I hurt you?"

"No. It's just—I'm not sure this is helping me get to sleep."

His touch changed to a featherlight caress and soon a languor stole over her. "You have amazing hands," she said lazily, struggling to concentrate on the binoculars.

"Women always tell me that." But his tone was teasing, and Holly laughed.

Somehow it was easier for her to say what she had to say when they were sitting like this, when his piercing blue eyes couldn't laser through her. "Jared?"

"Mmm?" He sounded drowsy, like she felt.

"I just wanted to thank you for all you've done the past few weeks. Really, you've saved me. You hired me when no one else would, then you posted my bail. Now you've traipsed halfway around the world to help me. I can't figure out why, but I do appreciate it."

His hands stilled on her shoulders.

"And I want to apologize," she continued, "for being so rude when we first met. I made a lot of judgments before I knew you, and you've proven me wrong."

When he remained silent, she added, "I know now

that you're a man of integrity, and I—I admire that." His hands left her shoulders, and she felt a sudden chill.

"You don't know me at all," he said roughly. "I don't do anything that doesn't suit me, so don't romanticize what's going on here. I'm no knight in shining armor."

Holly put the binoculars down and twisted to face him, saw his harsh expression in the moonlight. "I'm not romanticizing it, I'm merely—"

"Next thing, you'll be falling in love with me." He sneered.

"I will not! Just because I said I admired you." Holly couldn't explain the stab of pain that left her floundering for words. "I'd...I'd...I'd rob my clients blind and lie to the FBI before I fell in love with you, Jared. So you and your monster ego can take a running jump."

"Fine," he said. "So long as we're in agreement on that. Now it's time you went back to bed." He pointed to the binoculars. "While you've been berating me, Fletcher could have gotten halfway to China."

Holly thrust the binoculars into his hands. As Jared focused on Fletcher's house again, he heard her stomp back to bed. He grinned, but the satisfaction was hollow. Truth was, when she'd said she couldn't figure out why he was helping her, he hadn't been able to come up with a satisfactory answer himself.

Sure, he didn't want her to lose out to Keith Transom or to go to jail for something she hadn't done. But the easiest thing would have been to pay for the best damned lawyer in the country to defend her and have the case dismissed for insufficient evidence. He couldn't justify the time he was taking off on the basis that he needed her accounting skills. She was the best, but second-best would have done.

The only excuse Jared could muster was the explosive physical attraction between them. He'd been thinking with the wrong part of his anatomy every step of the way. Yet he hadn't even tried to get Holly into bed. Jared sighed in disgust. Lust dictated his actions right up until he and Holly got close. Then his damned brain kicked in every time.

Well, he was going to get what he'd come for. He wanted Holly, she wanted him. She'd just told him he was the last man she'd fall in love with, so there was no danger of anyone getting hurt.

Tomorrow night he would put the Colonel on watch duty for a few hours, and he and Holly would get down to it. Then she would know exactly why he was helping her like this. No mystery, no romance, just good old-fashioned sex.

CHAPTER SIXTEEN

DAVE FLETCHER DIDN'T go out at all the next day, which meant Jared and Holly didn't, either.

By dusk Jared was this close to going crazy.

Not that Holly was doing anything objectionable. But since he'd made his decision about their imminent greater intimacy he couldn't get the thought out of his head. Desire had plagued his sleep and grown more urgent this morning when Holly disappeared into the bathroom with her clothes to get dressed, dropping her bra en route. Jared had automatically picked it up. The silver mesh fabric put him in mind of very sexy chain-mail. He rapped on the bathroom door and handed it to her without a word. But the image of her wearing it stuck with him.

All day he alternated shifts with Holly, his mood fouler by the minute, and by the afternoon she'd lost any gratitude she'd felt last night and was snapping back at him.

It was hardly the ideal lead-in to a seduction.

At five-thirty Jared decided he had to get out of there, before he killed whatever attraction she might still feel for him.

"I'm going to the café," he told her.

Holly looked around from the binoculars. "But Dave hasn't left the house."

"I'm betting he'll eat there tonight. If I'm there ahead of him, he won't realize I'm following him."

"What if he goes somewhere else?"

"Call me when Fletcher leaves the house. I'll watch the window and if he goes past I'll catch him up."

"What if he takes a cab?"

Jared thought about that. "Call the Colonel and have him follow Dave." The Colonel had rented a cottage below Fletcher's. The older man would be sleeping now, prior to his night shift, but he could be wakened in an emergency.

"Okay." Holly put the binoculars down and sauntered toward him. With every step her knee-length wrap skirt, made of some clingy crimson fabric, parted to show an expanse of thigh.

Jared's mouth was suddenly dry. He realized he had to leave on a positive note, if he was to have any chance of getting Holly into bed tonight. Didn't they say there was no greater turn-on for a woman than a man saying he was sorry? It wasn't a tactic Jared had used before, but for Holly he was willing to give it a go.

She reached past him into the closet he'd left open and pulled out a white sweater. Dammit, what was he doing even *contemplating* sleeping with a woman who hung up her sweaters? Her breasts rose with the movement of pulling it over her head. Blind, she knocked into Jared's arm as she wriggled into the garment. He bit down on a wave of longing and croaked, "Sorry I was in a lousy mood today. You didn't deserve that."

She showed no sign of melting as she tugged the sweater down. Her eyes narrowed. "What do you want?"

Oh, hell. Jared gave up all pretense of contrition and took a hold of her upper arms. Her lips, colored a crimson that matched her skirt, parted in surprise.

"I want this," he said, and brought his mouth down to hers.

One thing about Holly, he thought raggedly, she didn't hold a grudge. After an initial squirm of indignation, her tongue welcomed his with an impressive fervor, and her body pressed into him so he could feel her firm breasts against his chest, her bare thighs against his jeans where her skirt parted.

It was all he could do not to make love to her right there and then. But the Colonel wasn't on duty until ten o'clock. If they were to succeed in bringing Fletcher to justice, Jared had to leave now. Still, Holly's soft sigh as he pulled away almost made him abandon his resolve. And when she licked her lips, he almost died.

"We'll finish this later," he said hoarsely, and ran out the door before he changed his mind.

Alone, Holly put a hand to her lips, traced the memory of his kiss with a finger. She knew exactly what he'd meant when he said they'd finish this later. No point denying to herself—or to him—that she wanted to make love with him.

No point denying she wanted more than that.

No point denying she'd fallen in love with Jared.

Just as he'd warned her not to. No matter that he was no more her type than she was his. No matter that he was irresponsible, rude, untamable. She loved him.

She should have seen it coming, should have realized she couldn't feel this kind of sexual attraction without it meaning something important. That Jared's intellectual capacity and quick wit would prove even more devastating than his physical charms.

Holly pulled a meal out of the freezer and set it to cook in the microwave. Normal life could carry on, even under the weight of this revelation. She just had to keep her emotions under control.

By the time she finished her meal, she'd narrowed her options: she could either fall out of love with Jared quick-smart, or she could convince him to love her back. The bond between them was already more than physical, whether he knew it or not. If he could just get over his anger about his brother's death he could free up some emotional space for something warmer, kinder.

Holly looked at her watch, already missing him, already wanting him back with her. Falling out of love seemed impossible. Which left the love-me-back option.

FLETCHER SAUNTERED into the café fifteen minutes after Jared and sat at the bar a couple of stools away. When his beer arrived, he raised it to Jared in the friendly fashion of well-disposed strangers. "Cheers," he said.

Jared saw a sudden flash of recognition in the other man's eyes. Jared kept his own expression carefully vacant as he replied to the toast. "Your health."

"A fellow American, if I'm not mistaken?" The question was light, but Jared heard the underlying hesitation that told him Fletcher was still deciding how to play this one.

"Yep. From Seattle. I'm here on vacation—I got to the island a few days ago."

"Pretty spot," Fletcher said absently, his mind clearly preoccupied.

Jared nodded. "Kinda quiet, though. I like more action."

"You've come to the wrong place." Fletcher hesitated a moment longer, then stuck out his hand. "Dave Jenkins, from Tulsa, Oklahoma."

Jared's smile came naturally, born of relief. Fletcher had obviously decided Jared's presence here had nothing to do with him. "Jared Harding."

"I thought you looked familiar," Dave said. "Harding Corp, right?"

"Right." Jared shook the guy's hand and, because he'd finished his beer, gestured to his half-empty bottle. "Buy you another?"

Three beers later, they agreed to have a meal together. Over dinner Jared mentioned he'd been traveling with his girlfriend, who'd gone home to the States to work, while Jared stayed on to do some business in this part of the world. Having sowed the seed, he quickly moved on to ask Fletcher which teams he was picking to make it to the playoffs. Fletcher would have to ask Jared about his business before Jared would say any more.

It was ten o'clock when they left the café, and Jared was desperate to get back to Holly and the night of hot sex he'd promised himself. It had been hard concentrating on Fletcher's inane conversation, but his efforts at camaraderie had paid off—Dave seemed to think of him as a newfound buddy.

They walked along the road together until Jared had to turn off to the resort.

"Might see you again," Fletcher ventured as they shook hands.

"Sure to. I have a few more days here and that place is the only restaurant within walking distance." Jared grinned, then ambled up the hill, barely refraining from breaking into a run. *Holly Stephens, here I come.*

Jared entered the room at full speed, as if he'd been running to get there, startling Holly. His arrival instantly raised the temperature by several degrees. He came to a sudden halt when he saw her in the ice-blue silk night-dress that shimmied over her curves.

"Wow," he said.

"How was dinner?" Holly kept her voice casual, but a tremor betrayed her.

"I forget." Jared took two steps toward her, and the next second she was in his arms, and the familiar passion ignited between them. She would never get enough of his mouth on hers, Holly knew. Flames of desire licked through her veins, lending urgency to her response. Their tongues clashed in a frenzy of longing. Jared walked her backward to the bed and eased her down. He pulled off his T-shirt and Holly sighed in delight at his naked torso.

He straddled her on the bed, his hands cupping her breasts through the silky fabric, making her shudder. The tiny movement drew a groan from him. "I want you more than I've ever wanted any woman in my life," he said hoarsely. His fingers shook as he began to undo the tiny pearl buttons at the front of her nightdress.

Holly gasped and fought for the breath to say the words she needed to. "Before we go any further, there are two things I have to tell you."

He chuckled. "That's my Holly, something to say about everything. What is it, sweetheart?"

She gulped. "This is my— This is the first time I've ever done this." His hands stilled and he stiffened, so she went on in a rush. "And also, I—I'm quite fond of you. In fact, er, it seems I love you. I know you said not to, but—"

"What the—?" Jared clambered off the bed faster than she would have thought possible. He stood glaring down at her, and, feeling at a distinct disadvantage, Holly scrambled to a sitting position.

"Is this some kind of joke?" he demanded.

She shook her head.

Jared cursed as he paced to the other end of the room, as far away from her as it was possible to get. "Why didn't you tell me before? What the hell am I supposed to do now?"

"I was supposed to tell you I'm a virgin, was I?" Holly was angry now. "And the bit about loving you— I only figured that out tonight. I had to be honest with you before we…"

Jared growled and ran a hand through his hair. "You had to be honest," he parroted. "Hell, Holly, couldn't you have lied just this once? No, you didn't even have to do that. All you had to do was *pretend* you wanted a great night of no-strings sex—but no, you had to be honest."

"And what would have happened when you realized I was a virgin?" she demanded.

He paused for a moment, then shrugged. "I might not have noticed. I wanted you so much I'd have been in quite a hurry the first time."

The first time. Holly forced her mind away from the thought of repeated intimacies with Jared. He'd said he "wanted" her. Past tense. "Don't you want me now?"

He turned aside so she couldn't see his face. "Don't you realize," he said, "that a virgin who's in love with me is the last woman I would ever want?"

The words scalded her heart like acid, corroding the preciousness of her feelings for him. Somehow she kept her voice steady, even cold. "Well, that's what I am. So I guess we both know where we stand."

"How the hell are you still a virgin, anyway?" He sounded more confused than angry now.

"I—I've never been in love before." She wished she wasn't now. "And I guess I never found a guy I thought was…good enough."

"And you thought *I* was?" he asked, incredulous.

"We all make mistakes," she said tightly.

Jared went to the closet and pulled out his overnight bag. Unlike Holly, he'd never unpacked, he just fished stuff out of it when needed. He hoisted the bag over his shoulder.

"Where are you—?" She stopped, refusing to be that needy.

"I'll spend the night at the Colonel's place. He's on watch so you don't need to worry about Dave. Get some sleep."

And with that he was gone.

A VIRGIN. In love with him.

Jared tossed in the spare bed in the Colonel's small

cottage, seething with anger at Holly's deception. She certainly didn't kiss like a virgin. And that underwear of hers shrieked "siren."

To his chagrin, the desire for her that had completely evaporated an hour ago began to return. He opened his eyes to rid his mind of the picture of Holly in her flimsy nightdress. "It seems I love you," she'd said. If he hadn't been so horrified he'd have found her hesitation, in stark contrast with her normal forthrightness, endearing. Sexy, even.

"I love you" is not sexy. Okay, now he had that straight, he could admit he still wanted Holly. Even though she was a virgin who was in love with him.

The virgin thing should be easy enough to deal with. Maybe she could hook up with someone else before she and Jared... Black jealousy stabbed him at the thought of Holly with another man, taking Jared by surprise. He could handle the virgin thing himself.

The love business was more difficult. But he wouldn't mind betting that Holly was confusing love with lust, given her inexperience. Once they'd been to bed the thrill would wear off and she'd be out of love.

Strangely, that thought didn't do a lot for Jared. He scowled into the darkness. Thank goodness Holly was due to leave Waiheke Island tomorrow, as their plan moved into the next phase. They needed some time apart, for him to get his head around what he really wanted from this...

It *wasn't* a relationship. He just needed to get his head around what he really wanted from Holly. And she needed time to adjust to the idea that whatever that was, it wasn't going to be a big love affair.

HOLLY PACKED HER BAGS in a fury.

Where did Jared get off, saying she should have pretended to be something she wasn't? If he didn't know her any better than that by now... As she stuffed her lingerie into the suitcase Beth had lent her, Holly recognized with dismal satisfaction that she'd been right about him all along. Jared was a jerk and a sleazeball.

It was clear what she had to do next. If she could fall in love, she could fall out again. It was only logical.

When Jared opened the door just after nine o'clock with something less than his usual confidence, Holly eyed him glacially. "What do you want?" She'd asked him that last night, and in response he'd hauled her into his arms and kissed her. Just let him try that now.

He looked her up and down, his thumbs hooked in the front pockets of his jeans. "Are you ready? The Colonel's outside. He'll take you to the ferry."

Holly dragged the case off the bed. "I'm done here." When he moved to take it from her, she tightened her grip and he stepped back again.

"I was a jerk last night," he said.

Against her will, she admired once more the peculiar brand of honesty that enabled him to admit his faults without apologizing for them. "And a sleazeball," she pointed out.

"That, too. But for what it's worth, I meant what I said about wanting you."

"That I'm the last woman you'd want?"

He winced. "Not that part. When I said...well, that I've never wanted a woman as much as I wanted you."

"*Wanted.* Past tense."

"*Want.* Present tense."

She could see it in his eyes, that wanting. But nothing more. "When I said I love you—" she pinned his gaze with her own, but he didn't even try to look away "—I meant it. But I was as surprised as you are that I feel that way. I'm a realist, Jared. I can see you and I wouldn't work out. So I don't intend to keep loving you."

"You think you can stop just like that?"

"I'm sure of it," she said, and she was. Though the tear-sodden pillow she'd woken up on this morning told her it might not be as easy as she made it sound. "When I look logically at what I feel, I can see it's part sexual attraction, part excitement at being with someone so different from myself, part intellectual stimulation, part gratitude—" he frowned at that, but she was saving the best for last "—and partly because I feel sorry for you."

"*You* feel sorry for *me?*" Jared said, outraged. *He* wasn't the one who'd just spilled his heart and been rejected. *He* wasn't the one who'd gone his whole life without getting laid. But he could see compassion in her gray eyes, and it was genuine. Baffled, he stared back at her. Then he figured it out. She meant Greg, his family.

He opened his mouth to tell Holly that her family situation was far more pitiful than his. But he found he couldn't say anything more to hurt her. Instead he said, "Let me get this straight. I want you, you want me."

"Ye-es."

"Like you said, you plan on falling out of love pretty

soon, and it sounds like you know just how to do it. So maybe we can do something about the wanting."

"I'm a virgin," she reminded him.

"I can handle that."

"That's big of you."

Jared grinned. "So what do you say to an affair?" One that would be conveniently terminated as soon as she knew what he'd done to Keith Transom.

"I say no."

FOR JARED, the next night followed the same pattern as the last, only without ending in an abortive attempt at seducing Holly. He had dinner with Fletcher, where he talked more baseball than he knew he could and developed an unpleasant fascination with the small balls of spittle that formed at the corner of Dave's mouth as he spoke. Fletcher was obviously conscious of the problem, for every so often he'd run a hand across his lips and the spittle would temporarily disappear.

When Jared got back to the resort he felt strangely desolate without Holly in their room. He wanted nothing more than to wrap up this business with Fletcher and get home to her.

Home and Holly? Jared shuddered. No way.

He'd arranged to spend the following day, Friday, on a fishing trip with Fletcher. The very idea of getting on a boat made Jared queasy, but it was the only place he could think of that would guarantee some seclusion, and enough time for the conversation to turn in the right direction.

He met Dave on the deserted Palm Beach at 6:00 a.m., doped up with seasick pills and wearing sissy-looking acupressure wrist bands. *The things I do for Holly*. They rowed out to the hired launch, where the Colonel was on board acting as skipper in case something went wrong.

As they sat on deck side by side in an open stretch of sea where the Colonel had promised the snapper were biting, there was nothing else to do but talk. Time for Jared to reel Dave in.

The first nibble wasn't long coming. Dave asked Jared how business was going.

Jared answered the question, allowing a hint of boastfulness into his voice. He was betting Fletcher was the kind of jerk who couldn't let anyone do better than him.

"I had a good business of my own." Dave jumped in when Jared paused for breath. "Accountancy practice, mainly technology clients, some real big guys."

"Really?" Jared paused. He didn't want to point out Dave's error, but he deemed it suspicious not to. "I didn't know Tulsa had many big technology players."

Dave stuttered over his reply. "You'd be surprised. It's amazing really, how many…"

Jared rescued him. "So you don't have the business now?"

Dave stared at him, still thrown by the Tulsa question, suspicion in his eyes.

"You said you *had* a business," Jared prompted him gently. "Did you sell it?"

Fletcher relaxed, and Jared felt his own shoulders easing. "I've moved on," Fletcher said. "I'm full-time on my own investment portfolio."

Jared gave a low whistle. "That must be some portfolio."

The other man nodded, his confidence restored. "I've done pretty well."

"My own portfolio needs a bit of work," Jared said. "I've got fingers in a lot of pies, but not enough liquid cash. My businesses are all geared against each other."

Fletcher nodded his understanding.

Jared's line jerked in his hands, and he busied himself reeling it in. It came up empty. He re-baited the hook and cast again. "But I'm about to solve that particular problem."

"Yeah? How's that?" Fletcher sounded almost uninterested, but Jared, staring out to sea, sensed his watchful gaze.

"There's a company in Hawaii. Not my usual hunting ground, but if this firm is the cash cow it looks to be, I'm willing to go out of my way. I'm stopping over there for a few days on my way back to the States."

"You're going to do the deal?"

Jared nodded. "But I won't be fronting it. If the owners knew I was involved they'd realize the business is worth more than they think. A lot more. I'm meeting a colleague in Honolulu who'll front up to them."

That was all he said.

THE NEXT STEP was planned for that evening in the Palm Beach café. He and Dave had each ordered a beer and were scanning the menu when the Colonel rang Jared's cell phone.

Jared pretended to listen, then cursed loudly. Fletcher looked up from his menu.

"You can't do this to me now," Jared said, conducting a one-sided argument with the Colonel. "I need you in Honolulu on Monday, Jeff. This can't wait."

He waited for the imaginary Jeff to reply.

"Of course I'm sorry about your wife, but where does this leave me?" He continued on in that vein for another minute, then ended the call with another curse and dropped the phone on the table.

"Problems?" Dave asked.

Jared grunted. "The guy who's supposed to meet me in Hawaii can't make it. His wife's had an accident. She's in intensive care." His tone made it clear he didn't think much of men who rated their fatally injured wives higher than his business.

"Can you get someone else to come down?"

Jared shook his head. "Not easily. This deal is...let's say, out of my usual sphere of operations. None of my regular people know anything about it, and I want it to stay that way." With his reputation, he knew Dave wouldn't be surprised to hear something shady was going on.

Jared cursed again. "I've spent months setting this thing up. The guy on the other side is pulling a fast one over his family, and he's already sweating about whether he can pull it off. If we don't go ahead on schedule, there's every chance he'll can the whole deal."

Silence reigned for several seconds. Just as Jared was thinking he was going to have to be less subtle, maybe speculate out loud about where he could find someone who could help him at this late stage, Dave leaned toward him, giving Jared a close-up of the ball of spittle, and said in a low voice, "If you need any help, say the word."

Jared faked a look of surprise, then gave Fletcher an

appraising once-over. "It's not a difficult job. I just need someone to front the deal, get the dotted line signed. Someone very discreet. And I'd pay to ensure that discretion."

Dave nodded. "No one would hear it from me."

Jared looked him up and down again. "I do these private deals occasionally. If this went well there'd be others you could help out on. I pay on a percentage basis. One percent of the purchase price."

"And, uh, how much is the Hawaii deal worth?"

"Four mil. Give or take a few thousand." Jared could tell by the light in Dave's eyes that the accountant's brain took only half a second to calculate one percent of four million dollars. Forty thousand dollars for a couple of days' work. Jared leaned forward and injected unmistakable menace into his tone. "But if you ever said anything to anyone about it, you'd regret it." He sat back. "You interested?"

"Very." Fletcher took a swig of his beer.

Jared let out the breath he'd been holding. He'd known Fletcher would be desperate for the cash he needed to start a new life, but he'd played a hunch the guy would have a passport in his new name. Otherwise he would never have agreed to fly to Hawaii. "Let me tell you what's involved."

At ten-thirty they shook hands on the deal, agreeing to meet at Auckland airport on Tuesday morning.

That left enough time for Fletcher to run some online checks into the existence of the quite legitimate business Jared was asking him to buy. And for Jared to place a call to the FBI.

CHAPTER SEVENTEEN

JARED DIDN'T WANT to get back on a plane, but there was no other way home. And he wanted to keep a watchful eye on his quarry, so it had to be the same flight as Dave.

Fletcher's passport, in the name of David Jenkins, attracted no attention at Auckland airport. Jared headed to the business-class section of the plane, thankful he'd bought Fletcher an economy-class ticket on the pretext they shouldn't be visibly associated with each other in case it jeopardized the Hawaiian deal. In reality, he couldn't stand another minute of the man's company.

Jared was one of the first off the plane in Honolulu. He knew Fletcher, who'd been seated near the front of the economy section, must be close behind. Jared headed into the men's room on his way to Immigration, and waited until he judged Fletcher would be safely in the line.

When he queued up, Dave was several places ahead. To distract himself Jared fell into conversation with the middle-aged couple behind him. He sensed rather than saw Dave reach the front of the line. When there was no commotion he looked up—and saw the customs inspector handing Dave back his passport.

No!

How could Special Agent Crook have failed to act on

the tip he'd received? Jared struggled to hide his dismay as Fletcher walked on through—then went weak with relief when a uniformed officer stepped forward to speak to him.

"I don't know what you're talking about." Dave's voice rose in panic, audible as far back as Jared.

Another uniformed man appeared and they escorted Dave into a side room.

Jared knew it wasn't over yet. He got through passport control, only to be greeted by the same officer who had taken Dave away.

"Excuse me, sir, are you Jared Harding?"

"That's right." Jared smiled pleasantly.

"Could you come with me, sir?"

"Certainly."

Jared found himself in the same room as Fletcher. He looked at the other man with disinterest.

"Jared, tell these goons I'm here with you." Fletcher must be desperate to think that was going to get him anywhere.

"Sir, do you know this man?" the officer asked Jared.

"Of course." Jared beamed, at his cooperative best. "It's Dave Fletcher. I believe he's wanted for questioning on fraud charges."

Fletcher paled. "My name is Jenkins, you know it is. You paid for my air ticket. We're here to do a business deal."

Jared turned to the officers. "That's what I told him." He shrugged apologetically at Dave. "I lied. I'm sure you understand that's necessary on occasion."

After a few more questions the officers decided Jared could go, on condition he stayed in Honolulu a few more days in case he was needed for questioning.

"Harding, don't leave me here." Fletcher's plaintive cry followed Jared out of the room.

HOLLY PULLED the EC Solutions files off the shelf above her desk in the penthouse apartment and tried hard to stay mad at Jared.

But it was difficult. For a start, against all odds he'd succeeded in conning Dave onto a plane and back to U.S. soil. Late the previous night he'd phoned to say Dave was in the FBI's custody.

And that wasn't all he'd said. When he'd finished telling her about Dave, he added flatly, "I miss you."

"You? Miss me?"

"Don't make a big deal of it," he snapped. "It's no fun sitting here waiting for the FBI to call me for an interview, and I've…gotten used to having you around."

"This won't make me sleep with you," she told him.

He laughed. "I never thought it would. I don't know why I said it."

Unable to help herself, she smiled. "Thanks, anyway." She missed him, too. That went without saying. "Maybe when I've fallen out of love with you and you've stopped wanting to go to bed with me—" he made a derisory sound "—you and I will end up friends."

She heard the frown in his voice as he said, "I'd rather work harder on getting you into bed."

"You're wasting your time." She hung up, exasperated that, where she should be furious at him, she was revitalized by the sound of his voice and foolish enough to hope that his missing her meant something.

This morning, she was ready to get back into the work that had been neglected while they'd traveled to New Zealand. She'd managed to wrap up the Wireless World paperwork before they left. Now it was time to make some progress on EC Solutions.

Next to the files on the desk in front of her was a newspaper clipping and, attached to it, a memo to Jared from his chief accountant. The concierge had handed them to her yesterday. Holly scanned the clipping. The in-house leak had been at it again, she noted grimly. Rumors of Harding Corp's interest in EC Solutions and speculation as to the smaller company's brilliant future had reached the press.

She grimaced. This could put the price of the acquisition up considerably if it attracted other bidders. And given that virtually no attention had been paid to EC Solutions by the media to date, it was doubly irritating. She read the memo, and saw her fears confirmed.

Jared, I hear Keith Transom is likely to bid for EC Solutions. Maybe it's a deal we should consider ourselves.

Jared's accountant obviously had no idea his boss was already working to acquire the company.

Keith Transom. Again. She knew from what Jared had said, and from her own recent research into the man, that Transom was drawn to anything Jared was involved in. If Jared showed interest in a deal, so did

Transom. A few times he had beaten Jared to some choice acquisitions. Now he was after EC Solutions.

"Not on my watch, buster," she attested, and her own voice startled her in the silence of the apartment. Her mind raced—what could she do to help Jared, to prevent Transom winning the deal?

Briefly, longingly, she wished she could resort to underhanded tactics—feed misinformation to the market, scare Transom off. But that wasn't an option. She would do this the old-fashioned way, working all day and all night, every night if she had to, to put together a deal Transom couldn't match.

She glanced at her watch. Nine o'clock. That would make it 6:00 a.m. in Hawaii. Not too early to give Jared a wake-up call with the bad news about Transom's interest in EC Solutions. He would want to know.

"Hey, gorgeous." His voice when he picked up the call was seductively sleepy.

"I hope you knew it was me—that you don't answer every early morning call like that," she said.

"I was just thinking about you, imagining you here beside me."

Holly swallowed, willed herself not to respond to his blatant flirtation. Then she heard herself say, "Beside you being, um, in bed, would that be right?"

"Sure would."

"You mean that place I'm never going with you?"

He laughed. "Wanna bet?"

"I never gamble," she said primly. Before she could think better of it, she added, "And, er, what were we doing? In your imagination, that is."

A sharp intake of breath at Jared's end told her she'd surprised him. She smiled.

"In my imagination," he said with soft intensity, "you had too many clothes on. So I took them off, one item at a time."

Holly squirmed in her chair, her files a blur in front of her. "Then what?"

He half laughed, half growled, and went on to explain to her in quite some detail what happened next. She should have been outraged, or at least embarrassed, but by the time he paused for breath, she knew she couldn't hear another word without exploding.

"That's enough," she said. "I get the picture."

"But, honey, I haven't even begun to tell you what you did to me…"

"Save it," she said. "This is a business call."

Jared groaned. "We can't stop now. You're killing me."

"It's Keith Transom," she said in a rush. "He wants to bid for EC Solutions." She told him about the memo.

Damn! All thoughts of Holly naked vanished as Jared took in her words. He'd been so preoccupied with Fletcher he'd completely forgotten about the work he was paying Holly to do.

"Where are you?" he demanded, trying to get context.

"At the apartment. I'm starting work on the EC Solutions bid."

"Take the day off," he commanded, desperate for some breathing room. "You need a break after all that flying."

She laughed, a honeyed, intimate sound that threatened to arouse Jared all over again. "I'm not tired. After that little fantasy of yours I couldn't be more wide awake. I may as well get started now, because if you want to beat Transom, you'll have to move fast."

For a second, Jared was tempted to tell her everything.

He couldn't.

Besides, he was ninety-nine percent sure she wouldn't find his time-bomb. His own accountants had looked over the EC Solutions finances a couple of years ago and found nothing amiss. Best to keep quiet, risky though it was. Holly would figure it all out later, of course, so either way anything between them was screwed.

He would go ahead as planned.

The decision left Jared strangely shaky. He took a swig from the glass of water next to his bed. This was no time to chicken out.

But he would feel better if he was with Holly when she went through the EC Solutions books. Being so far away, he had no control over what she found out and when.

"Leave it for now," he said. "We'll work on it together when I get back."

"It looks like a great business opportunity—you don't want to miss out," Holly objected. "And I have nothing else to do."

Damn again. Holly didn't like to be unoccupied... Then inspiration struck.

"I want you to take another look at Wireless World," Jared said. "Since you're so concerned about the fortunes of the Greerson family, why don't you see if there's some way we can keep them involved? Some way that'll be good for the business and won't hurt my interests."

There was a moment's silence. "Really?"

"Sure, why not?" He'd been thinking about it, anyway, after Holly's impassioned pleas during their flight to New Zealand, and if anyone could figure out a workable solution to keep the family involved, it was her.

"That's wonderful." To his horror, Holly sounded all choked up. "I—" he braced himself to hear another I love you "—thank you."

Jared exhaled his relief that she hadn't let slip those words again—words she'd never have uttered the first time if she'd known the truth.

"It's nothing," he said. "It really is nothing, honey."

After she'd hung up, he looked at his watch. Six-thirty. Another tedious day waiting for the FBI to work through due process. But at least he wouldn't have to worry about Holly going over the EC Solutions accounts.

IT DIDN'T TAKE LONG for Holly to figure out a proposal for Wireless World's owners. By lunchtime she'd pensioned off Bill Greerson Senior, shifted Bill Greerson Junior sideways from sales to human resources—the staff loved the guy, he just couldn't convince them to sell anything—and retained Bill Junior's brother on a six-month consultancy contract, renewable if his performance justified it. The Greersons would be happy, but Holly was even happier—a buzz of joy had enveloped her all day. Joy not just that Jared had done the right thing for the Greerson family, but that he'd done it for *her*.

Now she wanted to do something for him.

Another of those highly suggestive phone calls did

cross her mind. But that would be playing with fire when she had no intention of delivering on any steamy suggestions. Holly eyed the EC Solutions folder in front of her while she munched on her chicken and mayo sandwich.

Jared had said he wanted to go through the accounts with her, but she could make that process a lot easier if she did a preliminary run-through on her own. And faster, which would get them in there ahead of Keith Transom.

The thought spurred Holly into action. She downed the rest of her sandwich, poured a coffee and settled in for a long afternoon's work.

She worked nonstop, snacking on cheese and crackers when hunger pangs attacked, waking herself up with cups of iced water alternating with strong black coffee.

At nine o'clock that evening, Jared phoned to report that he'd had an interview with the FBI that afternoon, and they wanted to see him again tomorrow.

Holly told him what she'd worked out for the Greersons. He approved it in grudging tones, but she heard the smile in his voice and loved him for it. Then she told him she'd started work on EC Solutions.

At the complete silence from the other end, she wondered if they'd been cut off. "Jared? Are you there?"

"I'm here."

"I have plenty of time to do this," she assured him. "I finished with Wireless World hours ago."

"I told you to leave EC Solutions. You need to catch up on your sleep." Jared threw the sentence out as the first thing he could think of.

Holly made an indistinct sound of mingled surprise and pleasure, and for once, Jared could read her mind the way she read his. *How can he say he doesn't love me, yet worry so much about how much sleep I'm getting?*

Jared paced his hotel room, phone in hand. He should have known Holly wouldn't drop something just because he told her to. A sudden clamminess gripped his heart.

Every instinct told him to confess what he'd done, and to call a halt to his plan.

For once, he ignored his instincts.

He didn't want to be accountable to any woman, let alone one who set the bar as high as she did. He didn't love her, didn't want to be the kind of guy she loved. So why did he feel a sense of imminent loss that would be greater, even, than the loss of Greg?

The very fact that he cared about Holly's opinion told him he'd gotten too close to her.

So he said, "Do whatever you want."

After he ended the call, he imagined her sitting in the apartment, working her way through those files. She was thorough, yet fast. So fast she would overlook what he was hiding?

A crazy notion struck him. If she didn't spot the problem, maybe she'd never find out what he'd done. Transom wouldn't want his own idiocy made public— he'd pay up without a murmur. And if Holly never knew, she'd have no reason to despise Jared. Maybe when this was done they could start over.

No. The only thing he planned to start after this was his next round of acquisitions, for which he would not be employing the services of Ms. Holly Stephens.

CHAPTER EIGHTEEN

AT MIDNIGHT, Holly concluded that EC Solutions was a fantastic proposition. Undervalued, well-run, poised for major growth—it was amazing no one had tried to acquire it earlier.

She called Jared to give him the good news. He hadn't been enthusiastic about her doing the work today, but she wanted to tell him anyway. He picked up on the first ring. "Holly?"

"Hi." Her voice was tired but warm, and Jared found himself holding his breath.

"How's it going?" he asked.

"Great! I just wanted to tell you I'm really excited about EC Solutions."

Hope burgeoned within him. "You've gone through everything already?"

"Not everything. But it's looking good so far. I guess I just wanted to talk to you."

Against his will, he knew a stab of pleasure. He needed to enjoy what few hours he had left. "Me, too." They talked for a few minutes, but when Holly started yawning Jared said, "Okay, lady, it's time you went to bed."

"Maybe you're right," she said through another yawn.

"Get some sleep," he ordered. "Dream about me."

"You think that'll be restful?"

He grinned. "I hope not."

She said good-night, and Jared ended the call grateful to have one more day in hand. Maybe things would look better in the morning.

HOLLY RUBBED her tired eyes, and looked longingly toward the bedroom. Then she picked up the file of EC Solutions' customer contracts. Everything looked exceptionally well ordered, but she couldn't shirk her duty to examine every detail. She could put a little more time into this now, then sleep in late.

At two in the morning she shook her head to clear her exhausted brain. This couldn't be right. She must have misread this contract between EC Solutions and one of its clients, Java Code.

With a sigh of impatience at her idiocy, she read through the small print again. Only to arrive at the same conclusion.

There was no doubt about it. The contract featured an extraordinarily severe penalty clause for nonperformance by EC Solutions. Every other contract she'd read tonight had contained a similar clause, but involving far less money. With this one, if EC Solutions didn't provide Java Code with the contracted service, for whatever reason, it was due to pay a million dollars for every month of that service failure.

It was nothing short of bizarre. Holly tried to work out why the company would have entered into such a contract in the first place—but failed. She pursed her lips. If Jared bought the company, her first piece of advice would be to cancel that contract. Though that might not be easy—there was a twelve-month cancellation clause for either party. Another anomaly in an industry where one or two months was standard.

It didn't necessarily matter, as long as EC Solutions had been delivering on the contract so far, and as long as nothing prevented it from doing so for the next twelve months.

With a sigh, Holly pulled out the accounts receivable file she'd read earlier. She couldn't remember seeing copies of any bills sent to Java Code, but the monthly value was small, and dozens of other clients paid the same amount each month, so she may not have registered it. Best to check that EC Solutions had indeed been providing the service contracted.

At three o'clock in the morning, she sat open-mouthed and completely wide awake.

According to the files, EC Solutions hadn't delivered any service to Java Code for more than three years—thirty-eight months, to be precise. With that twelve-month cancellation period, EC Solutions owed Java Code nearly fifty million dollars, even if it canceled the contract today.

EC Solutions might be worth ten million on paper—Holly had already worked that out—but with this liability, it was worth nothing at all.

She laughed out loud out of nervous relief that she'd found the problem. She ought to double her fee—Jared would be eternally grateful to her for unearthing this contract.

Unease pierced her smug relief. EC Solutions

appeared such a promising business at first glance, it was odd that such a contract should even exist. Perhaps the original deal had been struck by people who were no longer with either company, and no one else was aware of it. But why would EC Solutions have stopped servicing Java Code without formally ending the contract? For such a well-run company, it was breathtaking sloppiness.

On one level it didn't matter how it had happened. She knew everything she needed to tell Jared not to go ahead with the deal. But maybe Java Code could be convinced to settle the contract in a way that would make the deal still affordable. After all, it could take a protracted court battle to enforce the penalty clause.

Jared might know something about Java Code. She dialed his cell phone, hoping he would still be awake at midnight.

Jared cursed loudly when he saw Holly's number come up on his phone, and waited for her to blast him to kingdom come.

She sounded a lot more tired now, but her tone was puzzled, not furious. "Jared, there's something odd about one of EC Solutions' contracts. Do you know a company called Java Code?"

He waited a long time before answering. *Tell her.*

"What about it?" he asked.

"They have a weird contract with EC Solutions."

"Weird?"

"I need to do a bit more digging, but I wondered if you know who owns Java Code."

What had he told her when she'd started work for

him? That he wouldn't lie to her, but he reserved the right not to answer any question. "Why don't you check it out with the Corporations Division tomorrow?" he asked. An evasion, not a lie, and it might buy him another day.

"I can check it online tonight."

Jared groaned as the net tightened around him.

A SEARCH on the Washington State Corporations Division Web site told Holly that Java Code was a wholly owned subsidiary of another company. The major shareholder of that company was a lawyer, who held the shares on behalf of a client.

Holly's unease intensified. It shouldn't be that difficult to find out who owned Java Code.

She looked at her watch. Three-thirty. In the morning—later in the morning—she would phone around and find out who the lawyer that technically owned Java Code was working for. But for now, maybe she could find out more by looking at the list of EC Solutions' directors. One of them must have signed the contract with Java Code.

Four of the company's five directors had been on the board less than a year. The other was a founding director.

Holly did a search on his name. He held no other directorships, and he was…another lawyer holding shares on behalf of a client.

Her frustration sizzled. Should she call Jared to ask him if he knew these guys? But it was twelve-thirty in Hawaii. The man deserved an uninterrupted sleep.

Holly yawned. Okay, she would sleep, too.

SHE WAS WOKEN at seven-thirty, almost as tired as she expected to be, by her cell phone trilling "America the Beautiful." Through bleary eyes she read Jared's name on the display, and answered the call on "for spacious skies."

"Good morning," she said, with more energy than she felt. Then it sank in. "Hey, it's only four-thirty in the morning there."

"I couldn't sleep." He sounded pensive. "How are you getting on with EC Solutions?"

"I'm not there yet," she said, "but I will be."

Invigorated by the sound of his voice, Holly showered quickly and ate a bowl of cereal before she got to work.

By eight-thirty she knew who owned Java Code.

Jared Harding.

It made no sense. Why would he buy EC Solutions when it had a punitive contract with Java Code, a company he owned himself? She would have thought he would exercise his contractual rights and sue EC Solutions. It would be the easiest money he'd ever make. And she assumed Jared was aware of the contract— she'd observed he was every bit as thorough as she was, due no doubt to his brother's misfortunes.

The answer must lie in the identity of the owner of EC Solutions. Perhaps it was someone Jared felt sorry for—Holly tried and failed to imagine such a scenario. She turned back to her screen, determined to get to the bottom of this.

By nine-thirty she was even more confused. She now knew that Jared Harding already owned EC Solutions, through other companies. It wasn't illegal for him to sell the company to another of his businesses, namely

Harding Corp, but why would he want to? And why hadn't he told her it was his company?

Holly felt as if some giant piece of the puzzle lay just out of her reach—a piece she'd seen, but failed to recognize.

She needed something to wake up her brain. Coffee. As she waited for the jug to boil she tidied away some of the papers she'd been too exhausted to clear last night. On top of the pile was the memo from the chief accountant, the one about Keith Transom.

Her anguished cry rang through the apartment. Suddenly she knew exactly what all this was about.

She paced the living room as she ran through it in her mind. Jared had known that if he showed any interest in a deal, Keith Transom would surely follow. Only this time Jared would let Transom win. And when the dust settled from the sale, there would be Jared, demanding his fifty-million-dollar compensation. Ruthlessly enforcing the letter of the contract, just as Transom had done to Greg nearly twenty years ago. Transom would be ruined—if not financially, then at least his reputation as an astute businessman.

The scale of the plan floored Holly. Jared must have been working toward this for years. The lucrative deals Transom had won—been allowed to win?—had lured him into the belief that if Jared was after something, it must be a good deal.

But why had Jared gotten Holly involved? Surely he'd known she would find the Java Code contract, and that she would never condone his planned revenge?

Or had he? It was so well hidden, maybe he'd hoped

she would miss it. And she might have—if she hadn't been out to do even better than usual because she loved him.

She halted in the middle of the room, sickened. Jared had used her to test how well the trap was hidden, before EC Solutions handed over its financial records to Transom for due diligence.

A wave of nausea hit her, and she clamped a hand over her mouth. It receded, only the bitterness of bile remaining. All this time he'd been deceiving her. With his professionalism, with his help in finding Dave, with his kisses. It had been a brilliant tactic. She'd actually started to think of him as a man who was honorable in his own way. *Fool*.

UNABLE TO BEAR the suspense another minute, Jared called Holly's number at 11:00 a.m. her time. She didn't pick up the phone.

She's in the bathroom. Or on the other line, or out at the store. He tried again ten minutes later, and again half an hour after that. Then every hour for the rest of the day, until midnight her time, when he knew she'd need to sleep.

So she knew.

SIMON CROOK phoned Maggie via the trailer park office on Thursday night and gave her the good news. Dave Fletcher had confessed; Holly was in the clear.

"Thank you." The simple expression held relief, gratitude and something deeper.

"I can't take any credit," he told her. "Holly and

Harding found the guy and brought him back." And hadn't Crook's boss had plenty to say about that?

"You gave them the chance," Maggie said. "You didn't have her taken in by the New Zealand police."

"Yeah, well…you made a good case for your daughter's innocence."

"It was more than that," she insisted. "Admit it."

Simon made a noncommittal sound. But she was right. If he hadn't believed in Holly's innocence all the persuasion in the world from Maggie wouldn't have saved her daughter's hide. It felt good to have relied on his gut again, and to have been justified.

"I guess," he said, "I won't need to visit you again." Damn, that wasn't what he'd meant to say at all. He'd meant to tell her he'd found a good reason to keep visiting Marionville. That he'd met a woman he thought he could love. "I had a great time with you last week," he added hastily.

Just thinking about the hours they'd spent together put a smile on his face.

"Me, too." There was warmth in her voice, and Simon wondered if she was remembering the lingering kisses they'd shared that evening. They had devised their own variation on Scrabble, using a set that looked old enough to have been Holly's when she was a kid. Every word they made had to relate to the other person. Crook had managed russet, curves and pretty, among others. Maggie had made sweet, agent and, best of all, with a triple word score to boot, I want you. Simon hadn't bothered to point out that was three words and therefore not allowed. Instead, he'd taken her in his arms and shown her the feeling was mutual.

Not sleeping with her had been torture, but he knew neither of them was ready to move any faster. "How about we—"

"I'm going away."

His mouth moved, but no sound came out.

"I'm going to Italy," Maggie said. She sounded apologetic. "It's time, Crook. I have to do it."

"You said you'd go when you ran out of ideas. Is that what's happened?"

"Not exactly. I feel as if everything's changing, and if I stay still and ignore it my painting will lack something. What I have here isn't enough anymore."

"But what about…" Crook didn't finish the question. Logically, there was nothing between them but a standing joke, a few kisses and a game of Scrabble. So he couldn't ask her not to grab hold of the dream she'd had for so many years. And she hadn't asked him to go with her—probably because she knew he would refuse. Which he would.

"I'd better go," she said at last. "I'll…miss you."

"Have a nice trip." *Meaningful, Crook, meaningful.*

MAGGIE WALKED BACK to her trailer, the evening breeze doing nothing to cool the heat she felt. Crook was the first person she'd told about her trip, and the telling made it real. Tomorrow morning she would go to the travel agency, confirm her booking and hand over the cash.

She began to prepare a sandwich for her dinner, but lost interest halfway through. What would Crook have said if she'd done what she wanted and asked him to come with her?

No.

She was sure of it. He might break out of the mold enough to kiss Maggie, to drive her around the country so he could spend more time with her, but unlike her he wouldn't trust a hunch that at some point down the line what they had would turn into a lasting love. He wasn't the kind of man to give up his neatly planned future. Just as, in the end, her husband hadn't been.

Maggie wasn't about to make that mistake again.

A FURY that hadn't abated overnight—not even when Agent Crook called and told her Dave had confessed and she was off the hook—propelled Holly to Sea-Tac Airport the next day.

Jared's purposeful stride faltered when he first saw her, then he continued toward her, not quite as fast as before, his chin jutting in an almost boyish gesture of defiance.

He walked right up to her, stopped close enough to kiss her, but didn't. Refusing to step back from his invasion of her personal space, Holly took a breath to tell him what she thought of him.

Before she could utter a word he said, "You found it."

CHAPTER NINETEEN

JARED SPOKE with a kind of grim satisfaction. Holly would never forgive him for this. Which made this crazy compulsion to return her love irrelevant. He felt a knife twist in his gut, and swiftly quelled the pain. This was what he wanted.

Holly nodded and turned on her heel without speaking. Jared followed her to her car.

When they were on the road, she said, "Am I right in thinking that you plan to con Keith Transom out of fifty million dollars through the contract with Java Code?"

"It's not a con. It's not like I'm forcing Transom to bid for EC Solutions. The information's all there, for anyone observant enough to read it." Why not split hairs?

"In the very small print of what appears to be a standard contract identical to hundreds of others in the file," she said.

"You found it. Transom may, too."

"You used me as a guinea.pig, to see how likely that is."

"I'm amazed you found it," he said conversationally. "You're very thorough."

"So now you won't go ahead?" she asked. "You'll assume Transom will also find it?"

Jared hesitated. That had been his original plan, but deep down he'd never thought Holly would find it. "Do *you* think he will?" he asked.

"Probably not." She eased off the gas as the traffic ahead of them slowed.

"Are you going to warn Transom off?"

"I gave you my word I'd keep this confidential," she said.

In other words, she wouldn't be his conscience.

"I thought," she said, "you were more than that."

A low blow. Jared steeled himself against its strength.

"I thought," she persisted, "*we* were more than that."

He forced derision into his voice. "On the basis of a few kisses? No doubt we'll both get over it."

He heard her gasp, but he wasn't prepared for her to come to a halt in the middle of the road.

"Get out of my car," she said.

Behind them a car screeched to a stop and the driver sat on his horn. Other horns blared.

"Are you crazy?" he demanded. But she was staring straight ahead, deaf to the commotion behind them. Jared cursed and got out of the car. Holly drove off before he could even get to the side of the road. He saw her pull over a couple of hundred yards ahead.

So she'd realized she was being childish. Jared ambled toward her, determined not to hurry. Then he saw her get out of the car, come around to the trunk and dump his bags on the roadside. With a squeal of tires, she was gone.

THE ONE GOOD THING about Jared's perfidy, Holly told herself, it had gone a long way toward killing her love for him.

She was now free to return to her condo, since she'd been cleared of the fraud. But she took no pleasure in its tidy conformity and the security it afforded. Damn Jared, throwing her whole life out of balance. She bit her lip to prevent the tears that threatened.

As if in answer to an unasked prayer, her cell phone rang. "Hello?" Her voice quavered.

There was a pause. Then a familiar voice said, "Holly? Baby, is that you?"

"Mom." In an instant Holly's need for comfort transcended the distance she'd put between her mother and herself. Crying, she said, "I'm coming to see you."

THE DRIVE from Seattle to Marionville usually filled Holly with dread as, with each mile, the mire of her childhood threatened to suck her back in.

Today, she was actually looking forward to seeing her mother. As she pulled into the trailer park Holly tried to see it through Maggie's eyes, tried to understand why Mom had refused her share of her inheritance from Nana's estate twelve years ago. That money could have bought her a small house, a regular home.

But even making a conscious effort to open herself to the joys of trailer park living didn't work. The park was just as depressing as it had been all those years ago. How could Mom not see it?

Holly parked alongside the trailer and made for the door. Before she got there it opened, and Maggie stood framed in the narrow doorway for a second before she rushed down the steps to enfold Holly in a hug.

Holly hugged her back, reduced almost to tears once

again by the sudden welling of need for her mother. At last she stepped back. "Mom, you look different. Your hair…"

Maggie's abundant reddish-brown hair had been pinned back off her face, rather than framing it in the usual wild profusion.

Maggie grinned. "No hope of getting a comb through it, but I gave it a good brushing in your honor."

"You didn't need to do that." Holly followed her inside. The old furniture was exactly as she remembered it, though the couch had perhaps lost even more of its stuffing.

"Didn't I?" Mom's grin was knowing, but kind. "Let me make you a cup of coffee."

It wasn't until Maggie placed a steaming mug in front of her that Holly realized… "You have coffee."

Maggie usually refused to have it in the house, on the grounds that caffeine was a mind-altering drug. A stance peculiarly at odds with her predilection for other mind-altering substances.

"That's not all." Maggie set a plate down on the table in front of Holly.

"Cookies." Holly eyed them doubtfully. As far as she knew there was only one kind of cookie her mother made.

"Chocolate chip." And when Holly still hesitated, Maggie added, "Drug-free."

Holly took one gingerly and ventured a bite. It was a bit overcooked, but unmistakably chocolate chip. "What gives, Mom?" she demanded. "Brushing your hair, buying coffee, baking cookies—what's going on?"

Maggie put her cup down and gripped the edge of the

table. "Honey, I've been waiting for years for you to need me. This FBI thing was the first time I can remember you needing help, and it killed me there was nothing I could do for you."

Holly made a sound of protest, but her mother shushed her.

"When you asked if you could come here today I knew I was being given another chance—*we* were being given another chance." She gestured to the coffee and cookies. "I've never even tried to understand why this stuff matters to you, but I know it does. It was the only thing I could think of to make you feel welcome."

Holly swallowed the lump in her throat. "Thanks, Mom."

"Well, don't hold your breath for any more baking," Maggie said gruffly. "Now, tell me what's got you so upset. Must be a man."

Holly started at the beginning, with how she'd always resented Jared's cavalier attitude to rules and regulations, and finished with the sad truth: she'd fallen in love with a jerk who'd been using her all along.

"Poor baby." Maggie pushed a lock of Holly's hair back behind her ears, a gesture of comfort Holly remembered from her childhood. It was strangely soothing. "I'm so sad for you. I don't know him beyond that one time I met him, but he sounds like a good man."

"Good?" Holly jerked her head away from her mother's touch. "How can you say that?"

"He went to extraordinary lengths to help you. He obviously cares deeply for his family, since he took his brother's death so hard. A man who can hold a grudge that long doesn't have a commitment problem. And, not that it matters, but I did happen to notice he's gorgeous."

Holly had to smile at that. "He is gorgeous," she agreed. "And he's done some good things. But dragging me into his revenge plan…"

"That was bad," Maggie acknowledged. "I'll bet he regrets that now."

"I don't think so. I think he was relieved to have it between us, to stop us getting any closer."

Her mother just listened, letting Holly talk on and on about Jared, which was more help than any amount of advice would have been. While she talked, Maggie made dinner, more the usual fare Holly expected of her, frankfurters with baked beans on toast. But that was okay. Her mother's gesture with the cookies had made the point.

Afterward, Maggie drank tea and Holly sipped at her coffee. It was time to ask the question that had been bugging her for years. "Mom, why didn't you accept your share of Nana's estate? And why won't you bank the checks I send you?" She'd even taken the risk of writing the checks out to cash on the assumption Mom didn't have a bank account. "Okay, so you want to stay living here. But surely you'd like a new couch or something?"

Maggie eyed the almost shapeless, faded blue sofa. "I'd love a new couch."

"Then…why?" Holly had always known her mother's flimsy excuses for not banking the checks hid the true reason.

Maggie sighed. "Sweetie, you might not like this."

"It's okay." Holly braced herself inwardly.

Maggie appeared to be groping for the right words. "Holly, your principles are very important to you, and I admire that."

I take after my father. She didn't say the words out loud, but, mortifyingly, Maggie read her thoughts.

"Actually, you get that from me. When I commit to something, I stick with it. And I won't do something, even something good, if it's for the wrong reasons."

In a way that was true, Holly supposed. Maggie never compromised her principles—with the possible exception of providing coffee today. Her commitment to organizations such as Greenpeace and Amnesty International had been dogged, long after others her age had matured into caring less. And the bizarre behavior Holly had found so humiliating as a child was a refusal to conform with a materialistic system her mother felt was wrong.

"Your father…"

Holly started. Her mother never mentioned her father.

"In a way it was my fault he left."

"He hated the mess."

Her mother smiled faintly. "That was probably the argument you heard most often, but there was more to it than that. When we met in the late seventies, I was a full-on hippie, flower child, whatever. He was only playing at it. He was never really comfortable out of middle-class suburbia. I'm not knocking him, it's just the way he was. We got married because of his conservative streak. I'd have been just as happy if we'd shacked up."

Holly blanched, suddenly knowing the meaning of being thankful for small mercies. She could have been illegitimate as well as everything else.

"I got to write the wedding vows, though," Maggie said. "You'd probably laugh at them—full of love for the earth and each other. And a promise that we would always cherish the things we held dear at that time. That we wouldn't change."

"Everyone changes," Holly said.

"That's what your father used to say. Only I didn't, you see. And if that makes me odd, well, that's what I am."

"But Dad changed."

"Big time." There was regret in Maggie's voice. "Three years later we were living in that house in Macken Street, hemmed in by a picket fence. I had you soon after we moved in, and then your father demanded that I give up all my old friends—I thought they were *our* friends— and conform to his suburban dream. I felt so…"

"Betrayed?" Holly suggested, feeling it on her mother's behalf. One thing about Jared, he'd never seriously suggested she should be less than herself.

Maggie squeezed her hand. "Betrayed," she agreed. "He let me continue my painting, but then he didn't want me to go out to work, so he could hardly object. I was so depressed I let the house get out of hand—my protest against the way we lived—but of course it just caused more trouble. We were heading for divorce, though neither of us wanted it. For me it would have been a betrayal of the commitment I'd made, and for him a disgrace. Then I found out I was pregnant with the twins, and we decided to try again."

"It didn't work."

Maggie shook her head. "He left. He threatened to take you away from me, but by the time he got established he'd changed his mind."

He did want me—at least a bit.

"Did he keep in touch?" Holly asked.

"He moved far enough away that visits were impractical, and when I moved here, I couldn't afford a phone. But I sent him your school report cards every year—it was the sort of thing he valued. And the occasional school photo. He sent checks. And the divorce papers when he wanted to get married again."

"So he's married now?"

Maggie shrugged. "I heard he had a couple of kids."

Holly winced. "You said he sent checks. So why didn't we have any money?"

Maggie hesitated. "I never banked them."

"Why not?" So none of it had been necessary—the embarrassment, the scrimping, the squalor.

"If we had parted on better terms, if I'd known he respected me," Maggie said slowly, "I could have accepted the money as my right. Looking back now, it was the wrong decision as far as you kids were concerned, and I'm sorry. But I was so wrapped up in my own grief. Knowing how he despised me, I couldn't take what was effectively conscience money."

"I don't despise you," Holly blurted, thinking of her own uncashed checks.

"I know you don't, sweetie, you're much too nice for that. But you don't respect me, either."

"I do." Yet she couldn't maintain the pretence, shameful though the truth was. The checks she'd sent her mother had indeed been conscience money. "I want to respect you," she amended. "I think I could learn to." The thought hadn't occurred to her before, but she knew it was true.

Maggie smiled. "That's good," she said. "Because I think I deserve your respect. Maybe not for everything I've done, but for some things."

"So that's why you wouldn't take Nana's money, either?"

Her mother nodded. "My mother felt she had a duty to divide her estate equally among her children. But she hated the way I lived and she couldn't stand that I'd let your father go. If she'd acted as she felt, she wouldn't have left me a penny."

It was dawning on Holly just how strict her mother's code of honor was.

"If you want to see your father, I'm sure I can locate him for you," her mother said. "Like a lot of guys who start a second family, he lost interest in his first one. But I would have insisted he see you if you'd asked. I wasn't sure if you wanted any contact."

"I was afraid to ask after…"

"After I destroyed all the paintings. I still loved him, that was the damned problem. I was hurting."

Holly swallowed. "I didn't know. I'm sorry."

"Honey, you were eight years old. It wasn't your job to comfort me. The trouble was I had no friends left and my mother wasn't speaking to me for losing my husband.

I think I went a little nuts." Maggie's face sobered. "You had to bear the brunt of that, and I'm sorry."

"There were good times, too," Holly ventured, and realized with a shock it was true. Times when they'd had a car and it was actually running, when they'd driven out to the woods and picked wild berries. Mom couldn't cook them so they ate them raw, juice staining their hands, faces and clothes. And with no TV they'd spent summer evenings outside, and winter ones playing Scrabble or silly card games in the trailer.

"I spoke to the twins last week," Maggie said. "I tried to persuade them to stay in college."

Holly stared. "What did they say?"

Maggie shook her head. "I couldn't budge Summer, and of course River won't do anything she won't do."

Holly smiled, resigned. "I probably pushed them into it in the first place." Her gaze fell on a travel agency flyer on the table. Cheapest Flights to Europe!!! it screamed in large red letters. "What's this, Mom?"

"That's why I called you this morning. To tell you I'm going away. To Italy."

"On vacation?"

"I'm going to paint there. I don't know how long I'll stay. I bought a one-way ticket."

Holly tried to digest that. "Are you going with someone?"

"No. I had hoped…" Maggie gave her head a small shake. "I'm going alone. I'll be fine."

"Why so sudden?"

"Honey, I've been talking about this for the past couple of years." Maggie's smile removed any sting from the words. "As soon as I heard you'd been cleared of the fraud, I booked my ticket."

"Can I— Can I come and see you over there?"

Maggie hugged her. "I'd love it."

CHAPTER TWENTY

JARED KNEW EXACTLY what he had to do.

He hit I-5 to Kechowa with a savage press on the accelerator and a sense of exultation that he could scarcely tell was fake.

"Hypocritical suburban paradise, here I come," he said out loud as, way over the speed limit, he blasted past a police car that had pulled another hapless driver over at the edge of the freeway.

He got there in record time, relief almost overwhelming him as he passed the Welcome to Kechowa sign. Five minutes in the bosom of suburbia and he'd be screaming for his freedom.

He wouldn't mind betting he'd be on the road back to Seattle by tonight, driven out of his mind with boredom and one hundred percent sure he'd thrown away nothing he actually wanted. *Bring it on.*

He gave a cheery blast of his horn as he pulled into his parents' driveway. But Mom and Dad failed to make their usual joint appearance in the doorway. He was slightly disappointed not to see them do their scuffle to see who could greet him first.

He checked his watch as he got out of the car.

Midday. A growl from the region of his stomach reminded him he hadn't eaten breakfast this morning.

Leaving his bag in the car, Jared walked up to the door, rapped lightly with his knuckles, then turned the handle. As always, the door was unlocked, so he walked right in.

"Mom? Dad?" He'd seen his father's car through the garage window, so they couldn't have gone out. He walked through the living room toward the hallway.

"Mom? Anyone home?" Puzzlement turned to alarm when he heard a stifled shriek. Adrenaline raced through his veins. He was halfway down the hall, moving at lightning speed, when Beth appeared in the doorway of the master bedroom.

She smoothed her skirt as she walked toward him. "Jared, honey, what a wonderful surprise." There was something about her bright-eyed smile that bespoke something other than just pleasure at her son's arrival. Before he could look more closely, she pulled him into a hug.

Jared returned the embrace awkwardly. "What's going on? Where's Dad?"

His unflappable mother actually blushed. "He, er, had a headache. He's taking a nap, and I thought I'd keep him company."

Jared wanted to believe her, he really did. With all his might, he fought the dawning realization of what his parents had actually been up to—before midday! But it didn't help when his father appeared in the bedroom doorway, his shirt tucked in carelessly. "Jared! We were just resting. Your mother had a headache and I—"

"You wanted to keep her company," Jared suggested.

Edward darted an anxious look at Beth, but nodded his agreement.

Beth hugged Jared again. "It's lovely to see you. A wonderful surprise." Then she released him and looked down the hallway behind him.

"Where's Holly?" his parents asked simultaneously.

"How would I know?" he snapped. At their obvious disappointment, he added, "She's probably off getting her skirt shortened."

Edward chuckled and fanned his face in mock over-heating. "Just as well she's not here then—I don't think my heart could stand it."

Jared glowered. If Dad was trying to suggest he was attracted to Holly...

"He's joking, dear." Beth took his arm and led him toward the kitchen. "We grew quite fond of Holly and her short skirts, as you know. But if you two aren't seeing each other anymore..."

"We never were seeing each other," Jared protested. Should he tell his mother her sweater was inside out? "It was business."

"Yes, dear," Beth soothed. "Let me get you some lunch. I haven't made bread today, but I have some rolls left over from yesterday and some cold roast beef. Then you can tell us what's brought you back so soon."

Great. He could hardly tell them he'd come here to be bored out of his skull so that he'd stop thinking about settling down with Holly. Settling down. Next thing, he'd be thinking the *M* word....

BY THE TIME they sat for lunch, Beth's sweater had found its way back to right-side-out, and his parents were giving a convincing imitation of two people who hadn't just been caught in the act of over-age sex in the middle of the day.

Jared sat tense, ready to blow at the first hint of judgment or reproach, or at any attempts to pry into his private life. But his long absences must have trained his parents well. They kept the conversation light, though not dull, he registered.

They were talking about what had happened in Kechowa since he left. Not much. Edward's dry commentary was quite amusing.

Out of the corner of his eye he saw Beth smile at Edward. His father, sitting opposite Jared, gave her a slow, meaningful blink in return. Holly was right. They did use a secret language.

"What was that about?" he demanded.

"What?" Beth was wide-eyed innocence.

"That look you gave him, that he gave you."

"Oh…nothing," she said infuriatingly. "Now, honey, tell us why you're here."

He hesitated. Why was he here? "To think," he said at last. "Just to think."

They had coffee after they'd eaten. Against his will, Jared's mind kept wandering back to the idea of his parents making love. Not in specific terms, of course. More the question of whether people that age could still have a good sex life with a person they'd been with more than forty years.

If he'd thought about it, Jared would have said he had every intention of having great sex until he was no longer capable—or preferably he'd die first—but it had never occurred to him it might be with just one woman.

"So how is Holly?" Beth asked.

"She's in the clear. The FBI caught her business partner and has charged him."

"Wonderful news." Beth couldn't have sounded happier if Holly had been her own daughter. "She's such a lovely girl."

"She's very uptight," Jared felt obliged to point out.

"But so sweet when you get to know her. She really warms up."

"She's got a big opinion of her own abilities."

Beth nodded. "I guess that happens when you've built a successful business from scratch."

"She dresses like a floozy," Jared said uncharitably.

"Doesn't she just?" The rumble of appreciation in Edward's voice raised Jared's hackles. "But there's a class act underneath all that," Edward said hastily. "Holly is the sort of woman you've got to respect, on all counts."

His dad was right about that. Holly was not the sort of woman you set out to use for your own ends. What he'd done hadn't damaged who Holly was, Jared realized. It had damaged who he was. In all the years of plotting revenge against Transom, he'd never breached his own ethical code. Until now.

"Honey, are you okay? You look pale."

He didn't want to talk about Holly anymore. He didn't know what the hell he wanted. On the other side of the table, Beth radiated the love and concern he'd thrown back in her face ever since… "Tell me about Greg," he said to his parents. "Tell me the truth."

Edward started to protest, but Beth took hold of his hand and put her other hand out to Jared across the table.

He took it, though it felt dumb, as if they were about to say a belated grace for the meal they'd just finished. But Beth clung tightly to his fingers, and they sat, the three of them physically connected, the circle broken between Jared and his father. The space where Greg should have been.

"We should have told you years ago," Beth said. "At first we were afraid. Later on we were too ashamed. And then it was too late to talk."

That was partly his fault, Jared knew. "Does the truth have something to do with the inscription on Greg's gravestone?" He remembered Holly puzzling over the words. "Forgive us our weakness?"

Beth let out a sigh that might have been relief. "I always told myself that if you asked about it I would tell you. But you never did. It was as if you never saw it."

"I didn't," Jared said. "All I saw when I looked at Greg's grave was my brother who shouldn't have been there in the first place. A good man with a great future that he'd choked out of himself, and no one seemed to care."

Beth flinched at the words but didn't let go of Jared's hand. "You don't believe we didn't care. You were angry, you still are, but you've never believed that."

"No," he agreed.

"Son, your brother suffered from manic depression," Edward said abruptly, his voice overloud in the small dining room.

It took Jared a moment to absorb this news. "You mean, he was depressed about the business?"

Edward shook his head. "Greg was diagnosed as manic depressive when he was fifteen."

"It's called bipolar disorder now," Beth said, "but we still think of it as manic depression."

Jared knew as much about bipolar disorder as the average person—next to nothing. "Who diagnosed it?"

"He had a number of psychiatric evaluations that all came to the same conclusion," Edward said. "It wasn't something everyone would necessarily see. But you'll remember Greg was always way up or way down. He'd either be working harder and playing harder than everybody else, or he'd be exhausted."

It was true. Jared had always assumed Greg's phases of exhaustion, where he would come home and stay with their parents for a couple of weeks and sleep around the clock, were the natural consequence of hard living and hard work.

"Greg tried to kill himself when he was fifteen, when you were just a baby," Beth said shakily.

"How— How did he—?" Jared's throat was painfully dry.

Beth closed her eyes. "He tried to hang himself from a tree in the woods behind the house. I found him purely by chance. I'd gone to pick some ivy to decorate the table because your grandparents were coming for dinner, and I—" She pulled herself up short. "I always say God gave me wings that day, because I have no idea how I got up there. But I guess I climbed the tree. Greg had used a sheet and he hadn't done a good job of tying it. It probably would have slipped undone in another minute anyhow. But I pulled it, and Greg fell down. He broke his ankle when he landed."

"Greg couldn't explain why he'd done it. He just said everything got too much for him," Edward added.

"Surely they treated it?" Jared asked. "Drugs or something?"

Edward nodded. "Drugs and counseling. Mostly they worked well. Greg had the occasional relapse when he stopped taking his medication—sometimes he'd say he couldn't feel properly when he was on them. He'd be on a manic high for a few weeks and then the low would hit, and we'd convince him to start the pills again."

"We need to tell Jared everything, Edward," Beth said gently.

Edward hesitated, then nodded. "When Greg was first diagnosed a couple of doctors recommended ECT."

"What's that?" Jared asked, though he was afraid he knew.

"Electro-convulsive therapy," Edward confirmed.

Electric shocks to the brain. Jared shuddered.

Beth noticed the movement. "That's how we felt," she said miserably. "We couldn't put him through that. Even though the doctors said it might be the most effective treatment, that it might even cure him."

"There were other doctors who didn't agree," Edward said quietly. "They said it might make no difference, or even have detrimental long-term effects. We chose to believe them. We nixed the ECT, stuck with the drugs."

It took a moment for his father's meaning to sink in. Then Jared realized this was the crux of his parents' shame. "You think that if Greg had had the ECT he might never have killed himself."

To their credit, both of them met his gaze.

"That's right," Edward said.

Jared raked his free hand through his hair. "But you don't know that. And presumably Greg could have elected to have the treatment himself when he was older?"

"He could," Edward said. "But deciding to put your own brain on the line is beyond most people. Greg couldn't himself bring to do it."

"ECT worked very well for many patients." Beth seemed determined to damn herself and Edward fully in Jared's eyes. "It might have saved him."

"So that's why you didn't blame Keith Transom for Greg's death—you blamed yourselves," Jared said. *Forgive us our weakness.* All at once he was angry again. "Why didn't you tell me this years ago?"

"We were afraid," Beth said. "You were fourteen when Greg died."

"So?"

"You were one heck of a moody kid," Edward said wryly. "We weren't sure if it was just puberty, or if you—well, like your mom said, Greg was fifteen the first time he tried to kill himself."

"You were afraid I might be manic depressive, as well?" Jared said, stunned.

"It can be hereditary, though it isn't always," Beth said. "We did actually get you a couple of preliminary evaluations. You remember those counseling sessions we took you to? The doctors said you were fine, but I couldn't quite believe it. I was terrified that if we dwelled on Greg's death too long, if we gave in to the despair, the grief, it might trigger a depression in you."

"And we didn't want to push you into football or any of the other things Greg had done," Edward said, "in case we put too much pressure on you."

"It sounds stupid," Beth said, "but…"

But. Jared was beginning to imagine what his parents must have gone through. Blaming themselves for one son's death, and terrified their other son might descend into the same hellish pit.

He thought about his brother, the golden boy—the football team, homecoming king, the adoring girl-friends, gaining his degree magna cum laude, the stellar career, the booming business…

Then he thought about what Greg might have been if he'd had the ECT. The same? Maybe. But maybe he wouldn't have brought that edge, that indefinable Greg-ness to everything he'd done. He might not have had the lows, but the highs might have proved just as elusive. Or maybe the ECT wouldn't have worked. Greg might have gone through that for nothing. The scale of the dilemma his family had faced overwhelmed Jared.

Jared cleared his throat and said what he'd never imagined saying. He absolved his parents. "You guys did the right thing for Greg. We all loved him as he was, and Greg loved what he was doing with the business. He wouldn't have thanked you for taking a part of him away."

"But he might still be alive," Beth said urgently.

"And he might not. We can't know." Though Jared wasn't sure what he was about to say was true, it needed to be said. "I would have done what you did."

He squeezed his mother's fingers and reached his other hand across the table to clasp Edward's garden-roughened hand.

They sat like that, each caught up in their own thoughts, Greg's memory in the center of their circle.

CHAPTER TWENTY-ONE

HOLLY'S CELL PHONE rang at eight o'clock Monday morning as she was clearing away the breakfast things.

Her mother picked the phone up off the counter. "How do I answer this thing?"

"Just hit any number key, Mom."

"Hello?" Maggie spoke hesitantly, listened for a moment, then dropped the phone with a squawk. "How do I turn it off?"

"I'll do it." Alarmed, Holly wiped her hands then switched the phone off. "Who was it?"

"It was some creep wanting to know what color underwear I'm wearing."

"The pervert." Holly held her hand out for the phone. "I'll see if his number's showing and give it to the police." The phone rang again as she took it, and she recognized Jared's cell phone number on the display.

Despite her anger, which hadn't abated one whit over the weekend, when she answered the phone she was laughing so hard she couldn't speak.

"Holly, is that you?"

His voice—sexy, demanding, confused—had a marginally sobering effect on her.

Still, a snicker escaped her. "Mom says to tell you she's wearing white."

Maggie was horrified. "Holly, are you talking to that pervert?" She relaxed when she saw her daughter's face. "I'll leave you to it." She headed into her bedroom.

Jared groaned. "Can we start over?"

Then Holly remembered she didn't laugh with him anymore. "What do you want?" she said abruptly.

"What color underwear do you have on?"

"I am *not* having phone sex with you—or any other kind of sex," she snapped. She hadn't heard from him since she'd dumped him at the side of the road, and he wanted to talk lingerie?

"Is it the lilac?"

"No."

"The red?"

"No."

"Is it the—?"

"Oh, for goodness' sake. It's the turquoise."

"Turquoise? You mean, that bluey-green number with little buttons?"

"That's the one," she said through gritted teeth.

He groaned his appreciation.

"You've never even seen me in it."

"I have a very good imagination."

She was quite sure he did. And the burning she felt in her cheeks had nothing to do with her anger. "Why are you calling, Jared?"

"Why are you with your mother?"

"Do you have to answer every question with a question?"

"Do you?"

She seethed in silence, and he capitulated. "I want to see you. To talk to you."

"About my underwear."

"No—well, yes, but not only that."

"Well, I don't want to talk to you. Goodbye, Jared."

Before she could end the call he said, "It's about work. You're still on my payroll, remember?"

"I quit."

"Not before you sort out the mess you've made with Wireless World."

"What mess? I do not mess up in my work."

"You did, and you have to clear it up."

"Jared," she said with a patience she didn't feel, "what I've done with Wireless World is perfect, if I say so myself."

"That's where you're wrong."

"I'm not wrong, I—"

"Will you shut up and tell me where you are?" he yelled.

"That's hardly logical," she pointed out. "I can't shut up and talk at the same time."

He made a strangled sound, and she said, "Okay, okay," and gave him directions to the trailer park. He hung up without a goodbye.

WHEN JARED HADN'T arrived four hours later Holly decided he wasn't coming. He must have realized he was wrong about Wireless World.

She looked down at the dress she wore. She'd gone into town on the weekend and stocked up on new clothes. She was sick of Summer's skimpy wardrobe, but she hadn't completely returned to her ultraconservative style. This dress was a cream linen shift, fitted to her curves and ending midthigh, rather than barely skimming her panties as any dress of Summer's would have done. It was sexy but understated.

She was thinking about changing into something less sexy when she heard a car pull up. Jared! She went to the window and looked out. But instead of the Saab, a familiar Ford Mustang was outside. "What now?" Holly groaned.

"What is it, baby?" Maggie called from her bedroom, which also served as her studio.

"It's that FBI agent, Crook. What does he want this time?"

To Holly's surprise, Maggie appeared lightning-quick. She checked her appearance in the mirror in the living room, running her fingers through her hair to tidy it.

"Mom?"

Before Holly could enquire further, a knock sounded on the door. Holly moved, but Maggie beat her to it.

As she opened the door, Maggie found herself praying for the first time in years.

There he was. For a long moment of silence she stared at Crook and he stared back. Then Maggie said, "Hello…" She paused.

"Simon," Crook supplied.

Maggie smiled. It was perfect. "Hello, Simon. Come in."

"Shall I bring these?"

Maggie noticed for the first time the two suitcases on

the porch beside him. She knew what they meant, but she didn't dare hope she was right. She nodded, and Crook followed her inside.

"Agent Crook," Holly said. "Why are you here?"

Simon looked at her as if he'd never seen her before, and Maggie stifled a smile at the puzzlement on Holly's face. "Simon's here to see me, honey."

"Oh." Holly continued to stand expectantly in front of Crook.

"So you might want to leave us alone," Maggie prompted.

"Oh!" Comprehension, mixed with mild horror, dawned on Holly's countenance, and she hurried out of the room.

Maggie looked at Simon, suddenly shy. He suited his name, honest and uncomplicated. She didn't know what to say, but he dispensed with the need for talk by taking her into his arms and kissing her. His mouth was gentle but insistent. Maggie closed her eyes and gave herself up to the warm reassurance and rising passion.

When the kiss ended he held her in a loose embrace. "Let me come to Italy with you."

Maggie swallowed. "You mean, a vacation?"

"No."

"How long for?"

"Until we don't want to be around each other any longer." He kissed her again. "Right now, I'm guessing forever."

"What about Florida? Your condo?"

He released her and took a step back. "That was the future I planned with Sally. If she hadn't died we would have gone down there, and it would've worked out. But I'm not the same man I was with her. I never realized that until I met you. No wonder I wasn't happy—I kept looking to replace what I had. But I want something different. I want you."

"I won't marry you," she said. "Probably."

"I didn't ask you to marry me," he said. "I asked you to take me to Italy. We've got a lot to learn about each other, Maggie, and Italy sounds like a great place to do it."

"You haven't got a work permit."

He grinned. "I'll let you support me with your illegal earnings." She swatted him, and he chuckled. "There's also my FBI pension."

"If you're not going to work, what will you do there?"

"I figure they have photography schools in Italy."

"That's a wonderful idea," Maggie said.

Simon's face clouded. "So how come you didn't think of it, Maggie? Why didn't you ask me to go with you?"

"I was scared," she said simply. "I've faced down Japanese whalers, I've stood on the front line in protests and taken a hit from tear gas, but I've never been as frightened as I was when we talked on Friday. When I knew you had no reason to come back here." She took his face in both hands and kissed him hard. "It's all to do with how much is at stake."

"So does this mean…?"

"It means we're going to Italy."

IT WAS ENTIRELY TYPICAL of Jared that long after Holly had given up hope of seeing him, long after she'd heard the plans her mother had made with Simon Crook and envied the older couple's attempts to steal kisses from each other when they thought Holly wasn't looking, he should pull his car up outside Maggie's trailer.

And this time, Holly made sure it was the Saab.

From the doorstep, Holly watched Jared walk up the path. As soon as he was within earshot she called, "What's the problem with Wireless World?"

He came right up close to her and the sight of him was almost a physical ache. "There isn't one. Wireless World is perfect."

"So you lied. What a surprise. Now you can leave."

He ignored her, pushed past her into the trailer, leaving her no choice but to follow.

"You look great. I like your dress." The hunger in his eyes told her he more than liked it. Then he looked around the small living area, at its shabby rug and the walls hung with canvases. Looking at the couch as he must see it, Holly realized it was even worse than she thought. Jared's jaw tightened.

"So this is where you were raised," he said.

"It's clean." For the first time she felt inclined to defend the choice her mother had made. "It's not so bad."

Before he could utter the sharp rejoinder she sensed was imminent, her mother came into the room. "Baby, there's a car outside—" She stopped when she saw Jared and advanced cautiously.

"Mom, you remember Jared Harding, my former employer." Holly had the satisfaction of seeing him wince.

"Hello, Mrs. Stephens."

Maggie withdrew the hand she'd tentatively proffered. "It's the pervert," she said. "I recognize his voice." She scowled at Jared. "I don't talk on the phone often. You might have put me off for life."

"It's not my usual opening gambit," he assured her with a level of patience Holly wouldn't have expected of him. "It's a standing joke between me and Holly."

"And what color underwear are *you* wearing?" Maggie asked.

Jared's draw dropped, and Holly had to stuff a fist into her mouth to keep from laughing. Maggie stood waiting, hands on hips, clearly expecting an answer.

"Black," Jared said with good grace. Then he seemed to recollect his purpose. "While we're having this cozy question-and-answer session, why are you—" he pointed a finger at Holly "—putting yourself in a position where this woman—" now the finger pointed at Maggie "—can hurt you again? And as for you, Mrs. Stephens, do you know how much you hurt your daughter? You're lucky child protection didn't take your kids—"

"Jared, stop." Holly's face flamed. It sounded as if all she'd done was tell tales about her miserable childhood. "Mom and I have been talking. Everything's fine." And when his thunderous expression didn't lighten, she laid a hand on his arm, the first physical contact she'd had with him since she'd left Seattle. "It's okay," she said. "Honestly."

"You can't get over years of pain in just a couple of days' talking." He looked distractedly down at where her hand rested on his forearm.

She smiled, knowing where he was coming from. "Some people can. I can. And so can Mom."

"I'll leave you guys to it." Maggie left the room.

"So who was right, you or your mom?" Jared demanded.

"Does everything have to come back to right or wrong?" she said, irritated.

"With you it does."

He had a point.

She blew out a breath. "Mom made plenty of mistakes. But I was wrong about why she did what she did." The admission came easier than she expected, so she added, "I judged her in a way I shouldn't have."

Holly couldn't tell what Jared thought of that. His blue gaze burned with an intensity she couldn't interpret. "Tell me why you're here, Jared." She waved him toward the couch, but he didn't sit.

He looked her in the eye. "I'm here to ask your forgiveness, to say I'm sorry."

Holly hardened her heart. "Oh, yes, I remember, apologizing is one of your seduction techniques."

"This is not about getting you into bed. I'm sorry I deceived you, I'm sorry I used you. I want you to forgive me."

If Holly had thought the way he acknowledged his faults without apology was impressive, his full-on repentance was nothing short of amazing. Still, she wasn't ready.

"There's something you're not telling me," she said. "There's no way you drove three hours from Seattle just to ask my forgiveness."

"Seven hours. I came from Kechowa."

"Oh." She absorbed that. "How are your parents?"

"They're fine," he said. "They send you their love. Do you think my parents are boring?"

His change of tack disconcerted her. "You know I don't."

"Can you see me ending up like them in thirty years?"

She thought about that. "No," she said at last. "Even if you mellow slightly—which is a big if—you'll never be as unassuming as your father. And you'll never be as polite and charming as your mother."

"Very funny." But his lips twitched. "Have you forgiven me yet?"

"No, I haven't," she said crossly. "What does it matter whether I forgive you or not?"

"Because," he said in a long-suffering tone that implied she should know this already, "if you haven't forgiven me, you won't agree to marry me."

"You're damned right I won't." The words were out before she'd comprehended. Jared laughed as her eyes widened. "I won't *what?*"

"Marry me," he said. "I'm offering the works—white wedding, in-laws, kids, till-death-do-us-part."

"This is a joke." She turned away from him in disgust.

He grabbed her shoulders with a force that made her yelp, and spun her around to face him. "Will you listen? This is not a joke, though I can hardly believe I'm saying it myself."

"Tell me what happened with your parents."

Jared didn't mind the non-sequitur—it gave him some breathing space. He told Holly about Greg, about his parents, about how they'd forgiven one another.

"And now you've realized you were wrong about

your parents you think you have to go out and get married," she said.

"I don't *have* to do anything," he snapped. "I care about you and I want to marry you."

"Would the wedding be before or after you sue Keith Transom?"

"I took EC Solutions off the market this morning," he told her. "I instructed my finance team to close the business down and offer the staff jobs in my other companies. That's why I didn't come here on the weekend. I couldn't until I'd fixed it. I also spent some time figuring out a new job for you."

"I don't need a job. I have my own business."

"But if you want to, you can head up the Greg Harding Investment Trust, to fund research into mental disorders. You get to invest loads of my money, and do some good at the same time. I wouldn't trust anyone else."

It was perfect. Holly's heart overflowed with love for his courage and creativity.

"I'll think about it." She returned to the more pressing matter. "So…you're not suing Transom for fifty million dollars?"

He shook his head. "I don't want anything more to do with the guy. I'm going to forget he exists."

"I'm so glad."

"Yeah, well, you should be. I did it for you."

Holly shook her head. "No, you did it for you."

He grinned. "It does feel good to be free of him. Maybe I didn't do it *for* you, but I did it because of you, because you make me want to be better than I am."

She blinked away tears. "Thank you."

"So can we get married, now we've agreed my motives are legitimate?"

"Actually, your motives are still regrettably unclear." She chose her words with the precision Jared hoped would be driving him nuts for the rest of his life. "You said you care about me. What exactly did you mean?"

"What do you want?" He groaned. "My heart on a plate?"

"Yes, please," she said primly.

"What I meant, Holly, is that I love you. I don't want to love you, and if you refuse to marry me I'm going to wish I didn't, but I love everything about you, from your gorgeous underwear to your beautiful face. From your uptight attitude to that honesty that forces me to face up to myself. *That* is why I want to marry you."

"Well, I guess that's reasonable."

"You love me, too," he reminded her. "You don't fall out of love that fast."

Holly put her thumb and forefinger almost together, to indicate just a pinch of love left.

Jared laughed. "I can work with that." He caught her up in a kiss more intimate, more precious than any she'd known.

At last she pulled away. "So you think you're man enough to cope with a virgin who's in love with you?"

"Oh, yeah. I know just what to do with one of those." He claimed her lips again. After a moment he lifted his mouth from hers. "But please," he said, "don't make me live in the suburbs. I know you want the picket fence and the garden—"

She waved a dismissive hand. "The picket fence is negotiable. We can stay in the city."

He sighed with relief.

"We can have children, can't we?" Holly asked. "Maybe a couple of them?"

He released her from his embrace, but kept her hands clasped in his. "I do want to have kids with you. But bipolar disorder might run in the family."

"That's okay, twins run in mine." More seriously, she added, "There are no guarantees with kids, Jared. But if we put half as much effort into our family as we both have into our businesses…"

He kissed her lightly on the lips. "You're right. Does this mean you'll marry me?"

"First I have to get one thing straight." His groan didn't deter her in the slightest. "Understand that I am madly, crazily in love with you, Jared. If you marry me, that's it for life. You'll be as tied down as it's possible for a man to be."

He hauled her into his arms with a suddenness that robbed her of her breath. Holly felt the wild beating of his heart against her breast. Wild. That about summed Jared up.

"So tie me down," he breathed against her mouth.

* * * * *

Happily ever after is just the beginning...

Turn the page for a sneak preview of
DANCING ON SUNDAY AFTERNOONS
by
Linda Cardillo.

Harlequin Everlasting—Every great love has
a story to tell..™
A brand-new line from Harlequin Books
launching this February!

PROLOGUE

Giulia D'Orazio
1983

I had two husbands—Paolo and Salvatore.

Salvatore and I were married for thirty-two years. I still live in the house he bought for us; I still sleep in our bed. All around me are the signs of our life together. My bedroom window looks out over the garden he planted. In the middle of the city, he coaxed tomatoes, peppers, zucchini—even grapes for his wine—out of the ground. On weekends, he used to drive up to his cousin's farm in Waterbury and bring back manure. In the winter, he wrapped the peach tree and the fig tree with rags and black rubber hoses against the cold, his massive, coarse hands gentling those trees as if they were his fragile-skinned babies. My neighbor, Dominic Grazza, does that for me now. My boys have no time for the garden.

In the front of the house, Salvatore planted roses. The roses I take care of myself. They are giant, cream-colored, fragrant. In the afternoons, I like to sit out on the porch with my coffee, protected from the eyes of the neighborhood by that curtain of flowers.

Salvatore died in this house thirty-five years ago. In the last months, he lay on the sofa in the parlor so he could be in the middle of everything. Except for the two oldest boys, all the children were still at home and we ate together every evening. Salvatore could see the dining room table from the sofa, and he could hear everything that was said. "I'm not dead yet," he told me. "I want to know what's going on."

When my first grandchild, Cara, was born, we brought her to him, and he held her on his chest, stroking her tiny head. Sometimes they fell asleep together.

Over on the radiator cover in the corner of the parlor is the portrait Salvatore and I had taken on our twenty-fifth anniversary. This brooch I'm wearing today, with the diamonds—I'm wearing it in the photograph also— Salvatore gave it to me that day. Upstairs on my dresser is a jewelry box filled with necklaces and bracelets and earrings. All from Salvatore.

I am surrounded by the things Salvatore gave me, or did for me. But, God forgive me, as I lie alone now in my bed, it is Paolo I remember.

Paolo left me nothing. Nothing, that is, that my family, especially my sisters, thought had any value. No house. No diamonds. Not even a photograph.

But after he was gone, and I could catch my breath from the pain, I knew that I still had something. In the middle of the night, I sat alone and held them in my hands, reading the words over and over until I heard his voice in my head. I had Paolo's letters.

* * * * *

Be sure to look for
DANCING ON SUNDAY AFTERNOONS
available January 30, 2007.
And look, too, for our other
Everlasting title available,
FALL FROM GRACE by Kristi Gold.

FALL FROM GRACE is a deeply emotional story
of what a long-term love really means.
As Jack and Anne Morgan discover,
marriage vows can be broken—
but they can be mended, too.
And the memories of their marriage have
an unexpected power
to bring back a love that never really left....

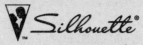

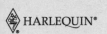

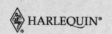

EVERLASTING LOVE™

Every great love has a story to tell ™

Fall from Grace

Kristi Gold

Save $1.⁰⁰ off

the purchase of
any Harlequin
Everlasting Love novel

Coupon valid from January 1, 2007
until April 30, 2007.

Valid at retail outlets in Canada only.
Limit one coupon per customer.

RETAILER: Harlequin Enterprises Limited will pay the face value of this coupon plus
10.25¢ if submitted by the customer for this product only. Any other use constitutes
fraud. Coupon is nonassignable. Void if taxed, prohibited or restricted by law.
Consumer must pay any government taxes. Void if copied. Nielsen Clearing House
customers submit coupons and proof of sales to: Harlequin Enterprises Ltd. P.O.
Box 3000, Saint John, N.B. E2L 4L3. Non–NCH retailer—for reimbursement submit
coupons and proof of sales directly to: Harlequin Enterprises Ltd., Retail Marketing
Department, 225 Duncan Mill Rd., Don Mills, Ontario M3B 3K9, Canada. Valid in
Canada only. ® is a trademark of Harlequin Enterprises Ltd. Trademarks marked with
® are registered in the United States and/or other countries.

52607370

HECDNCPN0407

REQUEST YOUR FREE BOOKS!
2 FREE NOVELS PLUS 2 FREE GIFTS!

HARLEQUIN®

Super Romance®

Exciting, emotional, unexpected!

YES! Please send me 2 FREE Harlequin Superromance® novels and my 2 FREE gifts. After receiving them, if I don't wish to receive any more books, I can return the shipping statement marked "cancel." If I don't cancel, I will receive 6 brand-new novels every month and be billed just $4.69 per book in the U.S., or $5.24 per book in Canada, plus 25¢ shipping and handling per book and applicable taxes, if any*. That's a savings of close to 15% off the cover price! I understand that accepting the 2 free books and gifts places me under no obligation to buy anything. I can always return a shipment and cancel at any time. Even if I never buy another book from Harlequin, the two free books and gifts are mine to keep forever.   135 HDN EEX7   336 HDN EEYK

Name _____ (PLEASE PRINT) _____

Address _____ Apt. ____

City _____ State/Prov. _____ Zip/Postal Code _____

Signature (if under 18, a parent or guardian must sign)

Mail to the **Harlequin Reader Service**®:
IN U.S.A.: P.O. Box 1867, Buffalo, NY 14240-1867
IN CANADA: P.O. Box 609, Fort Erie, Ontario L2A 5X3

Not valid to current Harlequin Superromance subscribers.

Want to try two free books from another line?
Call 1-800-873-8635 or visit www.morefreebooks.com.

* Terms and prices subject to change without notice. NY residents add applicable sales tax. Canadian residents will be charged applicable provincial taxes and GST. This offer is limited to one order per household. All orders subject to approval. Credit or debit balances in a customer's account(s) may be offset by any other outstanding balance owed by or to the customer. Please allow 4 to 6 weeks for delivery.

Your Privacy: Harlequin is committed to protecting your privacy. Our Privacy Policy is available online at www.eHarlequin.com or upon request from the Reader Service. From time to time we make our lists of customers available to reputable firms who may have a product or service of interest to you. If you would prefer we not share your name and address, please check here. ☐

HSR07

COMING NEXT MONTH

HSRCNM0107